Path of Sorrow and Wind

Book One of the Sorrowborn Trilogy

April Davis

Kevin A Davis

Inkd
Publishing

*For Family, born and found; in all their wondrous colors,
preferences, and identities.
For Love*

Path of Sorrow and Wind

Introduction

The Sorrowborn Trilogy is a character-driven YA Adventure Romance set in the area that once had been Georgia and the Carolinas.

Caitlyn is born shortly after the first effects of the Sorrow are felt, and she is one of the few unfortunates who demonstrate new powers, leading to the disastrous witch riots and the labs. When we join her, she has long since been moved to the quasi-military Camp Sparta, where she and others like her are trained to fight the cryptids that the Sorrow has unleashed.

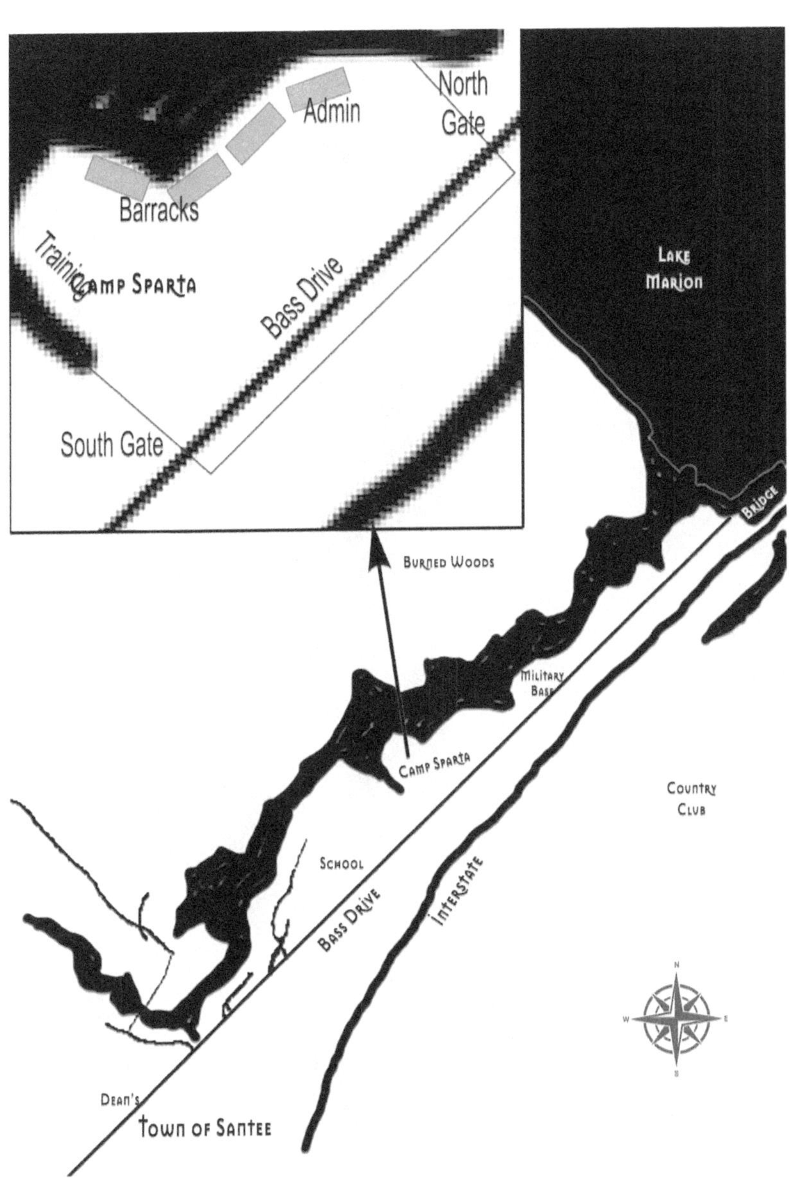

North Gate
Admin
Barracks
Training
Camp Sparta
Bass Drive
South Gate
Lake Marion
Bridge
Burned Woods
Military Base
Camp Sparta
Country Club
School
Bass Drive
Interstate
Dean's
Town of Santee
N
W
E
S

Chapter One

There were five known cryptids, none of which I'd ever seen alive, but what sat with its head cocked to study me certainly wasn't one of them. Sharp eyes peered down a foxlike muzzle, one of its too long ears flopped over while the other stood up, its sky-blue fur was tinged pink at the tips, and an outrageous tail curled above like an oversized squirrel. Worst, it blocked my path out of the tin shed I'd foolishly explored alone.

As a Youth Guard, I should have done my duty and tried to strike it down without a moment's thought; instead, I stood frozen in the musty shed, chilled even in my coveralls, staring wide-eyed at the creature.

When it lifted its front paws to stand on its haunches, I jumped back with my yellow braid swinging over my shoulder. I nearly fell when my heel dug into a stack of rotting cardboard. I could scream to draw the others in my patrol, Eric and Roxie. They'd gone in the abandoned house.

I sucked in a breath when the creature spoke with a clear voice and possibly a northern accent. "Caitlyn? That's an odd name."

His voice sounded like that of one of the younger, high-pitched boys at Camp Sparta. It took me a couple seconds before I slapped my hand to my name tag on my chest. "You can read?" I flushed, and my pulse started to race. One should never engage a cryptid. However, that he stood and spoke surprised me more than his ability to read.

"Of course." The creature tapped his chest in an all too human like movement. "My name is Moonjir."

I should capture it for the officers. That was my duty. Moonjir stood about four feet tall. All my training told me not to grapple with it. His bite could have an effect similar to a werewolf's, and that would just get me killed. The thought of wounding it with my machete caused me to frown. Reporting the sighting would be enough.

Getting additional information for my report would be the smart thing to do. "What are you?" I asked.

He tilted his head forward and spoke slowly. "My name is Moonjir."

Roxie would know what to do. She always did. "Step outside," I said. "We'll call the others." He seemed more snarky than aggressive. Vampires were said to be very charming in their daytime hosts. I had no intention of getting too close.

Moonjir ignored my suggestion. "You're awfully young for all this." With both paws, he motioned toward my military coveralls and the machete at my hip. "Fourteen?"

"Fifteen." I snorted lightly. "Two weeks ago." I clamped my lips tight. *Never engage*, I thought. Even this close to the camp, we were always supposed to stick with our patrol. I'd separated from Roxie and Eric. My report would not go well unless I brought back information. "What kind of cryptid are you?"

"Witty, fond of summer flowers, and overall just fabulous." Moonjir smiled, showing obvious canine teeth.

My earlier apprehension faded and my pulse slowed,

but I refused to smile. He mocked me in a charming way, but I had no idea how dangerous he could be. I reworded my question. "What are your type of cryptids called?"

"Some of us I name downright boring, though I rarely tell them to their faces." He turned, and I considered running around him, but he spun to pace at the entry. "This visit is all about you, golden-haired Caitlyn. You need to move up in this world." He rested a paw on his chin as he walked on his two hind legs. Again, the position and actions reminded me far more of a human than a fox with blue and pink fur, one floppy ear, and an oversized tail that, even curled, rose above his head.

He might think I wanted a higher rank in my unit; I didn't, though I'd likely be promoted during the monthly inspection. I was the oldest cadet at Camp Sparta; everyone my age was already a senior, but I was horrible at focusing on all the rules. I offered no response because he wasn't answering my question, and his comments didn't make sense.

"This military thing doesn't really match your skills." So, Moonjir didn't mean moving up in rank. He spun in the dust of the shed, continuing at a casual strolling pace. "Some are meant for it by their very search for some illusion of control. Not you, Caitlyn. Not you." He paused, turned to study me, and tapped a black nail against one of his teeth. "Which path will you take?"

At the moment, he blocked the only path I wanted — out of the shed. I would have little to report, but our trainers had never mentioned this type of cryptid, so I might have something useful. I shifted to a more demanding tone. "Move out of my way."

Moonjir grinned and continued his pacing as he studied the dust swirling around his feet. "The weather *is* growing warmer. Flowers are already starting to bud."

I peered at the yard outside the shed. We were patrolling the abandoned buildings of Santee, left empty from the Sorrow. The Sorrow began a year before I was born with people vanishing from their loved ones' sides, society collapsing, and deadly cryptids appearing in clustered zones. Roxie and Eric would come searching for me. "Let me out."

Moonjir never broke a stride, but pointed at my machete. "Or else?"

The other thing the Sorrow did was leave teens like me cursed with magic. I frowned and didn't move as I attached my will to the air around me. Weapons weren't necessary; I'd been trained to be one. The sense of the volume of the molecules of air in the shed came easily. The ever-present otherness growled to me. I focused on Moonjir's side. I didn't have enough air inside the shed to force him out, but I hoped to at least stagger him. The otherness joined with the air and my will in a surge, then I fired wind directly into him.

At his feet, dust billowed out of the musty shed in a cloud. Outside, leaves rustled away from the opening. The debris clouded my view beyond even as air refilled the vacuum I'd created.

Against the cryptid, my wind had no effect. Not a single long hair shifted, other than what normally moved as he paced. He tilted his head, glancing at me with one eye. "You appear disappointed." Moonjir let out an exaggerated sigh and faced me. "Very well."

Immediately his hair flattened on his body as if a storm gust tore at him from my direction. The chilly room had no more breeze in it than when I'd stepped inside. He leaned impossibly angled against a non-existent gale with arms outstretched and hind feet sliding back an inch. Tufts of pink and blue fluttered at his chest, and his lips peeled back to show canine teeth. His eyes were slits.

His feet shifted back a hair more, and he leaned so far forward that he appeared sure to topple over. I frowned at his mockery of me, but couldn't take my eyes from his performance.

All the fluttering stopped as quickly as it started, but he remained tilted, little paws near the ground. I swore he wore a smirk on that canine muzzle. Moonjir glanced in one direction, then the other, as if the gust might return.

One eye then the other opened fully, and he peered at me with a sly smile that seemed to come easily. Straightening, he brushed down his ruffled fur. "Very little is as it seems."

This much appeared true, as my wind had left him untouched, while whatever mocking effect he had caused impacted only him. I could admit to being curious, but not soothed. I didn't trust him.

"Let me out," I repeated and moved my hand to the grip of my machete.

"Ooh, the soldier speaks." Moonjir continued to pace.

I hardly considered myself a soldier, not even the Youth they expected me to be. None of it had been my choice. I wouldn't attack him, though Roxie would have shot him or thumped him with her quarterstaff.

Jumping, I feinted to the side, but didn't actually get closer to him. My clumsy feet nearly dropped me in the dust. Moonjir never flinched nor altered one stride of the pacing he'd resumed. My jaw tightened as I felt trapped. "What do you want?"

Moonjir stopped and focused his dark eyes on me. "To be friends, of course." He frowned, short pink and blue hair wrinkling at his brow. "We aren't that different, you and me, except

I have a breathtaking tail and you have blonde hair. Bonds connect dissimilar and the similar. One such as yourself can create new bonds or break them. Don't forget that." As his one floppy ear twitched, he held in the air a single nail as if to pause his monologue. "We're going to have to cut this short."

He bowed, backing to the side of the shed and giving me room to escape. I skittered out, so focused on him that I nearly tripped over the track for the shed doors.

Roxie, using her staff as a walking stick, stepped out of the old house onto a weathered gray porch. Her head snapped to follow my movement. She had short black hair, rich brown skin, and wore the same military-issued coveralls we all did. Eric, following her, had the same hair, but his skin leaned toward tan and his small nose turned up.

"What is it?" Roxie yelled, her grip slipping lower on her staff.

I stopped, embarrassed suddenly at my hurried retreat, and pointed back to the open doors of the shed. "Cryptid."

She launched off the porch without warning and landed on the winter-dead grass at a trot to reach me. "Werewolf?"

It was the only type we had ever heard of in Santee, despite all our training. "No, something different."

I chilled slightly when Roxie studied my hands and clothes. Once bitten by a werewolf, you became the enemy, or soon would be when you turned. Raising both hands, I rotated them to show no scratches or bites. Before this moment, I'd never had the sensation of being questioned or suspected by my own teammates. This felt worse, since I had been dating her just two months ago. Would she have killed me, here and now?

Roxie's face hard, she nodded, glancing back at the open shed.

Eric joined us, his machete in hand. "What happened?" His eyes were wide and his lips turned tight and pale.

I reluctantly pulled my own machete. "There's a cryptid named Moonjir in there."

Roxie cocked her head, still focused on the shed. "Named Moonjir? Did you talk with it?"

"He wouldn't let me out." I flushed. My report would make me sound like a coward. "I didn't want to get bit. I tried wind, but there wasn't a lot of air in there."

"Healing is your strong magic, not air." Roxie stepped forward, quarterstaff ready. "We should capture it. Watch my back." Her abilities with heat could leave Moonjir a charred corpse. Of the three of us in the Youth Guard, she was the deadliest.

"With my *weak* air magic." After letting her get two paces ahead, I started to follow her. Inside the shed, shadows hid the corners and made the lumpy cardboard suspicious.

Roxie paused a step from the opening and leaned forward to glance to one side then the next. I tensed as she straightened and walked inside. "There's nothing in here."

I stumbled on dead grass as I hurried to join her, jabbing the tip of my machete to the corner. "He was right there. He must have darted out."

She studied me. "I was standing on the porch. I saw *you* come out — nothing else." What had once been boxes of someone's belongings had melted to low wads of cardboard and debris with nowhere for Moonjir to hide. Roxie turned to study the area outside the shed, holding her weapon ready. "Describe it."

"About this high." I measured to my chest with my left hand. "It wasn't exactly a fox; the tail was too big and it had one bent ear. Blue fur with pink tips."

At my last comment, her eyes widened as her gaze flicked to me. "Are you making this up? It's not funny."

Eric giggled and relaxed his tense stance.

I pointed again to the side where Moonjir had moved to let me leave. "When I left, he was right there. This is no joke." I questioned my sanity at the moment, not my sense of humor. We trained daily to deal with cryptids at Camp Sparta; if the officers knew about something like Moonjir, we would have been schooled in it. Maybe they didn't know about all the creatures that had come to Earth during the Sorrow. "I don't know how Moonjir got out, but I need to report this to Tyrell."

"Moonjir," Roxie repeated. She gave the shed one more thorough gaze. "It spoke to you. You keep calling it a he, so it was male?"

"It sounded male. A young male."

Roxie jutted her staff toward the northeast and the road behind the sheds. "Let's get you back."

Our patrol this morning had been Sector A, including the abandoned neighborhoods along the Bass River, which some locals called Chapel Branch. Camp Sparta rested on the shore of the water, north on the crumbling Bass Drive. South led into the town of Santee. I usually enjoyed this patrol because of the little footbridge we crossed. We wouldn't make it that far today.

We headed past the rusting blue husk of a truck at the front of the house and climbed through a rotted fence to get to Bass Drive. Roxie started a slow jog, and we all fell into it.

Eric trotted to my right side. "Do we report to Selina first?" he asked.

I shook my head but waited for Roxie to answer. "Protocol on sighting any cryptid is to directly inform the superior officer on base," she replied. "In this case, it is Sergeant Major Tyrell. I can notify Selina of the situation."

Smiling, Eric bounced a step to catch my eye as he spoke. "I'll go with you, Caitlyn."

Roxie snorted. "We'll all be going to the headquarters. They'll want our reports after hers."

"Like when we spotted the white dog." He giggled, avoiding Roxie's eyes.

"A white, mottled *canine*," Roxie growled. "I was very clear about that."

"You thought it was a werewolf." I chuckled, looking to our left at the old motel sign with holes in its yellow plastic. There were no students or teachers outside at this time of the morning. The buildings had been refitted for young children who had shown magical abilities. We were the oldest, born before people even knew the Sorrow had started.

Roxie fumed as we passed the first building. "At least mine wasn't pink."

I tilted my head to the side and shrugged in agreement. My report would be difficult to believe. I barely wanted to talk about it, but they needed to know.

We reached the parking lot of the school where three old cars rotted in front of a row of little apartments. For two months, Selina and I had shared a room there when Tyrell first brought us to Camp Sparta. I'd been nine and she turned ten, though we didn't even have sweet cornbread to celebrate with. Over six years later, we still didn't have much in the way of parties. I remembered my last birthday with my parents. We'd had little chocolate cakes wrapped in plastic. There had been a tiny candle.

Far in the middle of the road, I could just make out the gate in the wire fence marking Camp Sparta. I could barely see the moving forms of the unlucky guards. "Maybe we'll miss guard duty." Tension tightened my chest, not that Tyrell would be mean about my report.

"That would be nice." Eric sounded hopeful.

Past trees and brush to our right, the tops of huge,

house-sized trucks rusted in a parking lot at the burned-out welcome center. The wide highway that led north to the large bridges was there, though I couldn't see it. The road was called Interstate 95 back when they had states, not just the Savannah Charter and the cryptid zones. We crossed it when we patrolled the old golf course.

Tomorrow we would have a real patrol with the whole unit in the outer area to the north. An armed soldier would join us. "Do you think they'll cancel the outer patrol tomorrow?" I enjoyed heading north over the bridges. On the other side of the lake, we usually got to explore places we hadn't seen a thousand times.

Roxie shook her head and took deep breaths between sentences. "I hope not. If we see actual action, we might get promoted during the inspection next month. You, at least."

I doubted seeing a pink and blue cryptid fox would get me promoted to senior, but I could hope. The rank didn't count for much, but I was the only fifteen-year-old still at cadet. I straightened and focused on the fence ahead. Tyrell would have to see a new cryptid as important; if he believed me.

Chapter Two

The cracked asphalt of Bass Drive led to a wire fence enclosure that surrounded Camp Sparta, except at the back where the river flowed. With steady footsteps, we jogged at a slow pace toward the south gate.

We'd already had our daily run this morning, so my thighs were beginning to burn. "I'm going to be sweating."

"Just be concise." Roxie huffed. "They're going to have a tough time believing it."

"Yeah, I am, too." My chest still felt tight.

Carrion birds plucked at a decomposing wolf hung on the pole at the corner; there were two at the north gate. The military decorated the fence with each one they killed, sure it helped keep the rest of their packs away. The breeze often carried the disgusting scent of rot across the compound. Summers were the worst, and I didn't believe it warned away werewolves.

Three members of the Hounds unit stood guard inside the fence, watching us with rifles ready on their shoulders. Cadets and above were allowed firearms at the gates and on the outer patrols. Between the stench and boredom, I dreaded the daily duty at the fence when it was our turn. Today, we were scheduled for midday.

The guards' expressions quizzical, they opened the gate before we arrived. Ben, a senior, nudged his chin at us. "Everything okay?"

"All clear," said Roxie. Evidently it wasn't regulation to alert the guards about a new cryptid, at least not before reporting to Tyrell.

We were all getting out of breath. She slowed us as we passed through. The gate portion had been built over the crumbling asphalt; on the left, the bottom wire was buried even into the water as the fence angled into the river until it submerged.

The camp had been a hotel or resort sometime before the Sorrow. Behind the buildings, the Bass River trailed through the forest on the west side, and decaying docks lined the shore. The four largest structures stood three stories tall with well-maintained staircases and balconies. The Youth Guard quarters only took the uppermost floors of the two southern buildings to my left. The northern buildings straight ahead held officers and some students who were too young to join our corps.

Breathing deeply, the three of us crossed dead grass to the first cracked parking lot.

"I'll notify Selina. You head directly to Tyrell." Roxie probably followed a regulation and could have quoted it if I asked. She took off for the southernmost building where our Wolf Squad unit was housed.

"Got it. Thanks." My pulse started to rise in my throat.

Eric stayed with me as we began jogging again, crossing the winter-brown grass. We passed what had once been a swimming pool that now held dead plants in a green murk of foul water. The faded gray concrete had traces of worn sky-blue paint. Behind it were the row of latrines and the burned-out shell of a small building that had served some purpose before the Sorrow.

"They probably won't allow me to stay," Eric said. "I'll have to come back when they're done with you."

"I know."

"You'll probably miss lunch mess."

"I know." Apprehension grew as we neared the northernmost building of the compound. They'd want to hear every detail over and over. Worse, they might think I had handled the situation wrong.

Eric slowed his jog as we crossed pitted asphalt bordering the front of the building. "I'll grab you something from the kitchen."

The officers' headquarters had a large American flag draped down two floors from the roof. The one white star on the top row shone bright compared to all the dead gray ones. We weren't the only state left after the Sorrow, but the Savannah Charter didn't include the Carolinas yet. Once we freed them, their stars would be added in white.

Painted in careful lettering over the center entrance to the stairwell was the army's motto, "For the nation, of the nation."

I stopped at the door to Tyrell's office, heard voices inside, and drew a deep breath as I formed a fist and knocked. As I waited for an answer, I resisted the sudden urge to draw my canteen off my belt and ease my dry throat. There had been other times I'd visited his office, but usually for failing some regulation or another.

A chair scraped inside. "Come in." Tyrell's calm voice soothed me a little. He could be emotionless, and thus rarely angry.

I stepped in, saluting. "Sir." The apartment had been widened into the neighboring rooms, and the walls were covered with maps and charts; one draped the tabletop.

Sergeant Major Tyrell stood at the table where one of the military officers sat. He wore his dark green service uniform with a dark blue tie and colorful medals pinned across his chest. Below his sandy brown hair and mustache, he had pale skin tanned lightly by the winter sun. He offered a light smile and nod to offset the fierce appearance of his broken nose and keen eyes. "Cadet Caitlyn."

I couldn't be sure if I should report in front of the other officer. The soldiers rotated in and out of the nearby military base so quickly that I knew few of their names. "I have a sighting to report."

Tyrell's eyes tightened and all his attempts at a fatherly countenance locked into hard lines. "Report."

The other officer, the same rank as Tyrell, stood.

"I spotted an unusual cryptid on patrol." The room felt warm, and the smell of sharp cleaning supplies hung in the air.

His eyes widened, then tightened again. "Situation?"

I faltered and swallowed. "I came to report to you. ..."

"Where is it now?" He'd never been this sharp with his tone before. Recognizing my reaction, he forced a grim smile. "Do you need to sit?"

After running all the way back to the camp, I glanced at the chair, but shook my head. "I'm okay. He disappeared from the shed. We searched for him."

"Him?" Tyrell's military hat bobbed as he lowered his head and studied me from under his eyebrows. With two long, quick steps, he moved to a roster and map to my left. "Where did you last see this cryptid?"

The roster had all the Youth units listed: our Wolf Squad, Hounds, Sburbs, Rose Buds, Cryptdead, and Sure Death. He checked a number there and stabbed his finger on a red trail marking our day's patrol route. I moved closer and pointed to the spot. "End of Huran Lane. Last house. In the shed."

Tyrell glanced back at the other officer, then nodded his head in a silent command. Even with soldiers of equal rank, he tended to have an unusual influence. The officer hurried to the door and left us alone.

"Sit, please." Tyrell motioned me to the table and chairs. He smoothly took a seat and waited.

Again, I thought of my water, but just sat stiffly. "Roxie and Eric were in the house. I had opened the shed and stepped inside to look at the debris."

"Had you heard a noise?" he asked.

I'd been bored. "No. Routine check of buildings." Unsure where to place my hands, I pressed one thumb to the other palm and tried not to fidget. "I was about to leave when he appeared in the doorway, blocking me inside."

Tyrell glanced at the machete at my belt. "Were you bit?"

"No, and he wasn't a werewolf. Moonjir stood about four feet tall on his hind legs, he has blue and pink fur, and his tail was almost twice as long as his body, curling overhead like a squirrel."

"Moonjir?"

"That's what he said his name was. I tried to get him to tell me what kind of cryptid he was, but he just made jokes." My quick grin dropped when I saw Tyrell's expression.

"He spoke. You asked questions?" His incredulous tone did not sound like I'd be getting a promotion during the next inspection.

"I tried to attack — with air. I threw everything in the shed at him, but it didn't even ruffle his fur, then he. .." Swallowing, I didn't think I could describe how Moonjir reacted, but I tried. "Moonjir made his fur bluster, afterward, and leaned as if he was in a storm, but there was no wind. He just mocked me."

With a sharp scrape of his chair, Tyrell stood and turned away, as if restraining himself from speaking. It took too long before he did. "Did anyone else witness this cryptid?"

Did he think I was making it up? It would be absurd to walk into his office with this kind of story. *Maybe he thinks I was hallucinating.* "No one," I said. "But it happened. All of it."

Tyrell tapped his right thumb to each of his fingers, twice, before he nodded and strode to a desk at the back window. The river showed through leafless trees outside the glass. "Let's get this conversation with the cryptid written down." He extracted a yellow pad and a pencil from the drawer. Both were as precious as Twinkies or a fabled Coke. Tearing off the top page, which he stored in the drawer, his face was expressionless as he returned and shifted the map on the table to clear me a space on polished wood. "Every word you remember. We'll go over the description again as well."

"Yes, sir." I couldn't tell whether he believed me or not.

As I started to write, Tyrell headed for the door. "I'll be back in a minute."

Trying to remember exact words, I glanced at the map on the table. It showed a coastline with a city named Charleston at the bottom. I had never heard of it. A red arrow had been drawn north to four circled locations marked with an "x" near another place called Myrtle Beach. Distracted, I studied a map ahead of me on the wall. This one included Santee and the bridge leading north. A red arrow led to three x marks at a place called Manning. I frowned at a dotted line leading farther away to someplace named Sumter where two circles had no x.

As I leaned back to see maps along the wall, I remembered my task and focused on what Moonjir had said. In all the excitement, it was a blur. Blushing, I wrote how he'd tricked me into giving him my age. I still didn't understand why he'd said the visit was about me and moving up in the world.

Anger bristled when I had to mention that he thought the military didn't match my skills, even if he was sort of right.

The door opened and I started. Tyrell entered with a woman I recognized from the clinic. She had black hair tied into a tight ponytail and wore the tan khaki uniform of the military, but smiled quickly as I studied her.

Tyrell gestured to me. "Stand up, Caitlyn. We're going to do a preliminary check now; you'll head to the clinic for a full exam."

I held my pencil tight, not moving. "I wasn't bitten, scratched, or even touched." Old panic spiked in my chest. The people at the lab had worn white smocks, but they smelled like sharp alcohol. I would never forget them. As different as our camp clinic appeared, I couldn't fight the old memories of the lab every time I entered.

He smiled, crouched beside me, and placed a reassuring hand on my shoulder. "I know what you remember. However, our medics are not those scientists, and our clinic is not their lab. You're safe." Tyrell had rescued us from that place.

Everything in the lab was white except the gray concrete walls. In the middle of the day room, Tyrell had removed the collar. Selina had been standing beside me, her face hard. The nasty shampoo they made us use every day reeked, lingering in our hair. I winced when the metal around my throat clicked as Tyrell used the white key. He had freed us, brought us outside into the summer heat full of real smells, and given us each a small, delicious cake wrapped in stiff plastic.

In a strange cart pulled by a horse, the three of us had ridden to Camp Sparta. I'd been happy to come here, once he'd convinced us we couldn't go home and risk our parents in another riot.

I put down my pencil and nodded. Tyrell eased back so I could stand. The woman was gentle when she lifted my blonde braid at the back of my neck, then lightly combed through to view my scalp. Tyrell read my notes while she pulled up my sleeves and inspected my hands and wrists.

I waited for him to chastise me for speaking, for telling Moonjir my age.

"Is there more?" He tapped on the pad.

"Yes." I faced the wall as the woman gently turned me.

One of the maps had a city I recognized, Columbia. Marked heavily with flat red lines enclosing a section of the city, it also had many red arrows pointing to spots along those walls. One mission of the Savannah Charter included liberating Columbia, and thus Carolina.

After she checked my cuffs and ankles, the woman left, though I still had to report for a full exam. Tyrell sat me back at the table to continue my writing and strode out the door.

Ignoring the maps, I focused on my retelling of Moonjir's conversation. I allowed myself a few sips of water while Tyrell was gone, but wanted to be done with my report. It was unlikely I'd get to avoid the afternoon guard duty at this rate. If I hurried, and Tyrell didn't have a lot more questions, I might make it to lunch mess after the clinic. I shivered at the idea of a full exam.

Chapter Three

When I stepped out of Tyrell's office into the chilly midday air, I found Selina sitting on the walkway leaning against the wall beside his door. I'd heard voices earlier while Tyrell had gone in and out. As unit ueader, she carried a revolver in a holster at her side. The rest of the Wolf Squad only got weapons when we went on outer patrol.

"How'd it go?" She pushed herself to stand, equal to my height and with a similar athletic build. Auburn hair peeked from under her baseball cap and highlighted her sharp blue eyes. Her skin, paler than mine with an abundance of freckles, didn't do well with sunlight.

I'd crushed on her in our early years at Camp Sparta, but that had faded. She'd always been a staunch lesbian, and I'd been embarrassed when she'd called out my bisexual tendencies. We'd remained friends, but grew more distant after she became our leader. I shrugged, pointing toward the door to the clinic at the next building. "Worst is yet to come. Exam."

Selina turned and led us down the shaded walkway. "It'll be fine." Her expression remained emotionless. None of us who were old enough to remember the labs enjoyed medics or doctors poking us. "You'll make lunch. I want to hear a report on this creature."

"Moonjir."

Her lips turned in a light frown. "You named it?"

"He named himself."

"Roxie told me you said it spoke." We crossed between the buildings, exposed to the sun, and she tilted her head to keep the shade of her hat's brim on her face. "What did it say?"

I sighed and began recalling what I could in one long retelling, slowing my pace as we reached the next building. At the point when I mentioned Roxie, I frowned. "Where are Roxie and Eric?"

Selina gestured south to our building. "They've been interviewed and sent back for lunch. We'll meet you there. Your patrol has gate duty at 1500."

No one needed to remind us of gate duty; everyone in camp dreaded it. "I know." My tone expressed just how excited I was for the task.

Her lips twitching at the edge of either a frown or smile, Selina saluted and corrected my response. "I know, sir."

Sighing, I lazily returned her salute. "I know, *sir*."

We both glanced at two soldiers jogging from the south gate toward the camp's headquarters. Neither of us commented on them, but I wondered if they'd been sent to investigate the shed where I'd met Moonjir.

Selina left me as I opened the door to the clinic. My pulse raced at the scent of antiseptic that clung to the air inside. The woman from Tyrell's office peered around a divider and gestured me toward her.

"Come in. We're alone." She kept a pleasant smile, even as she motioned for me to strip.

The area behind the screen had a metal bed with a thin mattress, but she hadn't motioned me toward it. I stood beside a shining tray on metal legs. Fresh cloth had been folded into a neat pile beside a bottle filled with clear liquid. Cabinets covered the upper part of the walls, and a counter sat below them at the far end. A curtain blocked the view of the river behind us. I crouched to undo my boots. "I wasn't bit, or anything."

"It's just regulations. Everyone has to go through a formal check."

I was fairly sure Tyrell wouldn't have to. His word would have been enough. Peeling my arms out of my coveralls, I exposed the tattoo on the inside of my left forearm. "1-8-43." I'd been unconscious during the tattooing, but the pain afterward had been a hint of what waited for me at the labs. I'd been seven. The memory had my heart racing. *This is just the camp clinic*, I reminded myself.

After ten humiliating minutes, I exited the clinic and jogged for our building. A breeze caught one of the rotting werewolves, and the reek made me hold my breath. Some members of the Rose Buds unit were on the second-floor balcony of their building; they paused and watched me as I passed. *Everyone knew.* Did they wonder if I was making it up or losing my mind?

Our building, southernmost in the line of five, bordered the training grounds. Several Youth Guards were practicing their heat magic. The river behind us split into a stagnant tributary toward the road, where it met the fence. The brush had been cleared to make a safe area to practice with heat. I found it difficult to control, as did the younger boy who had lit not only the target ball made of twined branches, but the pole holding it. His group was already running toward the flames with water. The acrid scent of smoke drowned out the rotting flesh as I slowed at the door to the mess hall.

The large space had been made from multiple apartments, much like Tyrell's office. Stained wooden tables with attached benches formed two rows of three down the room, enough for each of the patrols to have their own table. The Wolf Squad were at the rear right, and my whole unit waited there.

Outside the back windows, the trees of the river shaded a steep shore down to the water. A local in a yellow vest rowed his boat past, watching our building. The pendulum clock showed 1250, so the cook would still be serving hot food. Through the door I caught movement in the screened in patio, which had been built to handle his grills and stove.

Eric smiled and pointed at a plate. Finished with their meals, Roxie and Selina were holding hands. The youngest Wolf Squad, First Class Jordan and Second Class Yaz, turned to study me. Their dragonfly and flame patches were bright and new. My stomach growled at the sight of food and the scent of cooked chicken. I really dreaded when we had fish, which was nearly every other day in the summer.

Yaz, a fourteen-year-old girl with tan skin and black hair, smiled encouragingly. Pale Jordan sported his usual grimace, turning back to his food as I approached. I slid in beside him, across from Eric.

"What did Tyrell say?" asked Eric.

My plate had sweet peach slices from winter preserves along with the herbed chicken and cooked peas. The amount of the serving had me guessing he'd added his own portion. I grinned, then lowered my voice in a horrible imitation of Tyrell. "Were you bit?"

I glanced at Roxie; she likely had the most challenging time with the interview. She would've been stuck between our friendship and wanting to impress Tyrell with her precise details. She really wanted to catch up to Selina's rank and maybe get her own unit when the oldest students graduated into the Youth Guard. Jabbing a slice of soft fruit,

I spoke in my normal voice. "He must have believed me, even though he made me get a full exam."

"Do you believe you?" Jordan asked.

I didn't bother looking at his dour face and ate my peaches without giving him an answer. He wouldn't be the only one questioning me.

If we'd completed our patrol, we'd just be getting lunch now. I had time before gate duty to give Selina a full report. The rest of the time I spent talking with Eric behind the building, sitting on the least rotted portions of the ruined docks.

After collecting weapons, we joined Roxie at the south gate and positioned ourselves as far from the stench as we were allowed. It was a short while into our shift when three locals approached from Bass Drive. I recognized Dean from his leather jacket. He carried the damned thing over his shoulder in the summer when it was too hot to wear leather. With olive skin and black wavy hair, he caught the attention of plenty of us from Camp Sparta. He boasted that he had his own little boat, or his family did, and often paddled the Bass River to the north end of Marion Lake, where he had secret spots to fish.

Goofy Buck and his sometimes girlfriend, Francis, walked alongside Dean. All of them carried fishing gear.

Eric called out when they got close enough. "Bridge?"

Buck grinned, raising a fishing rod. "Of course. I knew we'd see your motley faces."

Dean's eyes flicked to each of us in turn, with an unreadable expression. A couple inches taller than me, I guessed he was a year older as well. He spoke with a calm authority. "Water's running cold out of Jack's Creek and Big Branch. The fish will be looking for warmer water this side of the lake."

Leaning toward the fence conspiratorially, Buck whispered. "Got a new batch done. Since y'all can get out now."

My stomach fluttered. At fifteen, we got nighttime gate privileges no matter our ranks. Selina claimed they just wanted us to end up at the Creche to have children, like Toni, our previous unit leader. I'd only been outside the camp twice since my birthday, but had no intention of getting pregnant. The others had gone out with the locals; I hadn't.

"Peach moonshine?" Eric asked.

"The best." Buck smirked and I had to wonder what he implied.

Roxie leaned against the fence. "Can Selina come?"

Buck shrugged. "Sure. Chapel Hill Baptist Church. About two hours past sunset." He frowned and straightened, peering into the camp. "Trouble?"

We turned as a group. Six soldiers escorted the Youth Guards of the Sure Death unit from the north gate. One of the unit's members, Talia, a senior, was being carried by four of her team on a stretcher. Her left arm had been wrapped in bandages spotted red from blood. My heart skipped a beat. If she'd been bitten by a werewolf, there was no saving her.

"Crap." Eric's voice was low.

"There's no cure," Dean said in a harsh, almost angry voice.

I glanced quickly at him, trying to glean if he thought we should just kill her. She had sixteen hours from the bite, sometimes up to twenty-four. Regulations were to cage her for the labs or dispatch her before she turned. In town, a wife had shot her own husband when he came home with a bite. Dean's eyes were hard under eyebrows that dropped in a grimace.

"It's not her fault," I said. "We don't even know if it was a werewolf."

Roxie let out a quiet breath. "The escort." She referred to the six soldiers.

Tyrell exited his office, and one of the guards ran over to report. Word had likely been sent ahead, while we were just seeing this. I had never witnessed a biting, but it supposedly happened to soldiers on occasion. They had their own infirmary at their base to the north of us.

"It would be better not to survive. She'll turn and be infectious, a danger to us all." Dean's voice changed from angry to a sadder tone. "Just shoot me. No regrets."

I shivered, never wanting to consider my choice. Talia had always been nice to everyone, and now she'd either be dead in a few hours or caged. What would I do if Roxie or Eric were bit? I couldn't kill them.

Buck sighed. "We should go."

I watched as Talia was brought into the clinic. She was sobbing. She knew.

"See you tonight." Buck's tone had lost any humor. "If they let you out."

Tyrell gestured to the soldiers. Dean and the other locals skirted the fence and headed north, stealing glances back into the compound. In a minute, the remaining Youth Guards of the Sure Death unit exited the clinic with an empty stretcher made of three cloaks and branches.

How would it feel to leave one of your members behind to die? Quietly, they waited as a group for Tyrell. They would have been inspected by the soldiers, but they would receive the same exam I had.

Lightning cracked near the interstate, and everyone jumped. Those who practiced electric magic wouldn't know of the situation with Talia. Their training field was out of sight. As dangerous as manipulating electricity with magic could be, they kept it very regulated. Selina might well be with the training group. She hadn't come out of the buildings as others had.

It was near the end of our shift and the sun had dropped low in the horizon when she returned with a small group and their adult monitor.

Roxie motioned Selina aside, held her hand, and leaned in to speak in her ear. "We think there was a biting." Nudging her chin to the two soldiers outside Tyrell's office, Roxie continued. "Talia. They took her inside the clinic. I think the rest of the Sure Deaths were examined. They went back to their quarters."

As she listened, Selina wrinkled her nose. I hated that I became used to the stench after a shift at the gate. My chest emptied at the thought of Talia's body, in wolf form, hanging on one of the poles. They wouldn't do that, would they?

"Let me check about tomorrow." Selina gave Roxie a quick kiss, then jogged toward Tyrell's office.

"Will they cancel our outer patrol?" Eric asked Roxie.

"Tyrell's discretion. We are being trained to handle exactly this situation."

"I didn't see them bring back a dead werewolf." Eric's lips turned into a weak smile.

"Neither did I," Roxie said.

It wouldn't take much of a bite to infect Talia. In less than a day after the incident she'd incubate, and her first strong emotion would trigger the first turn. Little was known beyond that. Many had never realized the danger when they'd been bit. Those often killed their family days later and disappeared into the wilds.

Our duty replacement was a lone soldier from the military with a rifle on his shoulder; they'd cover the dark hours.

We drifted off, uncertain whether to wait for Selina or head back to our building.

As the shadows lengthened, Selina exited Tyrell's office and met with us. "We're on for tomorrow." I couldn't tell if she agreed with the decision. Straight and rigid, she started for our quarters.

Roxie grabbed Selina's hand and tried to shake off some of the stiffness. "Moonshine? Buck has a new batch."

I walked behind and barely saw Selina nod her head in agreement.

She did come with us to drink moonshine, but Dean never showed. He was night fishing, according to Buck. I should have been excited at the novelty of drinking with the locals, but I couldn't get the werewolves off my mind enough to enjoy being out.

I'd seen a new cryptid, survived reporting it, and one of our own would likely be killed or shipped off to the labs for testing. As I drifted off with a buzzing head and dreary thoughts, I'd be happy to wake up in a new day. Tomorrow we were due to head out on outer patrol, where Talia had been bit. Maybe they'd cancel it after all.

The first of my dreams — nightmares left me hanging beside a very alive Talia on the fence. My ankles had been tied with wire as were hers, but her face had gone feral with sharp canines. Clinging to the fence with my fingers, I twisted myself away from her slashing claws and snapping teeth.

"Hold still," said Roxie. She held a rifle loosely.

My entire unit stood in the road, watching me. Jordan's evil grin nearly split his face.

"Don't shoot her," I called back, trying to orient on them upside down.

"We won't," said Selina, as she lifted her sidearm and aimed it at me. They all raised their guns.

Talia snarled and gnashed, catching shreds of my coveralls.

Wire biting into my ankle, I squirmed and dug fingers into the fence. "I haven't been bit." Pulling frantically up the links, I folded myself, trying to reach the wire and untie it.

Five shots rang like a bell.

Chapter Four

I woke with a sweaty jerk of my head as the bell rang inside our living area. My pulse raced, and my vision blurred in the darkness.

One of the soldiers or officers always woke us predawn for weekly outside patrol in the winter. I took long ragged breaths stinking of alcohol. My head thickened when I swung my reluctant feet off the bed.

Roxie rapped on my wall too loud, just in case I hadn't heard the annoying clanging. I searched for a candle and matches, clumsily knocking a pile of paperbacks off my nightstand.

"I'm up," I groaned.

The nightmare faded in the light of what we would have to do today. We'd eat breakfast and be off. Outer patrols exempted us from all the daily activities: martial, weapon, or magic training; the sprint down Bass Drive; whatever classes they had scheduled; local patrol, and most importantly, gate duty. I would usually smile at that thought, but remembering Talia tempered my excitement.

Would she be killed here, or sent to a lab? Tyrell

wouldn't allow us on outer patrol if he thought we'd be in danger.

I used yesterday's basin water, which I should have refreshed last night before we went drinking, to wipe my face and pits. My hair took a moment to weave into a short yellow braid. I dragged my body and backpack out of my room.

Roxie was dressed and waiting in the living room where the lantern flickered light on the walls. The furnace pipes had warmed the air slightly. It was night outside the back windows that faced west, toward the river. Unseen was the rotted back patio just below the window. Her room in the back had a window, which made it bearable in the summer.

"You barely even drank last night, and you look like crap," she said.

Pack on one shoulder, I grabbed my canteen off the table and machete from the wall by the door. "Remind me what a lightweight I am *before* I start drinking next time."

She led the way into the freezing night. "I'm surprised Tyrell is letting us go out."

Dull gray in the darkness, the compound appeared empty. I focused on the stairwell. "Maybe he wants us to engage the werewolves now since it's supposed to be our job." Each step jarred my clogged brain. A door opened above, maybe Jordan and Eric or Yaz. Selina would be waiting for us.

"With first and second class in the patrol?"

I didn't answer Roxie, but I doubted it. Why *had* Tyrell risked us? A blanket of stars covered the sky as we exited on the ground level. A muffled clatter sounded from the mess. Only our unit and the cook would be down here this early.

Selina and our escort soldier were already eating. The military man had on the usual dusky brown uniform appearing a shadow in the lamplight. A bowl of scrambled eggs and a plate of cornbread waited on the table.

I stowed my backpack, machete, and canteen on the table where the officer and Selina had left theirs. A stack of light gray cloaks waited for us along with the darker berets. Selina would bring her baseball cap and switch out for the extra shade if the sun grew too much for her skin. Tyrell had approved her exemption the first summer when she'd been left with a peeling burn.

"Morning." Roxie planted her face in Selina's red-brown hair and kissed the top of her head.

In her leader role and with a patrol ahead of us, Selina proved distant and more intense. "Running late. Eat."

The soldier, named Lance according to his name tag, had a pale scar under his left eye, which cut into rich brown skin akin to Roxie's, and tight curls trimmed close to his scalp. He smiled easily enough, but hadn't spoken more than a terse greeting in response to ours. To his right were cloth-wrapped rolls, which I assumed were our lunches.

Eric and Jordan trailed in as I piled my plate with cooling food. I wanted to eat it warm before I headed to the latrine.

"My teeth are chattering. When is spring again?" Eric sounded chipper for drinking as much as Roxie last night.

Lance nodded and grinned. "We had patrols going out two hours ago. I got the easy duty."

Selina frowned and spoke. "We need to be extra vigilant today. We're assigned a track on the north side of the lake, and the incident happened to the south of the bridge, but werewolves can cover a lot of ground overnight." I wondered if she reminded him as well as us of the dangers. I always took the outer patrols seriously.

Yaz skittered into the room when we were close to done.

Selina pointed her to the eggs and wrapped the last

piece of cornbread in a napkin. "Finish the eggs. You can eat this on the walk to the bridge."

While the youngest of the Wolf Squad shoveled food in her mouth, Lance handed out weapons; only cadets and above were assigned any. I took the old shotgun in my right hand, tossed four shells into my pocket, and loaded two. Roxie got the newer rifle, and Eric a battered pistol and holster. Jordan scowled but didn't complain. He'd be promoted to cadet soon, as he loved regulations and hated everything and everyone else.

We exited the mess to a ridge of gray that had formed on the eastern horizon while we'd eaten. Cloaks tied at our throats covered our backpacks, and berets our heads. The most unusual part of the morning was finding Tyrell waiting by the north gate, casually talking with the night soldier on duty. I'd never seen our commander outside for an outer patrol since he stopped escorting us years ago.

Lance saluted him, and Tyrell returned it. "Take it slow and careful. Turn at the four-hour mark instead of five. Keep to known paths since we have full squads out there."

"Yes, sir."

"Keep 'em safe, Unit Leader." Tyrell saluted the Wolf Squad as a whole and we returned it. He didn't appear worried, but unless he smiled, I couldn't gauge his expressions.

With the sky turning a brighter gray to our right, we cut through the trees to the interstate and headed north for the bridge over Lake Marion. The abandoned rusting cars and those burned-out into husks were all pushed off to the side, and vegetation had taken to climbing atop and inside them.

Wind started to whip at our cloaks, and Eric growled as he grabbed the edges of his. "Crap." The worst would be across the bridge.

"Too cold for that." I shivered and glanced at the lighter

gray-blue horizon. Shotgun on my shoulder, the best I could do was pin my cloak together with one hand. The temperature had to be near freezing.

We passed the first guard post, a box on a metal tower that people used to hunt from before the Sorrow. High winds ripped across the lake ahead. The shore dropped to rippling water splashing against the concrete posts. The bridge had been cleared, much like the interstate, but there were no bushes to push the debris into. We had one side clear, but the other was still dotted with vehicles. Occasionally a truck blocked some of the gusts, but my fingers ached for gloves. Those were reserved for below freezing temperatures to avoid excess wear and tear. It didn't warm even as the sun crested or when we reached the middle where ground held the road rather than concrete pillars rising out of the water.

"One more mile," Eric said.

We had a few more minutes of lake winds before we reached the trees and the nearly abandoned town called Summerton. "I don't understand why anyone would live over here." The cryptid zone was too close.

Selina walked ahead of us. "The Savannah Charter wants to repopulate the area."

Eric giggled. "I doubt they get any volunteers."

After so many had disappeared during the Sorrow, "Taken" my mother had called it, there was plenty of land available far from the concentrations of cryptids. "I wouldn't live out here."

We passed the last guard outpost on stilts, and the trees sprang around us on both sides of solid ground. The asphalt and relics of cars still left plenty of room for the wind. The sun added some warmth when we veered to the left for the northern patrol areas. The temperature climbed quickly as we crossed a short bridge and turned north onto a road close enough to the water to smell the marshy tones when the wind shifted.

More than an hour into our patrol, we passed the first populated complex on our route surrounded by fences bristling with razor wire. We never stopped there.

"Focus," Selina chided. I'd been studying the houses, searching for the people who lived there.

"I am," I said.

"Yes, sir," she corrected.

Eric exchanged a quick glance with me and joined me in an enthusiastic response, "Yes, sir."

"How do we know they're okay?" I asked Selina.

Lance spoke over his shoulder. "They are checked every week. We've got a few groups out here, some larger than this. Mostly along the water."

"I've never seen any others except the people at Summerton."

Lance chuckled. "South of that, and north of your patrol range. It's a big lake, over thirty miles long."

"How far is the graveyard?" Eric cleared his throat and tugged his cloak over his shoulder.

"Almost three miles."

Over an hour later we arrived at a peninsula littered with rusted out campers and a half ring of barricading cars. Tucked in the brush that had grown around the derelict vehicles were the bones. As a second class on my first trip out, I'd been pranked into treading into the "graveyard." It had taken me too long to register the snapping twigs as bones. A lot of people had died at the campground. The sign on the building barely read, "Jack's Creek Marina."

Out on the lake, two men rowed a small boat. Actually, one fished while the other held the oars; neither appeared to move.

"Look." I waved.

Eric, Roxie, and Yaz followed suit, but if the fisherman saw us, they didn't react.

Selina just frowned. "Stop it."

I smirked at Eric. "Yes, sir."

Eric caught up to Lance at the breezy shore. "How far are we going?" We'd all heard Tyrell's instructions to cut the patrol short.

Lance nodded toward the sun. "About another hour. Across Jack's Creek."

When we circled back to the road, all the Wolf Squad kept a good distance from the barricade. Our patrol would soon lead us off paved roads, and the way across Jack's Creek always made me nervous. As clumsy as I could be, I'd ended in the water three times over the years. Luckily, never during the winter.

Dirt roads cut north through an open area with few trees and an occasional rusted camper overgrown with vines. Jack's Creek was a wide river with a misleading name, which made it sound like an innocent trickle. The last section of our approach gave glimpses of the water and distant shore.

Long before the Sorrow, a dirt jetty had been built into the water with cutouts on each end. The water flowed heavier during this season than in the summer, unless it rained. The south edge had two massive trunks toppled over the running water from each side that formed a makeshift bridge. Lance trotted across it as if they were flat.

Selina gestured to Jordan and Yaz to follow. "Take it slow." She jabbed my shoulder with a finger. "You're next. Stay out of the water."

I scoffed. "Going to try." In truth, my chest tightened as I watched the two youngest take first one trunk down, and the next up, with carefree ease.

As I balanced on the log, Eric took a step downriver,

closer to the shore. My friends would get wet dragging my soggy butt out if I went in.

With each step, I took a moment for balance. The shotgun I held in my right hand at the stock just above the trigger, muzzle dangling toward the water. The water gurgled underneath me. No one spoke. The scent of growth and the reek of mucky shores mixed in chill air. A breeze flapped my cloak as I neared the bottom where the two trunks crossed. Water splashed onto the bark.

My right boot slid when I moved my left foot to the next tree. Roxie swore behind me. I managed to drop to my left knee and put my palm on the trunk rising toward Lance, while my muzzle dipped into the water below. "I'm good. I'm good," I promised to myself more than the others. Dragging my right boot back out, I stood.

Yaz watched me wide-eyed from the opposite shore while Jordan frowned with obvious disdain. When I made it up the next log and finally leaped off onto the incline of the jetty, I wanted to smack him.

As wide as a road, gravel and stones formed the slopes underwater while thick vegetation and trees had grown into the earthen barrier. The water from upriver splashed and eddied at the breaker. It had rained heavy enough once that it had all been inundated except for the tops of the brush and trees.

Eric nudged me as we walked a winding trail between groomed trunks. "You've still got your chance to swim on the way back."

"Thanks. Appreciate it."

"Maybe we could tie some rope to you."

I glanced at the shore ahead where it rose into bluffs. "That joke is getting old."

The next part of our passage across Jack's Creek utilized two stout trees, a metal cable, and a harness. I sucked at using it, but the harness kept me from falling in. Lance took my shotgun across for me when he went. This gap stretched wide and deep. Water rushed through, tugging along the shore in a strong current; otherwise, the rivers around Lake Marion were slow and lazy. I floundered, in danger only of Jordan's judgmental glare.

Patrols through this area were frequent enough that we had blazed trails to the bluffs above. Lance's posture changed, though, and he held his weapon ready. His sharp glances into the surrounding woods kept us all on alert. To our right, the bluffs dropped sharply to the river below. Ahead and on our left were thick woods. Selina positioned me at the rear and kept our youngest between herself and Roxie.

Eric spoke quietly over his shoulder to me. "Trying not to think of getting bitten?"

I shivered at the images of Talia's arm. "That's why we're out here hunting."

He snorted and slowed to walk alongside me. "They don't really expect us to kill anything. We're still training."

"I know." They never let us go out as far as the soldiers actually went. The only cryptids that came even that close were werewolves. At least, I'd never heard about the others, and they hadn't hung a winged Tuathua on our fence yet.

The woods ahead erupted into a flurrying shape of brown fur. Jordan yelled and slammed back into Roxie, causing her to stumble backward. Two deer leaped over brush, veering their path to lead them quickly away from us.

Roxie stumbled on a tree root. Eric and I both reacted to steady her, but I found my right foot betraying me. The misstep seemed only a shifting falter, then the earth began to crumble under my heel.

"Crap." I spun, my already outstretched left hand

flailing into Eric. As I felt my balance shift backward, the shotgun snagged into brush and slipped from my fingers.

Time slowed while I pivoted into a backward fall down the slope leading to the river. I stared at Eric's widening eyes as he tried to adjust, reaching for me instead of Roxie. My arms pinwheeled. In the canopy above, evergreens mixed with leafless branches from other trees, silhouettes against a blue sky. The view lasted far too long. It ended abruptly when my body slammed nearly upside down onto the steep slope.

Immediately, my legs lifted into a roll and all sense of any direction except down disappeared. I tumbled before I could grasp anything other than dried tufts of dead grass. My hips slammed into a trunk, and I twisted into an awkward spin. Dirt flew into my eyes. My machete and sheath bent under my thigh.

My eyes tried to open, blurred and scratchy. When my feet touched ground, I tried to right myself. The momentum catapulted the side of my head into a stiff branch, jerking my body sideways into the air.

In those seconds, I imagined my friends scurrying after me to carry away a broken body.

Our patrol would turn into me being carried back on a stretcher. My knees and hands drew toward my torso. All sense of direction faded.

Freezing water engulfed me.

Chapter Five

I gasped icy water into my lungs. Panic locked me in a frantic fit. My coughs were dull, surreal noises under water. I still had no sense of up until my flailing hand broke the surface.

Paddling hands and feet, I found sweet air. Gagging and coughing, I splashed in a current that spun me. I had to get back to shore. The cold would weaken my muscles, and I wouldn't be able to tread water. I'd drown.

My cloak untangled, floating half submerged behind me. I blinked and spared a quick swipe of my face to clear the sand and water from my eyelids. Through blurry vision, the shore seemed impossibly far away. The current swept me away from it.

Adjusting my paddles and kicks, the closer shore, where I'd likely fallen, came into my view. Movement at the top of the ridge didn't appear very high. The fall had seemed forever.

The current tugged at my cloak and pack as I shifted to see downriver. Gratefully, the shore jutted out ahead. The jetty to my left stretched back in the direction home. Unencumbered, and perhaps warmer, I would have swum for that side. Instead, I pounded my kicks and paddled for the closer bit of land. My cloak bunched under my left arm, I worked with the current.

I could make out the cable between the trees. They would see me and be running there. I lengthened my strokes, and freezing muscles ached with each movement. Panic began to rise as I shifted left, toward the opening in the jetty rather than in the direction I aimed.

The entire river, lazy in most places, had to exit either here or the smaller access on the other end. I dug into the water, pivoting to aim for the corner made by the truncated jetty. Overcompensating, I spun sideways to the opening and swam without gaining any ground.

My heart pounded in my ears, and I thrashed weakening muscles into the water. My hand brushed on some underwater grass, and I ceased swimming completely to kick my legs down for some purchase.

I sank underwater and when my toe did find something resembling a bottom, it slid through it like pudding. I'd just wasted any chance I had. Digging at the water, I fought to return to the surface.

The current spiked, suddenly forced into the tight opening. I broke the surface to see the cable nearly overhead. The dangling harness waited, hooked at the tree, seeming to mock me. The shore appeared so close, and I didn't give up, but the river was in control.

Relax, I told myself. *Focus.*

I swam sideways across the current and peered at the shore downstream. There were burned-out cabins at the end of Jack's Creek on this side, nearly opposite the marina with the graveyard.

The first rotted dock appeared as I was pushed through the opening in the jetty. My muscles burned, but I pounded at the water. The movement would heat my body for a little while. We were in the water every night during the summer. I could do this. Once they reached me, the Wolf Squad would heat me. I would have tried my own magic, but I couldn't expend any energy except to paddle and kick.

Despite everything, I expected to hear their voices. My ears had water in them, my heart thudded, and I splashed almost continuously. They would be running to find me. Except maybe the little prick, Jordan.

The sensation of the current releasing me made me grin. My strokes pulled me in the direction of the shore more easily, and I kept glancing to the rotted dock that promised to catch me if I didn't reach the shallows before it. Bones chilled to the core, I had to get out while I still could.

Each stroke brought the shore closer. The ground did not rise sharply like where I'd fallen, but inclined gradually to brush. The charred remains of buildings poked jagged remnants above the tan grass and plants. The dock tilted into the water, though it appeared sturdier where it leveled into the ground. There were lone rotting poles extending into the water, and a rowboat had been pulled ashore to rest in the tall grass. Perhaps it belonged to the two fishermen from earlier.

My foot tapped against underwater plants, but I swam without pause. Ignoring the bottom until I was a few yards from the shore, I tested a foot against yielding mud. The muck held a toe, and then the next. Exhausted, my body shivered as my shoulders rose from the water.

I stood knee deep in the river when the gunshot went off.

Stopping, I blinked. A second shot followed.

It was too close to be my unit. Even if they knew where I was, they'd have to run through the woods to get here. Besides, they would be coming more from my left than my right.

My chest hollowed as I searched the surrounding area. What if someone were shooting at me? Like an idiot, I'd paused long enough for them to finish me off. No one tried.

Unsure, I took another step forward. I needed to get out of the river and get warm, soon.

Ankle deep in the water, I heard a distant growl and froze. Too far away to be in the brush ahead of me, I imagined the two fishermen being attacked. My job was to protect. I'm sure Roxie could quote the regulation, but I took a long step, then another.

In a moment, I was running up the slope in the direction I'd heard the noise. Over my boots crunching through dried brush, there were closer growls, and some sounded human. Concern fought panic, and I wished desperately to have my weapon back.

I had magic; I'd trained for this, somewhat.

The incline ended at the edge of one of the burned-out houses.

Three mottled white wolves, werewolves, darted at a single man who brandished a long blade. One of the werewolves moved sluggishly with bloody fur down its side.

Wearing his familiar dark jacket, Dean swung a glancing slice at one of his attackers, forcing it back. I stepped forward. His right hand bled. A shotgun lay on the ground a few paces from him.

There were three cryptids, but trees encroached on the camp, close enough to hide others. They hadn't seen me yet.

One darted in and snapped at Dean's left calf. Another took advantage and leaped for a bite on his right forearm, worrying the jacket he wore. The third, the one with its side wet with blood, circled for Dean's back.

I couldn't think as my will called the otherness and it swarmed to my call. My magic reached out to the air around me, sensing the massive volume. In practice, I always knew the magic would be needed. I'd fretted on getting it right, staying focused. In this moment, all that I knew was the air, the wind it created, the man I protected, and the enemy werewolves. Focus controlled me for one surging moment.

Wind rushed across the brush, gales ripping at leaves and branches. Three tight streams smashed into the werewolves. Their bodies flew as though swatted by an invisible hand. Yelping and howling, they launched unexpectedly far; one into a blackened house, another into the brush far at the back, and the last into the trees, slapping against a trunk and limbs, toppling out of control.

Dean had dropped his knife and scrambled for it, glancing back at me with a double take. His grimace faded, and he barked a laugh.

He'd been bitten.

I knew what the regulations would call for, even without Roxie here to remind me.

The werewolves weren't returning; I heard one scampering away. My unit would be here soon. They had to have heard the shots as well.

"I'll heal you," I said, more to myself than Dean who didn't seem to hear. Hesitantly, I stepped toward him.

He studied the woods, then his arm. "I hate wolves." Blood flowed from a bite near his thumb, and the other side near his pinkie.

"Let me heal you." I spoke louder, only a few steps away.

"No cure. They killed my father outright. I hate wolves." He laughed, still studying his hand.

"I can try." I slowed, two steps away. "Before you're infected and turn. Has anyone tried?"

He finally lifted his head, locking eyes with me. "Nothing is easy." Dean shrugged. "Never give up, right?"

I sighed in relief. "Lie down." Healing required contact, but not with the injured area specifically.

Acting as if he were dealing with the removal of a splinter, he studied the forest as he eased himself down. "You're Caitlyn, right?"

Flushing, I knelt beside him. This was no time to think of him as anything but a wounded patient; one who might become deadly in the next day if what I tried didn't work. One who would be dead if my unit caught us. "Yes. Shh." Unsure, I placed my right hand on his neck and my left on his forehead. His eyes were deep brown and his nose wider at this angle.

I shut my eyes, pulling the otherness to me. Healing used everything. Air, heat, electricity, and water magic embraced singular elements, adding, moving, or removing them. Bonds were reconnected and sometimes broken. Usually, it didn't require as much effort as other magic.

Healing, or its converse, destruction, required an intuition, and it came easily to me. I felt his body living in all its millions of parts. The connections in structure were obvious. The wound on his hand sang loudest, so I pushed elements back where they belonged. The small effort drew away some of my energy, already sagging after nearly drowning.

Next his bruises on his forearm and calf rang dully, so I moved and adjusted. I leaned into him.

The seething mass of his blood shrieked tiny screams, and I found the infection. The wrongness baffled my magic. I tried and felt shifts as elements boiled and steamed. Energy drained from me with the effort. Dean stiffened under my fingers. "I'm sorry," I whispered. Bones often hurt, but this was deeper.

My body sagged, and the chill cut deep inside. I felt elements inside Dean's blood shatter and rebuild. Growing, foreign bonds had to be broken. Elements were connected which shouldn't be, and they fought me. My own muscles ached to shiver, but barely managed a shudder.

The infection had changed from how I'd first found it, but still the blood was not right. It begged me for more. My ears rang.

Dean shoved me upright. I'd slumped head first over him. "Hey, wake up."

Rocking back on my knees, I couldn't focus on his face. "I don't know. .." Had I healed him?

"Is that your unit?" he asked me.

It seemed a strange question, then I heard Eric calling me. "Caitlyn?"

I smiled, happy that they'd found me. They'd have to carry me. It took more strength than I had to sit beside Dean. Blood still covered his right hand, but underneath I'd barely left a scar.

Sucking in a sharp breath, I focused on him. Sheathing his knife, he'd risen to one knee to study me. The expression of concern was for me. He'd been the one bitten by a werewolf.

Roxie called out, closer than Eric had been.

"They'll kill you," I said.

"Probably." He cocked his head. "You going to be okay if I leave?"

"Run. Hide." I nodded, and the world spun.

"Well, now I feel like a coward. I should stay and fight them." He grinned as he stood. "Thank you. If it worked, I'll let you know. If it didn't. .." Dean moved past me and I heard him retrieve his shotgun. "Thanks. I feel damned good, considering."

Selina yelled my name. They were nearby. I wanted to crash to the ground and sleep, but they might not find me. I would never make it back alone. The werewolves might come back. I pushed a hand against the ground. Dean's blood had soaked into the soil and dried grass. With an effort, I got to one foot, then wobbled into a shaky stance.

I couldn't let them find Dean's blood. Stumbling, I moved in the direction I'd heard Eric's voice.

Dean had disappeared, as promised. What if he turned and killed someone in the town? My healing had done something, but was it enough?

I shivered in freezing wet clothes.

What had I done?

Chapter Six

I shuddered, lifting leaden, numb feet to take steps. Dead vines wove over the charred husks of buildings. My pulse beat slowly but filled my ears. I wanted to hear Eric or Roxie's voice.

A muffled sound reminded me of being underwater. My feet weren't moving at all. Dirt covered my palms, and twigs bit into my skin. Gray swallowed me, and it seemed an appropriate time to sleep.

I dreamed of being home with my sister, Marjorie. We nestled in the quilt Grandma had made for us. Someone had let the stove get too hot, and I needed to get out from under the covers. I pulled at them, but Marjorie held them tight.

"Wait, not yet," she said. Her voice sounded odd, like she'd grown up.

I yanked again, and Selina spoke. "Stay still, dammit."

"Yes, sir." My eyes were dry and scratchy, but they opened to silhouettes against a blue sky.

Selina held my coveralls in front of herself, focused on something. Eric and Yaz knelt at my head, peering at my face. "She's awake." Eric sounded relieved.

I tried to sit up.

"Not yet." Roxie cuddled against me, smiling when I turned to look at her. "I've got you toasty warm, but we need to keep you that way for a bit longer." We had two cloaks draped over us.

Roxie could use her heat magic with better control than I did air.

"You're heating me," I said. The memory of Dean almost had me bolt upright. I couldn't tell them. "There's werewolves."

Her smile disappeared.

The soldier, Lance, came into view over me. "Who fired the gun?"

"I don't know," I lied. "Truly. I found three werewolves. I blew them — away."

Selina folded my coveralls over her arm, glancing around us. "Roxie, that's all the time we've got. Get her dressed." She dangled my clothes toward us.

I couldn't stand lying to my friends, but they wouldn't understand. Not that I could explain why I'd tried to heal Dean or covered for him. Worst would be reporting to Tyrell. He could be so intense.

Roxie's heat faded and I shivered, cold to the bone and exhausted.

Eric leaned in, his eyes locked on mine. "My turn." His healing magic rivaled mine. He placed his hands on my cheeks and closed his eyes.

The cloaks came off as Roxie rose and freezing air brought goosebumps along my legs. Eric blocked my full view, but Yaz had moved away, and I guessed she helped Roxie put on my socks since the warm coziness wrapped each foot at the same time. Hopefully Jordan was polite enough to not gawk at me in my underwear.

I breathed deeply as Eric worked on me. Healing could

be used to regenerate energy, but that worked slowly. With werewolves nearby, our patrol would be heading back to report. Technically, that was our job: find cryptids and report. Many of the units bragged that they'd be the first to bring back a kill. I'd seen multiple cryptids in the past two days and didn't feel good about it. *And now Dean*, I thought. Even as I pulled toasty warm coveralls over my legs, I shivered. I didn't sense the healing, like when a tear in the skin itched. However, my mind had become less foggy.

Eric had to let go of me when they had my arms in the coveralls and needed me to lean upright. At my feet, Jordan stood a pace away, almost grinning.

"Sit up," said Selina, holding out my boots. They were mostly dry, though cold.

Lance stood tense, studying the surrounding forest.

"Where did the wolves attack you?" Selina asked.

I raised my hand, almost pointing where Dean had been. They couldn't find his blood. Wavering, I gestured to the left of Jordan, closer to the dock where I'd climbed out of the water. "Over there. I'd just come out of the water."

Flicking his eyes toward the area, Lance frowned. Selina studied me. I worked on my boots, keeping my eyes on my hands.

When Roxie helped me to my feet, I swayed slightly as the world spun. Despite Eric's magical healing, my thighs burned and I yearned to sleep. Yaz handed me my belt with a welcome canteen and a bent machete.

My shotgun hung from a loop on Lance's pack. Weapons were a precious commodity since most had been manufactured long before or during the first few years of the Sorrow, before the world collapsed.

Eric forced my right arm over his shoulder. "Can you walk?"

I staggered forward. Leaning on him did help. "Easy. We should jog."

He snorted. "I'm waiting to see how you handle the logs on the far side of the jetty."

I groaned.

After I'd crossed the jetty in my harness, I worked on my second refill of my canteen and felt much better. I crossed the dual logs safely, despite sore muscles. We stopped for our sandwiches at the shore, and food helped. The hardest part came with questions from Selina as Lance listened.

"How far out of the water were you when you saw the werewolves?" She studied me with such a tight face that I had to remind myself we were friends before she'd become unit leader.

"It's fuzzy, but I think a few steps." I'd have to remember all this for my report to Tyrell. I hated lying to her.

"You didn't see anyone firing the gun?"

I shook my head, taking a bite to stall my answer. "I was in the water." My lie sounded guilty or embarrassed. Splashing wouldn't cover the sound of gunshots, and denying they happened wouldn't matter. The Wolf Squad had heard it. "I thought maybe it was one of you, signaling me."

"How far away were you from the wolves?" Selina had stopped eating, focused on her questions.

Eric and Roxie barely glanced at me. From their reactions, they had to guess I was uncomfortable.

I laughed. "Not far enough." Pushing my guilt aside, I lied more casually. "The cold freaked me out. I thought I would die for being such a clumsy idiot. When I got out, all I could think about was getting warm. You know, before hypothermia. I saw three mottled wolf shapes, decided they were werewolves, and blasted them. I had to be pretty scared because I tossed them a dozen yards at least." I took a breath, rolled my eyes up as if trying to remember. "I'd guess the closest was ten yards away. They'd just started to move toward me, not even running. You know they hate water."

Selina had taken a bite out her sandwich during my long, rambling explanation. Her hurried demeanor had me thinking she had more questions.

"I don't remember much past that. I knew I had to find you all, or I'd still die. Did I yell out or anything?"

Roxie shook her head. "Lance saw you standing for a moment. You were on the ground when we got there."

"Did you see the werewolves?" I took another bite, flicking glances between Roxie and Eric. If they started talking, maybe I could avoid getting nailed down on specifics by Selina. Manipulating my friends made the sandwich difficult to swallow.

Eric snorted. "If we'd seen werewolves, we'd likely have left you behind." His smirk told me he'd do anything but abandon me. "I was worried someone had shot you. We were trying to search the shore. Thought you might be smart enough not to go for a long swim."

I managed to avoid any more questions from Selina before we packed, refilled our canteens, and headed back toward Camp Sparta earlier than they expected us. Dean would be hiding somewhere by now. In a few hours, he might become the enemy, a cryptid. He wouldn't transform right away unless his emotions triggered him. By then, he'd be contagious. I could hope that my healing worked, but it had felt too off, too wrong. If I saw him again, I'd need to be careful. He might be gone forever at this point, like Talia. Tyrell wouldn't likely inform us about what they did with her. They treated us like children, not the soldiers they wanted us to be.

Hours later, as we walked the last bit of the road to the camp, I dreaded every step. I never had been very good at lying. The scientists at the lab always caught me. I'd held my ground about the tech, but they'd known all along.

I'd gotten better at avoiding the truth by the time Tyrell brought us to Camp Sparta, and Selina helped. She'd been a master at it when we met.

I couldn't trust her with the truth now. We'd grown apart over the past couple of years. Her focus had become leadership while I just wanted to have a little fun amid a very broken world.

Eric bumped shoulders with me. "Tired?" he asked.

That was as good as an excuse for my mood as any. "Exhausted."

Roxie slipped to my other side. "Do you think this is good experience?" she asked.

I blinked and nearly stumbled, then realized what she was mulling over. "No. It was a horrible experience."

She sighed and rolled her eyes. "You know, for promotion. I need to be promoted before Toni comes back and gets a new unit."

We'd had this conversation nearly every day since the last inspection. Eric faked a pitiful tone. "You'd split us up?"

"I could ask to keep you."

"As minions," I said. Neither Eric nor I wanted any real command. We'd talked and both preferred splitting off with Roxie, if she didn't get all stiff like Selina had.

"Henchmen," Eric countered.

"Underlings," I said.

"Lackeys."

I smiled. "Our new unit name, boot-licking lackeys."

From where she walked ahead of us, Selina turned her

head back, eyebrow raised, but with a smile at the edge of her lips. "You know I can hear you, traitors?"

"Defectors," said Eric before giggling.

The four of us broke into a laugh, and for one moment it felt like we were our old gang again. It faded when the guards at the gate ahead waved at us. I'd lied to my friends, and would continue to do so, just to protect someone I didn't even know. Dean needed a chance to survive, even if he did return someday in the shape of a mottled white wolf to be hung on the fence as a futile warning to other cryptids.

My chest tightened. "I hope you get the promotion, Roxie."

I really hoped my healing had worked and Dean would not turn.

I prayed I could lie to Tyrell.

Chapter Seven

The sun still high in the afternoon sky, I held my breath as I walked through the gate so as not to breathe the lingering stench from the rotting werewolf corpses. Nervous, I fumbled with my nearly empty canteen and drenched my parched mouth. I imagined Tyrell waiting for me in his office. Where had Dean gone?

"Don't be nervous." Selina had dropped back to walk alongside me.

"Can I be embarrassed?" I shot her a glance, trying to joke, but my face felt tight. "Hey, thought I'd take a swim. You'll never guess what I found."

"This is a serious report. Don't try to make light of it." She focused on Tyrell's door in the center of the headquarters. "Especially not after yesterday."

Lance had remained in front of us, perhaps as an escort in case I decided to run or to make his report first. The latter proved the case as he motioned for the Wolf Squad to wait on the walkway before he knocked. He stepped inside and closed the door behind him.

"I'm too clumsy to be a soldier," I said.

Selina's gaze remained on the door. "Not your choice." She was right. When had I ever truly had a choice?

"Maybe when they have enough soldiers, I can just be a medic."

She snorted. "Should have thought of that before you sent three werewolves packing. You might get a promotion or at least recognition."

"Swim team participation award?" I started to shift on my feet. The urge to sleep still hung in my body, but my mind raced at the thought of lying. I'd lied to my friends, so I certainly wasn't about to tell Tyrell the truth about Dean.

"Hilarious. I'm serious. When the army comes out for their inspection of the camp, they'll have already read the reports."

We had almost two weeks before the monthly inspection. "Maybe they'll forget." They wouldn't. I did want to be a senior, just to stay with my friends, but not get a command position like Roxie wanted. She could have it.

I jumped when the door opened. "Both of you," Lance said.

Selina led the way, and Eric patted my shoulder as I followed. He offered me encouragement while I'd lied to him. I might have possibly loosed a danger on the town of Santee as well. Apprehension was slowly losing out to shame.

Lance stayed outside.

Tyrell rolled a map on the table, his back to us. The faint smell of cooked chicken hung in the air. "Grab seats. Thirsty?"

"Yeah," I answered.

Selina offered me a sharp glance. "No, sir." She pointed me toward a chair.

"Yes, sir." I corrected my response, but her frown didn't ease.

The hard, wooden chair felt luxurious, even with my pack on. Tyrell smiled, a warmer smile than I'd seen yesterday, as he headed off with the rolled map to his desk. The remodeling of the two apartments into one office had left a kitchen alcove with a counter and cabinets. He strolled casually toward the area, not turning toward us. "Rough day, I hear. How are you feeling, Caitlyn?"

I would have relaxed, but our conversations with Tyrell hadn't been this casual since the early days of Camp Sparta when Selina and I boarded at what eventually became the school for younger students. Back then there were fewer Youth Guard, and the military weren't as meshed into our daily lives. His demeanor made me nervous.

"Tired, I guess." Even if I hadn't tried to heal Dean, they'd expect me to be worn out from nearly drowning and fighting the werewolves. "Sir."

Tyrell grabbed two corked bottles which had once held soda, a mysterious concoction which bubbled, according to rumors. As students, it had been our job to wash them, fill them, and cork them for the camp's officers. He brought me one, then settled in his own chair. "Sorry to hear about your mishap in the river. I'm glad you survived. You've got a good unit backing you. So, tell me about the werewolves; and these gunshots."

I was happy to focus on the cork and bottle to avoid his eyes. "The gun — I barely heard. It seemed pretty far off, but I was still in the water. Just about to climb out. Close, at least." My tongue didn't seem to moisten, even with a sip. "I got out of the water, took a few steps, and realized there were three werewolves coming toward me. I didn't even think about it. I was surprised at how hard I hit them." That bit was true. I had decent control with wind, but three targeted strikes and throwing them for a fair distance was nothing like what I'd accomplished in training.

"You had just gotten out of the water?" Tyrell asked. "Do you remember where along the shore?"

"That's all pretty fuzzy. I was panicked about drowning. My thoughts were about the cold and how I could avoid — well, dying of hypothermia." I'd nearly drained the bottle. Shrugging, I glanced up.

He hadn't touched his water, just uncorked it. "I can imagine. You can bring heat, though, with your magic."

I chuckled. "Pretty badly. I'd as likely set myself on fire as warm up. I would have tried it if I didn't think the Wolf Squad were close."

Tyrell nodded, taking a sip and leaving a long pause in the room. "So, from the shore you see three werewolves. They're low, in the brush. How close did they get before you saw them?"

"A few yards." I felt a chill creep up my back. Did he not believe me? "I didn't get bit."

"I'll still have you checked out." He eyed Selina. "Brush pretty clear along the river? How far along the incline could she see from the shore?"

"If I were to guess, five to seven yards, sir." Selina kept an emotionless tone, but her phrasing told me she didn't want to commit.

Tyrell drew in a deep breath. "I'm going to temporarily suspend Youth Guard on outer patrols."

"Yes, sir."

"Anything else to report at this time, Selina?"

She sat stiff and unwavering. "No, sir."

Did Tyrell expect her to come back later when I wasn't here? My mouth was still dry and my stomach had started to flutter.

"You're dismissed, Senior. Spread the word to the other unit leaders that we're canceling at least tomorrow's outer patrol, and I'll let them know when to resume."

Selina stood smoothly. "Yes, sir."

I tensed as she was allowed to leave. What more did Tyrell have to ask me? He couldn't know about Dean, unless someone had seen us. Lance would have asked me there on the spot; instead, he'd asked if I'd seen who fired the gun.

"We need to get you over to the clinic. Twice in two days; you're having a rough week, aren't you?"

I nodded, swallowing. "Yeah. I'm beat."

"You'll have the afternoon off to rest. Gayle can get with you tomorrow."

"Gayle Simmons, the instructor? What does she want?" I relaxed as we moved off the topic of the werewolves.

"A drawing of this Moonjir cryptid. She'll work with you." Tyrell corked his bottle. "We may have some others coming out to interview you about the sighting. The ability to resist air is troublesome. From the dust and leaf patterns, you managed enough wind to knock something back. Especially considering the size you described."

Dust and leaf patterns? Had Tyrell gone out there himself? "Well, it wasn't a very strong wind, and I was scared."

"Strong enough. Today's encounter with three werewolves proves that. You've been given a gift."

More like cursed, I thought. I would have rather had the childhood my mother had, or Grandpa Patrick's. Most people hated us for our abilities and somehow blamed us for the Sorrow — and the cryptids. "That's exactly what I thought when they took me to the labs." I started, realizing how sarcastic and bitter I'd sounded. Those types of reactions were not acceptable at Camp Sparta.

Tyrell's face tightened. "The witch riots were unavoidable. A lot of children were killed, even those without magic. Getting you out of that saved your life and others."

I didn't remember the riots, but I did remember the panic on my mother's face as she held my sister Marjorie while the soldiers took me. Grandpa had yelled at them from outside our bedroom, then he had become quiet. The soldier who had broken the door had pointed his rifle at me. It had been my fault. I'd blown leaves at Ricky next door.

"I know." I forced a weak smile, since Tyrell had been the one to free me from the lab. Maybe he didn't know that I would have died there like so many others.

"It's okay." He didn't stand, but he shifted, and I knew my reporting was nearly done. "I've sent Lance back with a full patrol. We can hope that you injured one or more of the werewolves. They heal quickly, but they're just as killable as any other wolf."

I nodded as a chill tightened my shoulders. "Okay." Dean had to have gotten away by now. Lance and the other soldiers would find his blood. What if he headed back to his house?

Would they know I was lying? "I wish I could have been clearer, about all this. I'm so tired, and I'm afraid I panicked when I thought I would drown." They'd studied the dust and leaves around the shed where Moonjir had been. I wanted to roll into a ball. What if they did find Dean, and he told them the truth?

Tyrell stood. "Keep this incident within your unit, for now. Get some rest. Maybe you'll remember something else." I couldn't sense any emotion in his tone. "Send in the next in your team, then head over to the clinic."

I wanted to tremble and cry, but I stood. "Yes, sir." Stumbling on my first step, I caught myself and strode to the door trying not to appear like I was escaping.

Roxie and Eric eyed me as I exited and closed the door behind me. "I've got to go to the clinic," I said. "One of you goes next."

"I'll go." Roxie straightened. "You okay?"

"I just want to sleep." I wanted to know if Dean had escaped and if so, where he had gone. I hoped it wasn't back to town, but where else could he go? I'd been foolish trying to heal him. No one had ever found a cure that I knew of. Surely, they wouldn't let people like Talia die if they had another option.

Roxie passed me going into Tyrell's office.

Wearing a frown, Eric studied me. "You look worried."

I flashed a smile and said, "Sleeep," exaggerating the word into a long moan. Before he could question me more, I turned toward the other buildings and headed for the clinic. "Thanks for not leaving me out there."

I thought of the instructor, Gayle. She'd always been detached and cold, but she knew a lot about cryptids. I could poke around about werewolf cures while I described Moonjir. The incident with Talia would be an easy cover. *That's cold.* I really did need some rest.

When I stepped inside the clinic, my thoughts immediately went to Talia, but she was gone. Had I expected her to be chained to some table? They'd likely moved her while we were on patrol, or they'd killed her. As the woman called me back, I couldn't help but search for some sign of Talia's plight, but the room appeared the same as it always did.

My exam was about as exciting as the day prior. When I exited the clinic, the shadows were stretched from the building nearly to the pool and the latrines. Ben, from the Hounds unit, passed as I opened the door. His step faltered as he recognized me. His mouth opened, as if he might say something. Oddly, he hurried on his way without any word.

"Hi." My tone slightly sarcastic, I wondered why he had acted weird.

He didn't turn when he spoke. "Hey." His pace quickened and I followed slowly.

Written over their mess hall, the student building had some of the same mottoes our Youth Guard quarters did: "Courage and Discipline" and "Strong of Mind and Body, Void of Avarice." The rooms and balconies were quiet; they'd be at the school, learning about cryptids and the dangers they posed.

As I passed between buildings, two members of the Rose Buds on the second-floor whispered, and as I continued under the balcony, they laughed. Between Ben's hasty avoidance and their snickers, I had to wonder what they knew. Was it my clumsy fall into the river? That wouldn't be a surprise to anyone who knew me. Had word of Moonjir gotten out?

I glanced at the guards at the gate a good distance away, and it appeared they watched me. It was irrational, but I couldn't shake the fear they knew about Dean; and that I'd betrayed Camp Sparta. I turned, studying the building rather than anyone who might lock eyes with me and guess the truth.

The mottoes on the Youth Guard barracks included "Youth Guard Against the Sorrow" and "Gifted by God Against the Cryptids." Even my own Wolf Squad would believe I'd failed the latter motto, if they knew. I would have to continue lying to them. They could never know.

With his scraggly almost-mustache, Ben raced up the stairwell and had made it to the third floor before I walked the stretch between buildings. Because our residence angled sharply toward the river, the sidewalk here was the longest.

South, on the far lawn ahead, one of three Youth Guards blasted at a target with air, sending a heavy bag of sand flying off a pillar. Eric and I practiced at that station nearly every day. Healing practice we did weekly behind the clinic, and we both enjoyed those far more. Sometimes we knitted chicken bones back together or a slice in its flesh; other times we'd have a live volunteer with a scratch. The soldiers didn't trust us. They only came when their officers forced them.

Would we have been able to save Dean if we'd tried together? I couldn't even discuss the idea.

From a roaring splash by the river, others were practicing their water magic.

Out of habit, I passed the stairwell to our rooms and entered our mess hall on the bottom floor to refill my canteen.

Three members of the Cryptdead unit sat at a table, eating and talking until they recognized me. I waved before I felt the awkward silence creep into the room. They nodded solemnly and watched my quickening march for the water pail. I could feel their silent stares as I put my canteen under the spigot. When I turned the tap at the base of the bucket, water splashed on my hand. Their intense study of me wore away the last of my patience.

Leslie had been from Wolf Squad but moved over to lead the new unit when the Cryptdeads were formed. She had the longest braid in camp and always let her black hair dangle over her shoulder.

"What is it, Leslie?" I asked in a less than delicate tone.

Her posture stiffened. "I'd have thought you'd had your fill of water today." Her posse chuckled, encouraging her. "Or did you see a pink cryptid and join it for a swim?"

More water spilled as I closed the tap. "I stumbled on a rock. You know how clumsy I am." I turned, capping my canteen. "Amazing likeness."

Her face screwed into a confused expression. "Likeness to what?"

Smiling, I started for the door. "Your face." I tapped my

upper lip. "The rock had a little moss right above the mouth."

Leslie had an obsession over her facial hair. It really wasn't that bad. I normally wouldn't have hit so low, but I was tired and a little angry. Her reaction was satisfying. "Wacky bitch."

I didn't respond and closed the door as I left. She couldn't know it, but I preferred her questioning my sanity rather than my loyalty. Plodding up the stairs, I heard one of the military's motorcycles chugging into the compound. I paused at the second-floor balcony and walked to the end where I could see it. They used vehicles, or the biofuel that powered them, sparingly. Tyrell met the man on the dried out winter lawn. I slid back so I could watch without being easily seen.

They might be sending a report back to Savannah, one where I played a prominent part. If so, the motorcycle would leave through the southern gate and head toward town.

Instead, the rider left through the north gate, back toward the military base. My throat thickened. They were going to search the area where I'd tried to heal Dean. They'd find his blood.

Chapter Eight

My heart pounded as I entered our quarters. I paced a circle in the sparse living room then into my bedroom as I removed my pack, canteen, and clothes. A soggy pack should have been my first concern, but Tyrell would have a new report soon. Maybe it would be too dark by the time the soldiers reached the place where the werewolves had attacked.

I scattered clothes around my room before finding fresh ones to put on. Tyrell could come back with more questions about blood, but I'd just play stupid. He couldn't know who had been attacked, or when.

Where *was* Dean?

Our uniforms, coveralls buttoned down the back, had small insignias of our Wolf Squad unit above our names. I had two sets with my name and a single lightning bolt stripe indicating my cadet rank. After buttoning the coveralls nearly closed, I climbed inside before reaching behind my shoulder to finish. My feet were wrinkled, and I appreciated putting on clean socks. The familiar ritual of dressing had eased my mood for a moment, but it darkened quickly without a task ahead of me.

I killed a few minutes brushing my hair and tossing out random blonde strands. Braiding it took no time at all.

"Now what?" I asked myself. With a sigh, I marched out of my bedroom. I needed to do something to fix this.

The living room echoed my steps as I pushed away a mild panic with a lap around the two wooden chairs, the only furniture in the room. Roxie had a stained poster tacked on one wall with a sad-eyed woman whose blue hair draped over half her face and an angry woman behind her with red hair and a matching jacket. The picture was the most colorful thing in our quarters.

By the time Roxie arrived, I'd worked myself into a mild frenzy.

Her even tone contrasted my mood. "Tyrell wants us to keep the news of the werewolves to ourselves, considering Talia's encounter." She peeled off her pack as she entered. The contents of mine were scattered across the counter of what had once been a kitchen before the Sorrow. She raised her eyebrows at the sight. "Everything soaked?"

I bobbed my head in a nod, forcing myself to lean on the wall to stop pacing. "Yep. I was going to let it dry overnight."

She dropped her pack in the living room and pointed to the iron tubing at the back wall. "Maybe put the worst by the radiator? They should turn on the furnace tonight."

"Good idea." The radiator pipes had been installed three winters ago, keeping the winter's freezing temperatures bearable. I jumped to take her advice, more to keep active than over any worry of my equipment.

Roxie peered at me. "I expected you to be crashed out when I got here. Tyrell took forever with Eric."

My heart fluttered, but no one knew about Dean. "I can't sleep. I was thinking maybe we can go into town and see what Buck and the others are doing." What if Dean had gone home? Would he risk his family like that?

"Sure, if you're up for it. After dinner mess?"

I froze, my back to her. Leslie's comments would not be the only ones I'd have to endure. My guilt made it difficult to accept. Maybe in a day or two I'd be more comfortable. "I'm not sure I want to go there. Maybe sneak me out a bite?"

"Somebody say something?" Roxie's tone grew hard. She had a protective streak, and comments had likely already been made around her.

"Just some bullshit. I'm not in the mood." I focused on placing my wad of gauze below the pipe. The thread in my sewing kit was damp.

I hadn't realized how silent I'd been until Roxie spoke again. "What happened? Really." Her voice was calm and even, but I knew she meant the incident on the shore where I'd hid what happened with the werewolves — and Dean. She knew me too well.

My hands trembled slightly. "I. .." My lie died on my lips and I studied the line of equipment along the wall before I spoke. "What if I did something I shouldn't — something against regulations? Would you report me?"

"I should." Roxie's tone was pained.

I swiveled to sit on the floor facing her. "Would you?" She'd kept secrets before, even about things which she should tell Tyrell. We both had.

She knelt a few feet away from me, hands on her knees. I loved her warm eyes and smile, wrapped with her brown skin; I'd been infatuated with her last winter. We were back to being friends, and Roxie had Selina now. I didn't regret our short infatuation or her move to someone else, but it had left something awkward between us.

Roxie shook her head slowly. "I won't tell, if it bothers

you this much. What happened? I promise to keep it between us."

"You're going to want to report."

"I'll punch you instead." She smiled, but she might.

The truth spilled out, sentences rolling over each other. "The local, Dean, he was the one who fired the gun. The werewolves had bitten him. I did blast them, but then I tried to heal him."

She stiffened and her tone was quick and harsh. "Jeez, Caitlyn. You've got to tell Tyrell. What if. .." Both of her hands raised as if to emphasize her words, then she stopped, her eyes flicking between mine. "You know what might happen."

"I'm worried, but the healing might have worked. It was so weird, and I could feel how wrong it was. If Eric had been there. .."

"He would have been smart enough to run. What if Dean went home to his family? The town could be at risk. You can't *not* tell anyone."

I curled in on myself. "We can check his house."

Her head lifted. "That's why you want to go into town and why you can't sleep." Roxie's lips tightened. "If he's there, we tell Tyrell."

I stared at the floor between us. Could I? "No. Only if Dean won't go somewhere away from town. I'll give him a choice."

She groaned. "He's not a stray tabby."

I winced at the memory. We'd hidden the kitten in our quarters for three months before Tyrell found out. I suspected Selina had told on us. "You'll help, then?" I glanced to find her glaring at me.

"Why would you?" She put her palms out, as if to stop me from responding, then closed her eyes. "Of course, you would try to heal someone who's been bitten. Have you told Eric?"

I drew in a deep breath. "No, but I will now. He won't repeat it."

"From me, you needed a blood oath."

"You follow the rules."

Roxie stood, scowling. "Obviously not with you around." She stalked off to her room, mumbling.

Despite my friend's complaints, the weight had eased off my shoulders, and I managed a light grin as I rose from the floor. I still wasn't going to the mess hall to deal with the rumors, though. Eric would grab me food.

I fidgeted and paced even as Roxie stomped out to go eat.

"See if Eric can bring me something."

She acted as if she ignored my request, opening the door without a response.

"Please. I'll explain everything to him then."

The door closed crisply behind her, but didn't slam. I'd nearly gotten hungry enough to suffer the judgmental eyes, but I'd wait until I resolved the issue with Dean before I faced the other Youth Guards. The most uncomfortable part was that I wanted him to survive, even if I hadn't healed him. My feelings went against everything I'd been trained for. They weren't about him being cute and suave, or his black jacket; I felt as bad for Talia.

I shook my head to clear the image of him bleeding in the grass with his jacket torn. My meandering took me to the kitchen, which we used for our boots. I'd left my soaked cloak in the sink. The beret had been lost to the river. Before we'd ever moved in, equipment had been scavenged, leaving gaps under and between the counters. Before the Sorrow there had been electric, gas, and water available inside buildings. The labs had those things, but the camp didn't, and I had never heard of anyone having even water. We weren't even supposed to use the drains. I tried to imagine life before the Sorrow, before the cryptids, before people like my father just disappeared, faded in front of people's eyes, and before kids like me started making weird things happen.

When Eric arrived, he carried an open plate of chicken, beans, and potato. Someone had given permission to take food out of the hall. He studied me as he handed over dinner. Roxie followed him with a pinched expression and arms crossed over her chest. She'd obviously alerted him to some level of my news.

"Roxie said you needed to tell me something."

Fretting in our little apartment, I'd grown famished and stabbed a piece of grilled potato as I headed for one of our chairs. "I lied to everyone. I had to." Seasoned with onion and garlic, the food went down after barely being chewed. "I'm sorry."

Eric sat on the floor. "Is this about the gunshot?"

I paused, my second bite of potato dangling in front of my mouth. "That's where it started." After eating another mouthful, I placed my fork on the plate and lowered them to my lap. His brow wrinkled, and he took a deep breath while I chewed. "Sorry. Starving. It was Dean, from town. He shot one of the werewolves, but they had him."

"Bitten?"

I nodded. "I did blow them away with air magic, but then I tried to heal the infection out of him. That's why I was so exhausted — well, and the river and all that."

"Did the healing work?" Eric sounded curious.

"I don't know. I fought against the infection. I could feel it. I wish you'd been there; maybe together we'd have been sure."

"You let him go." Eric's comment wasn't judgmental or

disapproving. His tone made me believe he would have tried to save Dean, and possibly release him as well.

"And lied to you all. I'm sorry."

Eric shook his head lightly. "I understand. You're telling us now."

I hadn't planned to speak of what I'd done to anyone. "I want to eat and go into town. We can find out where he lives — lived, and make sure he isn't there. If he's going to incubate, it won't be until later. He can't stay in town."

"You think he'd go home and risk everyone?" Eric frowned.

I shrugged and lifted my fork. "I feel responsible. Shouldn't I make sure he doesn't, since I set him free?"

Roxie hadn't said a word until now. "Bit late to start thinking." It was the sort of comment we might make with each other as a joke, but her frustration and my guilt made it sharper. She glanced away, as if realizing that it hurt. "Eat. We'll hunt down the locals. We know Buck lives at the hotels with his family."

Many of Santee's surviving inhabitants had moved from the outer areas to a group of hotels in the center of town.

"Thank you." I began shoveling down my meal.

My hopes were that Dean hadn't returned, but that would leave his family worrying. I couldn't tell them anything. He might not even have anyone left. I knew nothing about him, but he had seemed self-confident and capable. If I was honest, part of me did want to see him to know if he was okay.

We grabbed canteens and machetes for our walk, and I had a knitted black cap that I used for winter nights. I touched the wet cloak, but discarded the idea of wearing it.

"You need to return that," Roxie said.

There was a limited number of warm cloaks, used

primarily for outer patrols during cooler weather. I grabbed it and bundled it into a wad. "Sort of forgot."

Eric gave Roxie a frustrated glance. "Give it to me. There will still be people in the mess."

I didn't want to see any of them, so I handed the bundle over gratefully. "Thanks."

The temperature had dropped, and a couple stars braved the gray twilight. Voices sounded below us with the usual evening chatter. I stiffened but followed Roxie to the stairwell. Two Youth Guards headed for the row of latrines, and a single soldier from the military camp watched the south gate. Trailing behind my friends on the steps, I cringed at the sight of Ben and two others from the Hounds unit standing outside the mess door.

Their conversation stopped as they spotted me in the darkness. Eric strode toward them. "Hey." He pulled their attention, and they mumbled responses.

Roxie and I exited the stairwell and headed in a slow pace for the gate. Grateful for my friends, I let out a breath.

"It'll be old news in a day." Roxie glanced back at the second-floor balcony.

"Are you looking for Selina?" I asked.

She nodded. "She might still be with Tyrell."

My pulse quickened. "Why?"

"He wanted a more detailed report." Her eyes dropped to mine. "It did all seem a bit strange. Now I know why."

"What do you think he believes happened?" I asked.

Her eyebrows raised. "I doubt he suspects that you tried to heal someone bitten by a werewolf, but he might think you saw more than you're telling." She raised her chin. "It's not too late to come clean and keep us all from digging the hole deeper."

Eric's footsteps jogged to us from behind. In silence, we walked the last few yards to the soldier waiting at the gate.

The rot of the werewolves wafted in the crisp night air. Voices from the barracks faded, and only our footsteps sounded as the guard moved to unlatch the gate. His eyes were focused on me, ignoring the others.

"Thanks," Eric said.

The man barely grunted in recognition, and the gate clattered closed behind us. Bass Drive was a darkness cutting into the trees ahead. We walked the broken road without a word.

"I would want you to try," said Eric. "To heal me, if I was bit."

I'd frowned at his first comment, then nodded slowly. "Same."

"Just stop my heart," Roxie said. "They've studied the infection. You can't cure it."

Eric tilted his head. "I've never heard of anyone trying magic on it. Caitlyn's probably the first."

"They don't consider healing an important magic, unless we use it to kill." I could tell from the beginning when we worked on my healing skills that the teachers always mentioned what I could do to harm. They didn't know I'd already done that.

We were approaching the school. I tried to imagine how buildings appeared with lights. The empty, dead sockets hung everywhere. We had lanterns at the camp. No one had electricity, except for the labs. I'd heard rumors about the government using electricity in Savannah, but supposedly it was reserved for factories.

Roxie turned to me. "If he's there — at his house?"

"I tell him to leave, or we report him."

She studied me. "And you'll follow through with the threat?"

I hadn't been too sure about that part, but I'd have to. "Yes."

Dogs barked deeper in the town. In the summer, there would be frogs and insects, but there was only silence tonight.

The stars had come out in full force by the time we reached the first buildings of the town. The burned-out husks to our left where no more than dark silhouettes biting into the night sky. On our right, the closest building had a dim light flickering behind curtains. A rusted carcass of a truck had been left on the asphalt in front. The only readable sign on a tower to the side said, "Pawn Shop."

Eric pointed to the words. "I still think they sold chess pieces there."

"Junk," said Roxie. "Pawn means junk. That's what Toni said."

"Why don't they just say junk shop then?" Eric snorted. "You might be right. A chess shop would have the word queen or king in it."

Behind the sign tower, one continuous building circled a large lot which reminded me of the school back by the camp. More cars rotted on the asphalt. The chill breeze carried the scent of fish, but we were far from the lake.

"The town looks so creepy at night," Eric said.

"Chicken shit," teased Roxie.

"Says the woman who can turn someone or something into a torch. Like you have any reason to fear anything." Eric glanced at me to join in their banter, but all I could think about was what I'd do if we found Dean.

At the intersection ahead, fires had leveled buildings on both sides of us. Desolate but intact, structures appeared abandoned on the far side. We didn't see any signs of locals until we'd crossed and gone down Bass Drive a little farther. Dim lights dotted a couple more windows ahead to the right. We would be heading to the left at the next intersection.

"How many people live at the hotels?" I asked.

"About a hundred," said Eric. "Almost half the population remaining in Santee. There used to be a population of over a thousand."

"Taken?" I shivered, thinking of my mother's screams when my father had disappeared.

Eric shrugged, his movement barely visible in the darkness. "I don't think any more than anywhere else. Percentage wise, more people died of starvation and fighting after everything collapsed. I imagine it was the same here."

"They might have evacuated," Roxie added. "This is close to the cryptid zone. Statistically the cryptids caused the most deaths."

We turned the corner, and I could see the first of the hotels, firelight flickering off glass windows. Two cats watched us from atop a rusting car. Someone had a campfire going. The scent of smoke and murmurs of voices drifted in the air. We walked without speaking, listening to the occasional bark of a dog. The local kids seemed drawn to come talk to us at Camp Sparta, but the adults avoided the camp and us, at every opportunity.

Silhouettes moved as the flames came into view, all partially hidden by vehicles. The fire had been built close to the street. Leafless trees stood along the sidewalk. The louder talking and laughter died as someone spotted us.

I waved. Eric and Roxie followed suit. The group around the fire were mostly Black adults. A teenage couple was sitting off to the side on stacked tires.

"Hello, do you know Buck?" Eric asked.

An older woman with tightly braided hair and oversized eyeglasses pointed down the road. "Last hotel. Second-floor, I think. Lives with his uncle, Jacob." The firelight lit her cheeks and smile. Most of the group eyed us warily.

"Thank you." I started along the road, and my stomach churned.

Their quiet murmurs followed us. In Savannah, people's fear of our magic had led to the witch riots. I didn't remember much of the trouble, except for the military coming and taking me away. When people saw me with the soldiers, they screamed at me and accused me of bringing the Sorrow. Years later, Tyrell explained that we were born after the troubles had already begun. The people of Santee tolerated us because the military here said they had to. Tucked inside Camp Sparta, I often forgot how people reacted around us.

"So much fun," Roxie said when we were out of ear shot.

I rubbed the back of my neck. "Sorry."

"Don't mind her," said Eric. "Remember she was out here hanging with locals the moment she turned fifteen."

"Not the adults." She sniffed. "They act like we've got some disease. Selina and I were hanging with Linda and her friends. Buck and Francis sometimes. Never here."

We had to ask two more adults before we found Jacob, who just grumbled and pointed to the end of the balcony walkway. Buck and Francis jabbered with five other teens on the far side of the building. They were nursing a small jar of peach moonshine. My stomach roiled at the scent.

Buck beamed when he spotted us. "Hey, back for more?" Francis smiled and motioned for the jar.

I waved it off. "Is Dean around?"

"Dean?" Buck's eyebrows raised and he smirked. "You looking for him?"

Heat warmed my cheeks, and I swallowed. "I. .." Words died in my throat. As far as the locals knew, I'd never really met Dean other than when he passed by the gate. They would guess why I would be looking for him.

Eric leaned an arm on my shoulder. "We've got some fishing kind of questions."

Buck frowned. "I fish."

"Where does he live?" asked Roxie in a neutral, yet firm tone.

Francis answered. "Over on the way to you guys. On Bass Drive. You probably passed it on the way here. There's a pawn shop sign."

Standing in the breeze rather than walking, I had started to chill. "We did pass it. Thank you."

Buck nodded his chin toward the others. "Hang out. He's probably night fishing."

I doubted that. "We've got an early day tomorrow."

The trek back to Dean's house took us a few minutes, and clouds had started sweeping in to cover the stars in the east. We all strode quickly, and I'd been wet enough for one day.

A tendril of smoke rose from the building where the pawn sign hung. In the back, a metal tube rose to the height of the roof.

Roxie motioned me to the door near the window with the flickering light. "Your mess."

Drawing in a deep breath, I knocked. Metal clattered inside, and light steps ran to the door. I stepped back before it opened.

A girl maybe a year or two younger than me opened the door, surprised to see us. She had Dean's tanned skin color and hair, but I'd never seen her before. "Oh," she said.

"Is Dean here?" I asked.

She glanced between us, almost fearful. I thought she might shut the door. Inside was a comfortable room with a soft couch and two stuffed chairs. The scent of burning wood and cooked meat wafted out.

"I'm sorry. I'm Caitlyn. Roxie. Eric." We all smiled.

"Bettina. Donna and Grandpa are out looking for Dean now. Have you seen him?"

My chest hollowed, though I should be glad he hadn't come home. "No. We didn't realize he was missing."

She nodded quickly and her eyes teared. "He was supposed to be home to run for water this afternoon."

I couldn't stand there, knowing I couldn't tell her more. "If we see him, we'll let him know you're worried."

Bettina sagged and offered a grateful smile. "Thank you. If you don't find him, come back tomorrow."

Unsure, I agreed and waved goodbye awkwardly. She closed the door, and Roxie tapped my shoulder when I didn't start moving.

I stumbled away from the door. Dean's family was safe, maybe, but it would tear them apart not knowing what happened to him. I groaned. What could I possibly say? I couldn't tell them the truth.

Eric whispered. "Why does she want you to come back tomorrow?"

"I don't know."

Roxie slipped her arm through mine. "It's not a bad idea. Just to be sure. We can slip over at lunch. We've got patrol in the morning."

Dean had done the right thing, and not gone home. What would happen to him? My legs wobbled, and I was grateful for Roxie's support.

Chapter Nine

The next morning, I fought my dread and joined Roxie when she headed to the mess for breakfast. The sky had plenty of clouds that darkened the gray morning twilight. The air smelled like it would rain.

"We're late." Roxie clattered on the stairs ahead of me.

I'd had nasty dreams about wolves and had taken a while to get moving. "Not that hungry." We hadn't talked about Dean, but he was on my mind.

Selina stood on the ground floor walkway, talking with Leslie and Yaz. I faltered at the sight, stumbled, and managed to grab onto the railing tight enough that I didn't roll down the last four steps.

"Crap." I straightened. Everyone had stopped and turned to watch me. Three of the members from the Hounds unit were coming down one of the other stairwells and snickered at my clumsiness.

Leslie already had the door to the mess open. Faint lantern light flickered inside, and there was dull racket within. Selina waited as the door closed, then opened it for Yaz to lead us inside.

The room quieted as we entered. Faces turned to study

me. Coming for breakfast had been a horrible idea. Whatever they were thinking, I'd done worse. I checked Roxie and Eric's expressions, but they didn't show the guilt I felt. Selina scowled. I headed straight for the back door and the screened in cooking area.

The oversized patio had been built over the furnace because the back of the building dropped nearly another story before reaching the steep slope to the river. Stairs had been constructed on the right side so water could be brought for the washing bins. We often spent evenings on those steps or by the river where the top of an old dock had been retrofitted into a pavilion. Layers of screen and mesh hung around the patio, creating a hazy filter to the trees and river behind our barracks.

The cook worked at one of the grills at the back, and the smoky air smelled of fried potatoes and eggs. I grabbed a plate from atop a barrel beside the sink and hit the first serving pan with scrambled eggs.

Eric slid in beside me. "Mmm, scrambled eggs this morning."

"It's always scrambled eggs," I replied.

"Yep." He took the serving spoon when I handed it to him, then he raised it in a salute to the frowning cook who had turned at our conversation. "And mighty good-looking eggs at that. Ooh, potatoes."

I smiled at his attempt to distract me from the attention of the other Youth Guards. My plate full, I handed off the spatula. "Your scepter, my picky prince."

The moment only lasted until I reentered and drew everyone's eyes again. Rounding our table, I sat with my back to the majority of the room. I could pack food away with the best of them and intended to beat them all out the front door so they could gossip in peace. Roxie slid in beside me, and Eric sat across from me.

Selina dropped onto the bench beside Eric and left her food untouched as she briefed us with our day's schedule. "Civic studies class at 0800; Caitlyn, you're meeting with Ms. Simmons instead. We'll run at 0900." She stifled Eric's groan with a harsh glance, then Selina studied me until I nodded.

This time of year we ate first, took patrol, gate, training, or class, then ran after the sun started to warm the air. Come summer, we'd have runs in the morning or evening, depending on the schedule. I'd be happy to skip Civics and possibly the run for a leisurely chat with one of the instructors.

Selina continued, "Roxie, take your patrol on Sector C at 1000. Yaz and Jordan, meet me at the north gate; we have Sector E. Then we'll be at the south gate at 1300, while Eric and Caitlyn have air practice and Roxie heat practice." She pointed at us. "You three have north gate at 1600. Yaz, you have water practice at that time, and Jordan is in martial training down the road."

I stuffed another chunk of hearty potato into my mouth and tried to memorize my schedule. I'd likely end up asking Selina or Eric to repeat it at least once; another reason I tended to get low scores on my reviews. Missing even a couple minutes of class or training earned demerits.

As I ate quickly, Jordan babbled with excitement about going to the military base for training. I didn't enjoy it or the bruises from sparring.

The conversations at the other units' tables were lower than usual, and I assumed they were talking about me. I'd be happy to head over to Gayle Simmons this morning. Moonjir's appearance seemed like a week ago, not two days ago. The werewolves and Dean's healing hung fresh in my mind. The desperate expression on his sister's face haunted me.

I paused with a forkful of eggs as chills ran up my spine. What if his family found Dean? He might have an abandoned house along the river where he regularly stopped, and they knew where he might be. How could he refuse to come home without explaining it all to them? If my healing hadn't worked, he only had hours before he would turn. I ran a panicked scenario where he told them the truth so they'd go away, but then his family told Tyrell about my involvement. Hunching over my plate, I focused on my half-finished breakfast. My appetite was gone.

"Caitlyn?" Eric asked.

I flashed a smile. "Wild two days, huh? I wonder what Ms. Simmons will want." Forcing down more eggs, I tried to keep the dread off my face. My stomach churned.

He tightened his lips and nodded, appearing unconvinced. "Yeah, it's been a rough couple of days." Eric knew me well and likely guessed that I was worried about Dean.

We'd been friends since the day he'd arrived at Camp Sparta. Selina, Roxie, and I had just moved into the barracks. Eric arrived scared witless from the labs, and he stuck to the three of us the moment we said hello to him. Tyrell hadn't set the units yet, so we got Eric moved to our floor within a week.

I ignored some of the snickers that joined the murmurs around the room and scraped my leftovers onto Eric's plate before heading out back to clean it. Roxie wasn't far behind me. We had plenty of time before we had to get to our scheduled activities and duties.

"You okay?" she asked.

The washing area was adjacent to the back door and stairs on the right. I rinsed my plate and fork in the first bin, glancing back at the cook. "About as expected." My face tightened at her concerned expression, and I placed everything in the last bin with sanitizer. The younger students would come by to finish. I nodded toward the outside screen door. "Do you have a minute?"

Roxie followed me out, and we descended to walk across the dead grass to the makeshift pavilion by the river. The stairs still led down the bank, but the dock had been removed when kids had fallen through rotten boards. I could handle the mix of earthy, fishy smells near the water. It didn't look as green today. We sat, and I faced the building, watching as others came out to clean their dishes.

"I'm worried about Dean and his family. Myself, as well."

Roxie frowned lightly. "He didn't come home. That's good, right?"

"What if they found him?"

Her eyebrows raised. "On the other side of the lake?"

"There was a boat. He fishes, so he has a boat. Right? What if he came back to this side and just holed up in one of the abandoned buildings? Maybe they know where he hangs out."

"Doesn't mean he'd go back home with them."

I sighed, feeling selfish. "Would he tell them the truth to make them leave?"

She shrugged. "Maybe. Why does it matter, as long as he doesn't come back?"

Part of me wanted to believe I'd healed him, but I didn't think so. "Yes. It would be best if he didn't come back. But if they knew what I'd done — that I'd been there. .."

Roxie's lips pinched tight. "I get it. Word would get out. Someone would talk, and Tyrell would learn about it."

On cue, I spotted Selina peering through the screened porch at us, her plate in hand. A hollow ache grew in my chest as I focused on Roxie, keeping Selina in my peripheral vision. I wanted to believe Selina's friendship was stronger than her duty to Tyrell and the camp, but I couldn't be sure. We were talking about an enemy of humans who had killed our soldiers, possibly Talia indirectly, and many of the people of Santee. She might not be able to overlook that.

"Don't look, but Selina's watching us. I'm just talking to you because I'm upset about the rumors."

Roxie didn't budge, but smiled. "Wimp."

"Exactly."

Selina moved into the darker shadows and passed back through the door into the mess. I sighed.

"We can check back in with Dean's family tonight," Roxie said.

I bounced my leg. "Maybe today, on the way to our patrol."

"No."

"I can't wait."

"No."

"If I found out his family knows, then I could go to Tyrell first and admit everything."

"Do that now." Roxie's eyes were firm. Is that what she would have done? Yes, she would have followed the rules in the first place. Then Dean might have been dead by now, or shipped off to wherever they'd taken Talia.

I jumped when Eric opened the screen door. Roxie's glare faded as she turned. My decision to help Dean had been little more than a reaction at the time, but I'd choose the same option even knowing what stress it might bring. Maybe I'd make Dean promise not to go home.

"You want to know some of the gossip, according to Jordan?" Eric asked.

I shrugged. "Sure."

"The officers think you're lying about the wolves. That maybe they didn't exist or something. They sent soldiers last night and again today to investigate."

They'd find Dean's blood. "So, Tyrell will question me again."

"Everyone thinks you're lying about the other cryptid, too." He jabbed his thumb toward the mess. "They think you want a promotion and are making up stories to get some credit." He broke into a broad grin. "This is great. I mean, I don't know what Tyrell will find, but no one thinks you let loose a werewolf."

"Dean's blood. That's what's out there." I patted the bench beside me. "I need to find out something."

Roxie glared. "No."

"I could go alone. You two go on the patrol. It's just busy work anyway, training us for the real work out there." I pointed to the north.

"Look how well that's working out." Her voice was on the edge of a growl. "You're not going to Dean's house."

"Why? We went there. He's not home." Eric asked, "What am I missing?"

I leaned in, locking eyes with Eric. "What if his family found him?"

"That would be bad."

"Exactly." I ignored Roxie and hurried into my argument. "What if he didn't come back with them, but told them the truth, and they told someone like Tyrell."

Eric's forehead furrowed. "That too, would be bad. Not as much — but for you, yes." He raised his palms up to Roxie. "We should check it out. Make sure he hasn't come home, at least."

She rolled her eyes. "No."

"Let Caitlyn go on her own, like she offered. We can do the patrol together."

"We don't split up. Rule number one." Roxie held her finger to emphasize.

"Then I vote we go together," Eric said.

I held my smile back, even as Roxie stood. "No," she said.

Eric elbowed me. "We can talk about it on the walk down the road."

Roxie marched for the screen door. "No."

I stood, and Eric joined me.

"Well, that went well," he said.

Laughing, I pointed to the back of the other buildings. "Thank you. I'm just going to go between the buildings rather than back through the mess and all those people."

He tapped my arm with his fist and jogged to the stairs for the screened in patio. I strolled across the back lawn toward the end of the building. Roxie might give in. No one had ever been punished at Camp Sparta, but what I had done and the lies to cover it might bring Tyrell to consider it. I'd deal with that if it happened. I wished I knew where Dean was.

I stepped into the cryptid classroom as we called it, but Gayle wasn't there yet. The room, like Tyrell's, had been enlarged by cutting into the neighboring apartment and filled with folding chairs. The long wall to the left had elaborate life-sized paintings of the known cryptids with their stenciled names. The werewolf was first with its short and stocky form, white and mottled fur, and a menacing growl. In the text books, their human form could be anyone.

Next was a tall, male Tuathua with his thin, not-quite-human form and six insect-like wings sprouting from his shoulders to his lower back. The perspective highlighted his side and angled so we could see his butt cheeks but none of his junk, as Roxie called it. They didn't seem dangerous at all, despite Gayle's warnings.

The third was an oversized, blood-sucking bat attached to the back of his victim who was a teen male with no shirt. Black wings tucked under the arms, short feet and claws grabbed the boy's sides, and the tail trailed past his belt. Gayle had more detailed drawings in books, but this image prompted a visceral effect. The tentacled tongue embedded into the boy's spine at the base of the neck left a trail of blood, which always made me cringe.

The Onikai, with their hulking seven-foot furry forms, appeared to be screaming with their mouths open and long lower cuspids jutting up. The Naak beside them were shorter than humans and reptilian bipeds with scales and fins. I never found them intimidating, but they reportedly had only been found in the sea.

Only the werewolves were seen here at the edges of the cryptid zone except for Moonjir, who appeared to have no problem sneaking in to chat with me.

As the door opened, I turned and smiled at Gayle. An older woman with light brown hair, she had a quick smile. I didn't trust her, though; she reminded me of the scientists at the lab who acted friendly.

"Caitlyn. Thank you for coming. How are you feeling after your accident?"

I shrugged. She didn't really care. "I'm fine. Tyrell said you wanted to see me." The comment came out more like a question.

"Yes. Come back to the desk. I want to do some drawings, with your help. This new cryptid sounds quite — unusual."

At least she hadn't said unbelievable. I followed her to the massive desk at the back window. I'd never actually seen her sitting at it.

From a drawer, she pulled out a pad of paper with a rough surface. Pens came out next along with pencils. It was a treasure of equipment compared to what I'd ever seen at school. "Grab a chair."

I obliged and spent the next hour commenting with

additions and corrections to her pencil drawing before she got to the point of adding color with pens. Moonjir appeared a little comical in this format, but correct.

"You are very lucky," Gayle said as she stroked lines of pink at the end of Moonjir's fur.

"How's that?"

"First sighting of this type of cryptid." Her tone hung between excited and jealous.

"I'm probably luckier that it didn't kill me."

"That, too."

She had written "Moonjir" at the bottom. I glanced over at the paining of the Naak closest to us. "What will they name it?" I pointed to her drawing.

"I don't know." Gayle lifted her pen and smiled at me. "Suggestions?"

I shrugged and pointed to the Naak. "How did you come up with that name?"

Gayle's lips tightened as her smile vanished. She shook her head and turned back to her work. "I don't know."

She seemed to be holding something back, but I wasn't too surprised. Gayle had been nice enough. I appreciated that she never made me feel foolish and took each comment of mine seriously. Whatever secret she had about naming the Naak, or the Onikai for that matter, she could keep.

The picture finally reached a point where any adjustments would be repetitive coloring of the fur on Moonjir's back and oversized tail. Gayle stood. "Thank you. I appreciate your help. If I have more questions, would you be willing to return?"

I was pretty sure Tyrell would not be giving me a choice. "Of course." Smiling, I rose and headed for the door. After being ridiculed by some of the Youth Guards, being taken seriously made me calmer. I still wanted to find Dean, or at least make sure no one else had come in contact with him. We were nearing the twenty-four-hour mark when he surely would show signs of being infected.

The lawn in front of the building was clear, and the whoosh of wind magic broke the near silence. I'd missed the units' morning run, which only seemed fair after having to swim for my life in freezing water the day before. Heading back to the empty mess hall, I refilled my canteen. The clouds still threatened to rain, but hadn't.

I climbed upstairs to our apartment and affixed the sheath for my machete to my belt while I waited for Roxie and Eric to return. We retrieved the patrol watch to keep the time and headed for the gate. The guards from the Sburbs unit gave me sideways glances, but didn't say anything.

I'd worked out a reasonable argument for Roxie by the time we were all headed south on Bass Drive. "If we were going by the regulations, what would Tyrell do about Dean?" I strolled the road at a leisurely pace, not wanting to reach the area before the town where we branched off to patrol. At least, not before I had time to convince her.

She eyed me suspiciously. "What are you getting at?"

"Let's say Tyrell knew it was Dean who was bit; what would he do?"

Her frown grew into a scowl. "He'd have to find Dean, or make sure he hadn't gone home, but none of this is by the book, and you know it."

"I can't risk Tyrell sending me back to the labs because I made one mistake."

Eric and Roxie both turned to me sharply. "You think he'd do that?" she asked.

"Usually I only break a regulation or two. I think I outdid myself on this one."

"Four." Her response came so swiftly that I knew she'd been stewing on it for a while. "And they don't even have one for trying to heal a werewolf, but they would if they found out what you've done."

"So let's say I go to Tyrell, admit everything, and let him kick me back to the labs. Then what would he do?"

Roxie nearly growled through clenched teeth. "He'd try to track Dean and capture him." She emphasized the last part.

"So, let's say Tyrell finds out from Dean's parents and kicks me back to the labs."

She glared at me. "This is why. .."

Roxie didn't have to finish her comment. When she broke up with me, it had been because I talked her into getting in trouble. We'd sneaked out of the camp and gotten caught. I'd rescued the cat, and Tyrell found out. There were plenty of examples, and she'd cataloged them all for the breakup. I was doing the exact same thing now, but this mattered. I couldn't back down.

"I have to do this. It's probably best if you two go on the patrol without me."

She stopped in the road. "I'd be breaking a reg that way as well. If we're separated, I'm to return immediately so the camp can organize a search party. Don't you read these things?"

I usually made a snarky joke at this point, but that would only make her resist more. "Please?"

She closed her eyes and stood silent long enough to make me squirm before she spoke. "I'm never getting promoted."

My smile blossomed. "Thank you." I skipped forward.

His footsteps following, Eric called from behind. "Don't I get a vote?"

Roxie sighed. "You'd just agree with her; you always do."

"Still."

We walked in silence for a while, and I hoped they weren't rethinking their decision. The air remained cool as the sun hid behind growing clouds. I hoped Dean wasn't at his house and that his family hadn't found him, yet part of me wanted to know if the healing had worked. If it had, would I admit everything to Tyrell? It might mean the end of killing soldiers or other people who'd been bit.

More likely, Dean and I would both end up at a lab.

I made out the chimney behind Dean's house as we approached. A thin trail of smoke escaped from a metal pipe. Some of the houses we'd explored had fireplaces. For a couple structures, all that remained was charred wood and the chimney. "Wait here," I said.

"Why?" Eric asked.

"I'm just a lovesick girl, looking for a hot guy. I just happen to be a Youth Guard, not half a unit."

They stopped, moving to the side of the road so as not to be seen from the door or windows. I strode slowly to the front. It might be just Bettina again. I shivered at the idea of no one answering and a slaughtered family inside. We'd heard plenty of horror stories in cryptid class.

I tapped three times and stood back. Did I expect a werewolf to open the door and come leaping out?

The woman who answered had white hair in a kerchief and a wrinkled, ancient face. Wide-eyed, she studied me. "Is this about Dean?" she asked with a distinctive croak from age or panic, though I couldn't tell which.

"Is — is he here?" *Dumb question*, I thought.

She appeared to relax. "No. Angelo's out searching for him in the Thompson's boat." Her eyes closed for a second and her hands trembled. "I thought you were bringing us news. Bad news, I feared."

They hadn't found him, and he hadn't come home. The

weight on my shoulders didn't ease. "Oh, okay. I'll check back later, maybe tonight."

She reached out. "You tell those soldiers he's missing. Maybe they'll — see something."

I wouldn't. "Of course." My throat thickened and I forced a swallow. "Of course." I turned to go.

"What's your name?" she called out behind me.

I turned and smiled. "Leslie."

Continuing slowly, I waited for the door to close before marching to Roxie and Eric. "They haven't seen him."

"Yay, you got away with it."

I frowned as we headed back on Bass Drive. "What if the healing worked?" The nights weren't dropping below freezing this late in February; maybe he'd survive a couple nights out, not turn, and then come home.

Roxie tapped the back of my head. "Stop thinking. Whatever it is, it's bad."

Forming a sheepish smile, I gave her a one shouldered shrug. "Nothing I can do about it; he wouldn't hide nearby."

"You want to go find this werewolf?" she asked.

"He might not be infected anymore."

Roxie snorted. "Don't believe you're all that."

"Whatever, let's just go do our patrol."

"We won't even make it over the little bridge at this point. But yes, we'll give it a quick poke, then head back."

A breeze brought the scent of rain, but there weren't any signs of it from the clouds forming above. It would come though, cold and bitter.

"Crap," Eric said. We all faltered for a step, then Roxie groaned.

Only a dozen yards ahead, Tyrell walked onto the road ahead of us. He came out of the neighborhood which led to the Sector we were supposed to be patrolling. His face, already dour, turned into a full-blown scowl as he focused on us. Facing us, he didn't move to intercept; we were already coming to him.

I'd gotten us in trouble, as Roxie feared. She wouldn't forgive me soon. Dean wasn't in the town, so part of the morning had gone well. The rest of it would be turning to shit.

"Let me do the lying." I strode forward to meet our impending doom. We'd be in some sort of trouble no matter what I said.

Chapter Ten

The wind blew Tyrell's sandy brown hair away from his face as he watched me approach with dark eyes. His broken nose made his expression darker. He seemed out of place wearing his usual dark green service uniform sparkling with metals out on the barren forested road. We both knew I was the one misplaced.

"This is my fault," I said as soon as I believed he could hear me clearly. I continued walking toward him and rubbed my eyes, as if clearing them. "I lost it and started walking along the road. I wouldn't listen to Roxie. She finally talked sense into me." My voice loud, I assumed she could hear me. "It's too much. Everyone's saying I lied, but I couldn't bring myself to go into the woods. What if those werewolves come here? I got lucky. I'm not that skilled. I just lashed out. .."

"It doesn't matter what your excuse is." Tyrell's voice had low rumbling harsh quality. "You don't abandon patrols."

I stopped and hung my head, afraid that my relief would show. "I know." I'd rather he think I was a coward than know what I'd really done.

"Would you have reported this?" he asked.

I shrugged slowly and pointed behind me. "Roxie said she would." The most I'd seen for punishment was extra duties, which I'd gladly take on. My friends didn't need to pay for my obsession over Dean.

"She should have reported it as soon as you deserted your patrol." His tone had gentled, slightly. "All of you. What do you have next?"

"Training, sir." Roxie had stepped beside me.

"Drop off your weapons and head to your training stations early. Full run to the camp. Explain what happened to your instructor. Not one minute of free time. We'll talk about this later."

"Yes, sir." Roxie glared at me. "Go."

We raced away from Tyrell, and I had to force myself not to laugh. Eric had a grin on his face. Roxie was visibly seething. My amusement over hiding our actual actions faded. When we a good bit down the road, I started to tell her I was sorry.

"Shut up."

I did, and fought trying to explain myself. She knew why I'd gone to Dean's house, and I was glad he hadn't been there. I still wanted to know if he'd been healed, no matter how much I doubted it. I couldn't just cross the lake and go check on him.

The same group was guarding the south gate when we returned, and they didn't ask us why we were early. Roxie split from me and Eric as soon as we entered, but she'd have to return to the patrol watch anyway.

"Roxie's pissed," Eric said.

"You think?" We walked west toward the river where three Youth Guards practiced blasting air at sandbags. "I am sorry. I had to know. What if I'd unleashed a werewolf on his family?"

"Roxie's right."

I paused, not wanting to bring this conversation to the practice area. "About?"

"You shouldn't have lied when we found you. If you'd said Dean had been bitten, his family would have some closure and so would you."

Thinking of him being hunted bothered me as much as whatever they'd done with Talia. "If it were me, would you tell them?"

"Maybe, to keep you from that nightmare." He rubbed his ear and wrinkled his nose as if unsure.

"What if you knew they were going to send me to a lab, like they probably did Talia?"

"No, then I wouldn't. But you barely even know this guy."

"Dean. If I'd do it for one of us, I should try to help him, too."

Eric shook his head and started walking. "I can't believe I'm saying this, but you think too much."

Kyle was the instructor today. It always seemed odd to have an adult too old to have magic teaching us kids who did. He pulled aside when we approached.

"I screwed up," I said to him. "We have to join this practice and continue into ours afterward. Punishment."

He shrugged and pointed to the line. One of the younger boys from the Hound unit attempted to topple a sandbag the size of me off a post, but I could tell by the rustling dead grass that he'd kept it too loose and wide. Air was easier to control than heat, unless you had a fire nearby. The trick was to tunnel it close to you, then match the final location's size to the target. A gust the size of my fist could be powerful, but might not move the object where you wanted.

When it came to my turn, the otherness and the air

around me blended smoothly into a diminishing corridor I manipulated to a point a foot from the sandbag. My magic whistled in a low wind as I drew air from yards around me and condensed it toward the distant point. The bag flew three yards before landing with a skid. I hadn't used a tenth of the effort I used against the werewolves attacking Dean.

Eric jogged with me to retrieve the heavy target. "Roxie's back."

The heat practice range used a large square of burned asphalt at the river where the trees and brush had been cleared. Roxie had her back to us, but I recognized her. "How long do you think she'll be pissed at me?"

He grunted as he lifted one end of the sandbag. "Depends."

The bag drooped between us, and we had to walk it sideways to the wide pole. "On what?"

"Whether or not she gets promoted. She'll blame all this if she doesn't."

"Damn." I shoved my end of the sack onto the hip high wood. "She would."

We jogged back to the line, a good twenty-five paces away, and Eric focused for his turn. He could move wind and water equally and said river water was easy because you had so much to work with. Water in the air was way different.

I had difficulty with finite control, though I could make splashes. Condensing a cup of water out of the air took too much effort. I'd managed a couple tablespoons at most. They kept me to air and heat, with only the odd week when I'd work on healing. Most people with the ability to call the otherness found that too complicated as you moved cellular matter, electricity, air, water, and heat by an instinctive symbiosis with the target body. It was all about bonds and connections. For much of our practice we used dead or inanimate objects, chickens mainly. I was far too young when I learned you could destroy a body far easier than heal it.

Eric groaned when we retrieved our next bag. "I'm going to fall asleep during gate duty. We still have three hours of this."

"I wish we were healing." I snorted as we lifted the bag.

"Agreed. I'd only be tired, not bored."

Our best healing sessions required volunteers from the military, and wounded or sick were better. Few had grown to trust us over the years.

Leslie was the only Youth Guard they'd found who was willing to use healing to kill animals with a touch. I would never be able to bring myself to do it again. Manipulating heat could burn or freeze, and a few had trained with live pigs. Roxie had joined the testing group, but couldn't bring herself to kill something.

Selina had electrified three pigs so far. She was the only one in our unit to kill during the tests, but we all knew that we might have to use our abilities against the cryptids some-day. I hadn't hesitated when it came to defending Dean, but I hadn't tried to kill the wolves.

My mouth tasted sour, and I glanced along the row of buildings toward Tyrell's office. Would he tell me if they found blood? I hadn't seen him return to the camp, but I hadn't been watching, either.

When the first training ended, Kyle didn't let us break for lunch and instead put us at the head of the line for the next group, which only had two boys from the Cryptdead unit. The rotation would move even quicker than before. I'd be hungry and tired by the time we were done.

The two Cryptdead boys were talking together and eying me when Eric and I ran out to retrieve his sandbag. He noticed my expression. "Ignore them. It'll blow over."

"Maybe." If Tyrell's soldiers found blood, the rumors might change, but I doubted they'd disappear. "I'm the new gossip." It had all been about the tall, black-haired Toni getting pregnant for a while. Her position and fire magic had meant nothing when she'd been sent off to the Creche.

We all paused as a soldier ran toward our group. He pointed at me as Eric and I jogged back from placing the target back on the pole. "Tyrell wants Caitlyn to report immediately."

Kyle tilted his head for me to follow the soldier. Pulse racing, I left Eric and ignored the smirking expressions of the other boys. The pale, freckle-faced soldier was young, but he had a hard expression as he turned and escorted me.

"What does Tyrell want?" I asked.

"For you to report to him."

My shoulders sagged. They'd found Dean's blood. I just had to stick to my story. Tyrell might not believe me, but he couldn't prove otherwise. One thing was for sure, I wouldn't be ranking to senior at the next inspection.

When I noticed the first squad of soldiers marching outside the gate, I stumbled on the grass. The line trailed down Bass Drive. There had to be a couple dozen. They walked outside the fence and none were coming in the north gate, so they likely were headed to town. My panic rose as I imagined Dean coming home and turning. If I had caused the death of his family, I wouldn't be able to forgive myself. Roxie might even consider reporting me.

"Keep up."

I'd dropped a few steps back, hesitant to meet with Tyrell. The guilt would be all over my face. My head shook more than nodded as I jogged to the soldier's side. The marching men were armed with rifles and grim expressions. Nightmare visions of the mangled bodies of Dean's family flashed in my mind. I didn't want to be a

Youth Guard; I never really had. Camp Sparta had just been a better option than the labs, and I'd made friends here.

Selina, Yaz, and Jordan were on the north gate. They were focused on the troops and didn't see me.

As we neared Tyrell's office, I fought the urge to run. He'd tell me about the blood they found, or bodies in town. *Maybe both*, I thought.

My escort rapped three times, and Tyrell barked from inside. The words were too muffled for me to hear, but the soldier opened the door and gestured me inside.

An officer from the military base, dressed similarly to Tyrell, stood with him at the table. They leaned over a map; both turned to study me.

"Reporting." I choked on the word, my throat thick. "Sir."

Tyrell straightened and his expression never wavered from a hard stare. He moved a chair sideways to the table. "Caitlyn. Have a seat." His voice was as hard as his face.

Uncomfortably close to his legs, I slid into the chair with my heels tucked underneath. "Yes, sir."

He glanced at the map then back to me. His finger dropped to a line. "This is the shore where you came out of the river."

I leaned forward. The map started to make sense. I could see the large lake and the peninsula of land that formed at the wide mouth of the creek. "Okay."

"Is that correct?" he asked.

"I think so." I kept my focus on the map rather than let him see my terrified expression. When my hands began to tremble, I shoved my fingers between my thighs. "I'm not great at maps."

His finger traced to a red dot marked on the black and white map. "Here is where you reported defending yourself against the werewolves, as detailed to your escort when they found you."

"Yes." I had no idea if that had been the location. "I think so. It's hard — the map. I could go back out there and show someone." Acting as if I were helpful and not lying was my only plan. I had promised not to change my story.

"Did you see anyone here, perhaps from where you were in the water?" He moved his finger to a second red dot. "Maybe when they shot at one of the werewolves?"

He was giving me an opportunity to change my story. "No, sir. Nothing." I almost smiled. Dean's family was not lying mangled in their house. He hadn't gone home. Tyrell had found the blood. I relaxed my face and turned to them. "Is that who the soldiers are looking for? The person who shot the gun?" He hadn't mentioned the blood, so I couldn't.

Tyrell glanced at the other officer, then nodded to me. "They're scouting the town now, going building by building. Nobody has reported anyone missing. We have patrols going to each homestead in the north area."

Dean's family would likely admit to his absence, then Tyrell would know who they were searching for. They might tell the soldiers I'd been there, asking about Dean. I should have hidden my blonde hair.

My expression must have changed as Tyrell frowned. He tilted his head. "Do you remember something?"

No, I just have the worst control over my expressions. "No, but why all those soldiers?" Maybe it was the wrong thing to say, but I couldn't think of anything else to explain my concern. I straightened in my chair.

The other officer finally spoke. "We have concerns."

Tyrell flashed the man a glance, and the military man stiffened, as if reprimanded. "There's a lot of people to interview, and we want to finish by dark," Tyrell said.

I was sure he was lying. They'd found the blood. If

Dean's family mentioned me, I'd have to explain that. I'd just play the lovesick teenager and start crying if they told me Dean had been bitten. I could handle this.

The lines of Tyrell's face softened, and he rested a hand on my shoulder. "Do you want to tell me what happened when you were supposed to be on patrol?"

I blinked at the sudden change in topic. "Everyone's giving me nasty looks, saying that I lied about all this." Drawing in a deep breath, I acted relieved. "But you believe me, don't you?" I gestured to the front of the office. "The soldiers are proof that I didn't make all this up."

He offered me a warm smile and patted my shoulder. "Of course I do. You're going to have to be stronger. You won't be able to run away every time things are tough here at the camp. I'm proud of you, fending off three werewolves. Keep that in mind when they're giving you a rough time."

I smiled, relaxing. "I will. I'm sorry about today."

"You heard the gunshot?"

"What?" I swallowed. "Yes. Somewhat."

He left his hand on my shoulder and the smile on his face as he pointed to the creek with his finger. "Where?"

"Where?" If I had been in the water when I heard the shot, would I have turned and seen Dean? I didn't know the layout well enough. "From where I was in the water?"

"Yes."

They both peered at me, drilling into me with dark eyes. "I don't really remember. I barely heard it — all the splashing and coughing." I focused on the map to avoid their stares. "It was less than a minute before I could put my feet down and climb out. I don't know, exactly. All I could think about was getting warm."

Tyrell straightened and his smile disappeared. "Understand." He took a deep breath.

I couldn't tell if he believed me or not. I'd gotten us all

in trouble going to Dean's house and given him a reason to be suspicious of me.

Meanwhile, Dean was out there somewhere. He might be waiting to see if he turned, and when he didn't, he could come back after the bite healed. That would be the best scenario, except now Tyrell would be searching for him. I wanted to warn Dean, if he wasn't turning into a werewolf already.

"Back to your unit." Tyrell focused on my eyes.

I stood a little too quickly, obviously ready to leave. "Yes, sir." I made for the door a little less rushed.

"Caitlyn." Tyrell called behind me. When I turned, he continued. "Leaves are canceled for the day and tonight. I've let the gate guards know. You'll keep to your barracks after your duties."

"Okay." I hadn't planned on going out. What was I going to do, search for Dean?

Chapter Eleven

The next morning, I braved the rumors and odd glances to have breakfast with my unit. Eric and Roxie had both been quizzed by multiple people the night before at every chance meeting before and after dinner. I, it appeared, was the cause of all the ruckus and the leaves being canceled. No one talked to me except the Wolf Squad, which was fine. Roxie's grudge over being caught off patrol had diminished to an occasional sharp remark.

I'd started to glaze while stuffing down potato chunks seasoned with more garlic than usual as Selina detailed our roster for the day. "Caitlyn, martial training at 1000," she said.

"What?" I swallowed. It surprised me because I'd been to the army base already this week. If they wanted to do something about me talking to Dean's family, they didn't need to do it at a military facility. I hoped they hadn't found out, but the timing was suspicious.

She frowned, ignored me, and continued. "Roxie, your group has the gate at 0100 after lunch. Yaz, Jordan, meet me at the north gate for patrol."

I poked my eggs, trying to figure out why I'd be in

martial training twice in one week. There had to be a reason. With all the soldiers going up and down Bass Drive yesterday evening, I would have thought they'd cancel all training at the base.

Selina coughed to get my attention. "Roxie, pick a weapon at Tyrell's office for patrol along with the watch. Standing order until otherwise notified."

"Okay. Sector A? We just did that patrol this week." Roxie glanced at me, as it had been where I'd seen Moonjir.

Selina jabbed her fork into her eggs. "Not my call. That's the roster."

The strange schedule bothered me, but I couldn't see any reason it should, other than it wasn't the normal weekly routine. Assignments always rotated each week, except Bible study with the army's chaplain replaced classes on Sunday.

I still caught all the strange glances as Eric and I went to clean our plates at the sink. If anything, they studied me with more curiosity than derision.

Eric led the way out of the screened in porch and headed down the stairs for the pavilion. It seemed that while I was still in the spotlight, this would be our place to talk after breakfast. "Do you think they know?" he asked.

I rolled my eyes. "Know what?" We were hiding too many secrets to be sure what he meant.

"That we stopped by Dean's. They'll find out he's missing, if they haven't already."

I slid onto the bench beside him. "Yeah. I'm worried about that."

"What's your plan?"

"I'll be heart-broken when I find out my crush has disappeared." I rubbed under my eyes. "I'll work on the tears." I cringed at my comment, suddenly feeling callous.

Taking a breath, I peered upriver. Nothing had caught my attention, but I sensed something there.

The clouds still darkened the morning, but it hadn't rained despite the foreboding sky. Gusts whipped branches and rippled the water, but I couldn't see anything beyond leafless branches and the river.

"What are you looking at?" Eric asked.

I shrugged. "Nothing. I felt like something was there."

"Dean sneaking underwater to get us?"

"Stop. He didn't ask for this." He either was running as a wolf with his new pack by now, or huddled somewhere trying to live through the cold nights.

The screen door banged as Roxie headed for us. A frustrated expression flashed on her face when I smiled. "I'm still not good with you. You know I won't be promoted now, right?"

"You can't be sure," I said.

"Oh, I'm sure."

Flashing an apologetic smile, my shoulders sagged. "You could turn me in. Tell them you just found out what I did."

She sat and frowned. "Don't tempt me. No more bullshit, though. Right?"

"What do you expect me to do? Can I make this any worse?"

Eric laughed. "Probably."

I punched his shoulder. "Shut up."

"She's seeing bogeymen in the river now." He laughed and shied away as if I'd hit him again.

"What?" asked Roxie.

"I — felt something." I nudged my chin upriver. "Don't ask me. I'm a mess."

Roxie turned to study the river. "Just don't find anything else to get us in trouble. Maybe that's why they have you doubling up on martial training. I'd like to give you a few bruises." When she faced us, she smiled. "I'm just kidding. Don't mope."

"Sector A again," I said.

"With a rifle." Eric snorted. "I'm not getting what's going on."

Roxie rested forward with elbows on knees. "I pulled Ben aside before I came out. He's got a weird roster as well. He thinks it's because they've canceled the outer patrols for us. Too much werewolf activity. First Talia, and then Caitlyn."

That did make more sense as to why our schedule had been skewed. I was being paranoid keeping all these secrets. Tyrell would find out about Dean missing, or already had. I turned upriver again with a nagging feeling, but straightened before they noticed. My unit didn't need to worry that I was acting even more strange. The other units already thought I was lying, which I was doing, just not the way they believed.

Our class was with Gayle, studying cryptid behavior and how to kill them. I kept waiting for her to bring up Moonjir, but gratefully she acted as if we hadn't discussed it. The Tuathua were the focus this morning, with their biology similar to humans except their low-density bones where we should focus our blows. I had to believe they existed deep in the cryptid zone. She rarely had any anecdotal reports to relay about them. The werewolves had numerous detailed examples. The vampire stories were scarce, and the most horrifying of all to me.

I kept waiting for one of the others to make a snide comment about Moonjir, but they didn't. Disruptive behavior in class or training meant demerits or a meeting with Tyrell.

After our studies, Eric walked me to the south gate for our morning run. "Now they think you've got Tyrell and the military searching the town for your cryptid." He giggled. "I haven't dissuaded them from the idea."

All the units were heading for the road, some already stretching their legs on the asphalt. No matter where I turned, eyes were focused on me. I groaned. "Great."

When we stepped through the gate, Ben approached me. "Hey, Caitlyn."

I fought a smile. "I can't talk about it." Shrugging, I nodded toward the camp. "Tyrell's orders."

The result was satisfying, as he nodded. "Understand." Ben paused, his eyes flicking to the others watching us. "Probably best. I'm sure we'll be briefed when it's all worked out." He took too long between his words, as if he wanted people to think we were discussing something. "What do you have today?"

"Martial," I said and began stretching. "Later."

"Yeah." Ben smiled and headed for his unit.

Eyes followed him now.

"Everyone will be on him, then they'll act like they got something juicy. Nice." Eric reached to his toes. "Who knows, maybe Tyrell *is* searching for your cryptid as well."

Selina approached with the rest of the Wolf Squad, so I spoke in a whisper. "Moonjir, and he's not mine."

Our runs were two laps from the south gate of Camp Sparta to Pickney Road where the patrol for Sector C began; the intersection where Tyrell had caught us. Running at full tilt, I could make it in twenty-five minutes. We usually did it in thirty. We passed the school and the area we'd be patrolling. The nagging sense of being watched crept up on me again. It came from the side of the road with the river. Goosebumps crawled along my arms, despite the exertion.

After the run, Roxie paired off with Selina, holding hands as they headed for the buildings. Eric joined me to head for our barracks. The other units kept watching me, but their expressions weren't as harsh.

"Introduce me to Moonjir today?" Eric smirked at my frown.

His comment had me wondering and glancing over at the river. "I'd gladly have a witness, just to get rid of *that* gossip." Surely something with bright blue and pink fur couldn't hide in the woods and watch me.

When I filled my canteen on the way to the military base for martial training, Leslie tried to play nice. In one day, people had turned from labeling me a liar to mining me for details. I blew her off as quickly as I could and headed for the gate.

The sky threatened rain and the air carried the smell of it. Summer would bring more frequent storms, and I'd always be wet. Only two other Youth Guards were on the road heading north.

The military base on Bass Drive had a fence around it leading into the water, much like Camp Sparta did. One werewolf carcass hung from the fence, but the winds blew the scent away. The fence stretched across the road, coming to corners where guard posts rose on the inside.

The soldiers recognized me, or the uniform, and opened one side of the gate before I arrived. "Beta building."

I groaned, but he remained indifferent. "Thanks," I said. The middle building contained the gym, which meant I'd be doing dumb crap like rope climbing, close quarters grappling, or kickboxing.

Behind me, a dozen or so other Youth Guards had left Camp Sparta and were following me down the road. The gym would leave us standing in lines for our turns and give them plenty of time to dig for information. I'd rather be on gate duty.

Each of the buildings was larger than our barracks,

though they had a similar style of stairwells leading to balconied top floors. Flags flapped from a pole, and military vehicles were parked close to the center building. The motto "For the nation, of the nation" was blazoned on bricks above the main entry.

Noisy soldiers were inside the offices that had been built into the existing structure. The smell reminded me of Eric and Jordan's musty quarters mixed with something that reminded me of wet clothes. Stairs led to the bottom floor of the middle building.

The structure had been cleared out to form an open area with sections of padding. Rope ladders and climbing ropes had been distributed into one of the army's obstacle courses. None of the soldiers gave an awkward glance, so I joined the other two in line and kept my distance.

During my first attempt, I managed to fall off each challenge, causing a bottleneck with the others. Clumsy and rope ladders don't mix. I stopped apologizing by the fourth obstacle, a knotted rope stretched between two wooden braces. We had to pull ourselves upside down without releasing our legs.

Leslie maneuvered herself into line behind me and tried to start a casual conversation. "Sucks that they shut down leaves."

I tilted my head over my shoulder just enough to catch her expression. "Saved me swimming around with pink cryptids."

Her pale skin flushed and she snapped her head back with a shake of her black braid. "Screw you."

I faced forward, smiling at the instructor halfway across the room who had glanced in our direction at her outburst. "No thanks."

A few more Youth Guards tried to ease into conversations, and I kept my non-committal responses politer. After two hours of proving myself lacking an ounce of grace, I jogged ahead of the others to get to lunch without any more opportunities for prodding. It would be best if they came up with their own conclusions on what my situation with Tyrell was. He hadn't deemed it necessary to share news of my encounter with the werewolves yet, it seemed.

Gray clouds hung low in the sky. As I opened the door, thunder growled outside. Roxie and Selina were holding hands in line for cold cornbread and chicken. I ignored the few already sitting, except for Eric and Yaz with their plates.

"Have fun?" Eric smiled from our table.

"Call me Grace." I pinched a corner of Eric's cornbread before he swatted at me, and I got into the queue.

The odd sensation from the morning returned to me, and I peered out the windows at the trees and water. I'm not sure what I expected to find. In the past few days, my life had become bizarre. I couldn't be blamed for a little paranoia.

When I returned with my food, the last seat available was beside Jordan and across from Roxie. "It's going to rain on us." I tilted my head toward the front of the hall. "Guard duty."

"Probably." She locked on my eyes, and I could tell she had something to say.

I glanced at Selina and Eric, but they didn't appear concerned. Taking a large bite of chicken, I noticed Roxie hurrying as well. I'd grown hungry when I stood in line; now I just wanted to finish and talk with her. We'd need to go upstairs to get our weapons anyway.

We exited the mess with two members of the Hounds unit, so I had to wait as we climbed the stairs. The gloomy day hadn't helped my declining mood over the past couple of days.

Roxie went in ahead of me, and I closed the door. "What?" I asked.

She grabbed her staff from the corner. "Tyrell knows it was Dean."

I paused, ready to clip my machete and sheath on my belt. "How do you know?" A panic rose. I'd assumed he would find out. Did he know I'd been asking about Dean?

"Selina. She was at the gate when the word went out with Dean's description. They'll likely brief us when we show for guard duty."

"We'll be hunting him?"

"If he's dumb enough to come around, yeah." Her expression softened. "We're not hunting anyone. We just have to report anything we see."

I'd assumed he'd stayed on his side of the lake, since he hadn't come home. "Okay."

She walked to me and forced us to lock eyes. "Meaning, we report him if we see him."

"I said okay." Pulling back from her gaze, I focused on my weapon. Hopefully, he was far away by now. I knew what my duty should be, but if I saw him, I would yell at him to leave.

Someone should have come to bring me to Tyrell's office. Since they knew about Dean missing, the soldiers had to have talked to Dean's family. Tyrell either knew about my visits and didn't think I'd answer truthfully, or they hadn't mentioned me. My blonde hair and pale skin would mark me in an instant.

Rain slammed against the building. Wind blustered it under the balcony, and heavy drops tapped at the window. Roxie drooped at the sound. Last winter we'd still had rain gear, some brittle plastic jackets, but they hadn't survived the summer.

Surprisingly, the downpour lasted all of half an hour as

we huddled at the fence. The next couple hours we stood soaked, guarding the gate. The heavy clouds remained overhead, threatening more rain. The winds brought alternating scents of fresh rain and the rotting wolf corpses.

"Do we bother changing our clothes before patrol?" Eric peered at the gray clouds.

Roxie snorted. "I'm going to. It'll get colder near the end." She turned to me with a smile, which faded as her eyes flicked toward the buildings. "I'm never getting promoted."

Tyrell had been walking toward us across the lawn, and when I turned, he stopped, pointed at me, and motioned to follow him. His expression unreadable, I guessed that he knew about my visit to Dean's family. What else could it be?

My chest tightened so I couldn't breathe. The whole day had been tense waiting for this, dealing with peers, and whatever I sensed out by the river. I had to face this. Tyrell might suspect I was lying, but he couldn't prove it.

"I'm not telling him anything," I said to Roxie.

Chapter Twelve

I started toward Tyrell, and he turned away without waiting. His dismissive action made my heart race faster. He had to be angry with me and may even believe I was lying about what I'd seen on the other side of the lake. There wasn't anything to lead him to believe I'd attempted to heal Dean. However, the family had to have described me.

As Tyrell approached the door, a soldier hidden by the stairwell appeared and walked over with a sharp salute. They spoke in low voices, so I barely heard a murmur.

When I was three steps away, the soldier snapped another salute. "Yes, sir." He darted off without giving me a glance.

Tyrell stepped into his office and left the door open for me. He walked over to his table, empty for the first time I'd seen, and waited for me. "Close the door, Soldier." His tone was flat, barren of any hint about my situation.

"Yes, sir."

"We've identified the person who fired the gun before he was bitten by the werewolves that tried to attack you. Dean Valdina, a local boy who's nearly a year older than you." Tyrell paused, giving me a moment to twist. "Did you see him out there?"

I could see no choice but to lie; otherwise, I risked Roxie and Eric getting caught in this. "No, sir."

He studied me and I tried a feeble smile.

"Water?" he asked, then, without an answer, headed for his partial counter in the back of his office.

Did he believe me? "Yes, please." I still had half a canteen. Maybe the family hadn't mentioned me. Tyrell could be telling me because I'd been involved with the werewolves. He could have just told me on the lawn, but had brought me into his office instead. My eyes flicked to the river behind the building.

He came back with two corked bottles and a small white bowl with pecan halves in it. His familiar, warm smile on his face, he placed them on the table and nodded toward them. "Pecans. Savannah harvests have been growing. There will be more coming next fall."

We'd had the pecans last year for our birthdays. There hadn't been this many. I took one of the halves. "Thank you."

He handed me the bottle of water. "Ever met this Dean?" he asked.

I tried not to choke on the nut. "Yes. I think. Older than me with a jacket? All the locals drop by the gate on their way to the bridge to fish."

"Have you met him outside the gate?" Tyrell slowly uncorked his water.

"I've never met him outside the gate, sir," I lied, and chattered a bit too quickly. "Truly. I just turned fifteen, so I've only gone out on leave a couple of times."

He motioned me to have another pecan. "Inspection is coming. March second."

I obliged, taking another of the delicacies, but I'd barely

tasted the first nut. My mouth dry, I worked out the cork before eating. "Yes, sir."

He studied me over his bottle as he finished his water, took a moment to swallow, then spoke. "We have two new ranks we'll be filling soon. Specialists, who will have exemplary martial or healing skill sets above others. Section Leaders, who will work directly with me to lead two or three units. They will also be tasked with coordinating the first deep, overnight patrols into the cryptid zones with their units."

That sounded horrifying. "Yes, sir." I held the nut, waiting for him to mention Dean again.

Tyrell motioned me to one of the maps I'd looked at before, depicting the city of Columbia. Flat red lines enclosed the city. He pointed to the red arrows leading to those walls. "The primary goal of the Savannah Charter is to liberate Columbia."

I wanted to ask what the people were being liberated from, but this discussion had turned strange enough. He hadn't pushed, but he knew there was something between me and Dean. "Yes." My tone suggested I knew that, and I did. We discussed the priorities in Civics regularly, though in theory and rhetoric more than details.

He moved to a more local map with Santee at the bottom. At the top, a town called Sumter had two circles on the west side. A dotted line led there while a solid red line led across our bridge to Manning, where three circles had been marked with x.

"We pushed into the cryptid zone at Manning without too many incidents. We'll be hitting Shaw Air Force Base soon." Tyrell tapped my sternum. "I'd like to have you and some of the others travel with us as observers." He tilted his head toward the first map. "When we move for Columbia, we'll have an elite unit and their Section Leader, maybe even a Specialist, from Camp Sparta, along with others from five other camps joining the army. It will be our test of the Youth Guard program."

He seemed proud of his plan, so I tried to sound impressed. "I'm sure it will be an honor for those who make it, sir." I finished the pecan, studying his maps and waiting for him to continue. The silence that followed had me chugging the last of my water.

"You're due on patrol next." His tone dried to a crisp command. "Keep an eye out for this local, Dean."

"Yes, sir." I took his words as a dismissal.

When I left and jogged toward Roxie and Eric; their expressions varied from curiosity to concern. My own emotions calmed with the exertion. Whatever Tyrell knew, he hadn't pushed or condemned me. I could live with that. Dean was gone, and no one would know about my help except for my closest friends.

"So, he knows it's Dean," I said.

Roxie's lips tightened. "And our visit?"

"Never mentioned."

"He could know," she said.

"Yep." I took a deep breath, trying to let go of my anxiety. "I also got a tour of all the army's upcoming plans for some air force base and Columbia."

Roxie frowned at my comment.

"Are they going for planes?" Eric asked with a smirk.

"I don't know." It was still unbelievable to think of machines in the air. "Roxie will be excited about the new ranks."

Her expression grew curious, and her tone intense. "What new ranks?"

"Section Leader, boss of some units. Specialist." This position actually interested me, and I turned to Eric as I spoke. "Like healers and people who specialize in fighting.

I'm not sure exactly." We could end up doing what we liked with our magic.

I pivoted my head, glancing upriver, but there was only brush. What had I expected?

They both turned to study the area. Eric asked, "That feeling again?"

"Paranoia. My nerves are raw. Ignore me."

He turned to Roxie with his brow furrowed. "Have you seen Caitlyn lately?"

I rolled my eyes and forced myself not to glance in the same direction again. Our patrol would take us into those woods in a short while. The Sector began at the edge of our camp, led south toward the town, encompassed the buildings by the river, and stretched to the tiny bridge and the west shore of the water. I hoped something wasn't watching me from the leafless trees.

We stocked our canteens and changed into dry coveralls before Roxie ran to collect a rifle and the patrol watch. I waited with Eric at the stairwell.

"From what I told you of Tyrell's comments, what do you think was going on?" I asked Eric.

"He knows. The rest was just to remind you to be a team player. His next little talk will be about forgiveness or some such so you know it's okay to break your little lie. Don't."

I scooped yellow strands of hair from my cheeks and wrestled with my braid. "I'm not going to admit anything. It's over. I'll not have him wondering if you and Roxie were in on it."

A door above us closed, and we grimaced. Waiting for footsteps on the stairwell, we straightened. Someone knocked on an apartment, and a moment later Jordan grumbled about wet boots before his door closed.

Eric mouthed. "Selina."

I could hope she hadn't heard us, but we'd been stupid to talk about anything close to the barracks. Rifle and staff tucked on her back, Roxie jogged from the other buildings at the same time Selina, Yaz, and Jordan came down the stairs.

Roxie smiled and moved to give Selina a kiss.

Eric and I stiffened but twitched like guilty squirrels.

Selina took a moment to study us before smiling and kissing Roxie. "Be careful on patrol."

"Dean. Tyrell told me." Roxie touched her rifle, and I blinked in horror.

The orders might have been to shoot on sight. He wasn't stupid enough to stay this close to the camp.

Selina tilted her head. "Caitlyn, everything okay?"

"Fine." I patted my hair. "Damp, but who isn't?"

The awkwardness lasted a moment longer as Roxie frowned, then our two groups started in opposite directions. We remained silent until we were outside the south gate.

"What?" Roxie asked.

I led the way down the trail into the woods just south of Camp Sparta. "I was talking about keeping secrets, and Selina might have heard."

"Did you say what secrets?"

"Nope."

Our path led into the woods along the inlet of water that carved toward the road from the river. On the opposite side was the back of the air training area with its thick posts. A trainer already had a line queued.

We were to search for anything unusual. Disturbances on the ground such as tracks were our focus here.

"Are you supposed to shoot Dean if you see him?" I asked Roxie.

"Only if he approaches." She unsnapped her staff and used it as a walking stick.

As we approached the river, our trail turned. A small log over at the camp burst into flames as someone focused enough heat into it. Fire magic was harder than blowing something with air. Pulling together all that heat from the surroundings and ground proved difficult, at least for me. Untrained, you could inadvertently draw from human flesh and cause frostbite. During the killing tests on pigs last fall, one had been purposefully frozen. I turned from the training at the camp with a shudder.

"Do you think Tyrell would actually just let me be a healer, a Specialist?" I mused over the idea like a childish dream.

The lazy greenish river stretched wide ahead of us to a shore dotted with barren trees and a spattering of evergreens. We turned upriver toward the back of the school.

Roxie snorted. "If you could stick to healing us, not the enemy."

"Roxie." Eric's tone pleaded and chastised.

I couldn't have not tried. Roxie took her rank and position seriously, but she would have tried to help as much as I did. The only real difference is that she would have told Tyrell afterward.

The wind gusted drops of water out of the branches. The clouds hadn't gotten any lighter. When children laughed in the distance ahead, I jerked my head to search. The feeling of being watched hadn't diminished, and the sound brought it to the surface. It did seem to be ahead rather than from the river.

Roxie pulled out the patrol watch. "Last class of the day."

"I sort of wish we'd gotten to go to school there. Like all day long." Eric strained to view the buildings through the winter woods. The forest looked barren, but the dead brush still made it hard for me to see through.

"I enjoyed moving to the camp," I said. Everything had seemed pleasant after the labs. The apartment with Selina had felt like a vacation.

The first of the homes along the river started to take shape. Two stories high, it had an upper balcony. Selina and I had slipped out numerous times to sit there and watch the stars. It had rotted now, but the skeleton of railings still showed. The school had a fence around the back, and the kids bunked at Camp Sparta when they opened the school.

Eric picked up a branch, snapping off twigs to make a walking stick. "I mean, they get to come here and focus mainly on classes, with just a little magic training here and there. We had to do it all right away."

Across the river, abandoned houses lay along the shore. Our patrol would take us there in an hour, but to get there, we'd have to go closer to town where the river nearly dried up and the footbridge crossed.

We reached the first building behind the school and spread out, searching for tracks or disturbed property. The storm had pulled down more branches, littering what had long ago been a someone's front yard. I veered nearer the river while Roxie went around behind the house and Eric the front.

A full neighborhood stretched from Bass Drive, tucked behind the school housed at the old hotel. No one lived here; they all had moved into town to build gardens and chicken houses. The townsfolk came here to fish, but no one was out this afternoon. They probably kept away when they learned Dean had gone missing.

"Do you think Tyrell told the family?" I asked when Eric came closer.

"Told them what?"

"About Dean being bit."

He thought for a second, poking leaves with his stick.

"Probably."

"They must be freaking out." I turned toward him as the shore curved.

"I'd say so."

Thunder rumbled off to the east. We both groaned at the idea of getting wet again. The patrol wasn't halfway done. We subconsciously picked up the pace, lapping the next house with Roxie.

I winced at the idea that Dean's family would be afraid of him now, and also mourn him as if he were already dead. A few of the locals had disappeared over the years. Each time, everyone got upset and nervous all over again. One man had come to the camp drunk and demanding that we do something about the werewolves. Tyrell said they'd been pushed back to the other side of the lake, but some people still lived and fished there.

"Maybe your buddy is home."

I turned to see what Eric meant, and he pointed to the building where I'd been cornered by Moonjir in the shed. "Funny."

Roxie let out a low whistle, and we turned to the house we were circling. She pointed to a newly broken window on the side. Other windows were broken, but we knew them by heart.

"Keep watch," Eric said as he jogged to the front door with Roxie.

My pulse began to quicken. Dean wouldn't be so stupid as to pick a house behind the school to hide in. Across the river would be smarter, and staying on the other side of the lake the best idea.

Roxie pulled out her rifle, leaving her staff leaning against the door jamb. I could hear my breathing as she checked her weapon. I wanted to shout for her to stop, but this is why we were on patrol.

Eric turned the handle, pushed, then leaned against the front door to force it open. Roxie raced past him into the darkness, and he drew his machete and followed.

My right hand trembled. "Please don't be in there." I didn't want Dean to be killed, not after I'd saved him. If the healing hadn't worked, though, I didn't want him to attack my friends.

The minutes wore on with only the occasional sound from inside. Birds called to each other, and random voices from the school drifted along the wind. Each moment I didn't hear a gunshot gave me hope.

Roxie emerged first, and I sagged with relief. Eric followed her and tugged the door closed. Before taking her staff, she slid her gun into the sheath strapped on her back.

"All clear," she called out as she strode toward me.

I bobbed my head and turned away, knowing I couldn't hide my expression. "Good."

"Probably a branch from the wind broke the window," Eric said.

We continued our patrol of the abandoned neighborhood, Roxie dipping behind the next building where the road drew close. The river thinned, and the houses across the water drew closer. I paused to study the opposite shore. The sense of being watched didn't come from there, but from ahead.

"Still got the creeps?" Eric asked.

I shrugged, feeling foolish. "Somewhat."

He nodded. "You have to expect to be a little on edge, after finding your cryptid and then the werewolves."

"I suppose." We were turning the corner along the shore where a brightly painted house had faded, leaving only protected patches of bright blues and reds. I glanced beyond it, where the house I'd found Moonjir waited.

Roxie curved toward us then back out to the road. The

area opened up, and Eric took the shore while I stayed in the middle. My nerves were shaken. After they'd searched the house, I hadn't fully settled. My stomach fluttered, and I drank more than usual to quench my dry mouth.

We reached Moonjir's shed, and I studied it as we approached in our spread out patrol. I veered toward the two wooden buildings, faded gray from weather, which had been built against the side of the house facing toward the road. Tensing, I forced a deep breath and circled both sheds.

Roxie glanced back at me from the road but continued. The doors were closed to Moonjir's shed. We'd left them open in our hurry to report.

I paused, too nervous to open the doors, but unwilling to move on. Tyrell's soldiers had likely searched it and closed it.

My paranoia screamed at me as I yanked open the left side, stepping back as I did so.

Thinking I should have drawn my machete, I stared at the empty and familiar space. I laughed at myself and closed the door. Eric was right that the jitters I felt were the result of multiple days of surprises.

I had worried about Tyrell, and it had worked out, whether he knew about my visit to Dean's family or not. Dean hadn't returned and killed his family. Whatever Selina heard, I could make up an excuse to explain. The worst part of the day had been the soaking at the gate. I could relax, have dinner, and go back to my normal life.

A little less timid, I went to the next shed. The bushes stunk like a latrine. I opened the door.

The shadows moved. A shape lunged for the opening, and I gasped. Brandishing a short, wooden handle, Dean stopped in his tracks when he saw my face.

Chapter Thirteen

Numb and dizzy, I stumbled a footstep back from Dean. He shouldn't be on this side of the lake. Blinking, I stared into the darkness.

Dark shadows marked his deep brown eyes, and he appeared gaunt and sickly. He wore the jacket and jeans I'd left him in. His expression slackened. "Leave. Close the door," he said.

"What — what are you doing here? Are you alright?"

Dean stepped deeper into the shadows, crouching beside a wall of debris. "You should go. You never saw me." His eyes dropped to the ground. "I haven't turned into one of them, but something's not right."

"You shouldn't be here," I said.

"I can't go home."

At least he had that much sense. "The soldiers are searching for you." If he knew he couldn't go home, he should have stayed on the other side of the lake. "Why did you come back here?"

"Nothing is ever easy. The wolves came back."

"They want you to join their pack. It's what happens when. .."

"You get bit and turn into a werewolf. I know." His expression tightened. "I've *always* hated them." The emphasis he put on the sentence made me believe he'd had experience with them before.

"The healing — it didn't work?" I asked.

Dean shrugged. "I can feel them — in the northwest. They're getting closer. I think — I can feel you, too."

"Why did you come back here?" He should go before the soldiers found him.

"I told you. The wolves came back. I crossed the lake at first, then I hid out at the campground west of here."

That didn't explain why he'd gotten closer to the town. "You need to go back there. Even farther."

"I am going." He held his palm toward me as if to stop my demands. "I need to leave a note for my sister. Tell her I hadn't turned, but had to leave." Dean focused on my eyes. "I'm going north. I promise. Fishing is good. The soldiers rarely patrol there because of the muck."

His eyes widened and he focused over my shoulder.

I spun to find Roxie, rifle stock to her shoulder, aiming at Dean. "Don't!" I yelled.

"Back away." Her jaw was tight. "I've got him."

I stepped in front of her, protecting him. As I faced her, my back was to Dean. My reaction surprised me. I just stared at her open mouthed. I'd chosen Dean over my duty, just as she'd feared. "I'm sorry." My hands were up, as if to hold her back.

She pulled the muzzle aside so as not to have it pointing at me. "Dammit. He's one of them. Get that through your dense skull." Her eyes flicked back and forth, glaring at me and into the depths of the shed.

Eric skittered around the corner of the shed, machete drawn. He nearly went down in the mud.

"He hasn't turned." I could sense Dean behind me.

Whatever I had done had created a connection between us. One he also felt for the werewolves. "But he's not okay, either. He's going to leave."

Peering into the shed as he walked, Eric came behind Roxie. "Why is he here?"

"A note for his sister." I glanced back into the shed. He hadn't moved. "Which I can deliver."

"You won't," Roxie said. "He comes in with us now."

I stiffened. "So you can get a promotion?"

The flicker of her eyes told me I'd been right. "We have a duty to protect people from his kind."

"He hasn't turned," I repeated. "Maybe what I did helped in some small way. We all know he can't go back, but does he deserve to end up in a lab or wherever they took Talia?"

"You're being irrational."

Eric coughed. "Actually, it is interesting that he hasn't turned into his wolf form while we've been standing here. Even more so that he didn't tear Caitlyn's throat out the moment she opened the shed. It's long past incubation." He flashed a half-smile at me. His machete pointed toward the ground as he stepped beside Roxie. "Maybe we do just let him go. Give him some time. Head back to the camp after a couple hours and report him so you can get some special patch."

"You're taking her side?" Roxie pinched her lips, which meant she was considering his advice.

"A rational direction would be to study him, in a humane way. What if we could heal the infection?" Eric motioned between me and him. "That would be far more important than anything." He sighed. "However, they want Youth Guards, not healers."

"Bullshit." Roxie's tone wasn't confident. Her brows pushed down farther.

Eric's portrayal of the program seemed a little harsh, but essentially correct. I wanted Dean to survive. The healing might not be complete, but he would have attacked us by now if it had failed. I shivered but spread my arms to hide it from the others.

"Can we agree to let him leave?" I asked. "But just hold off on reporting him until tomorrow."

"Tomorrow?" Roxie shook her head and narrowed her eyes. "Why would we possibly wait?"

I didn't dare smile, but Roxie hadn't bypassed the argument and gone directly to shooting him or bringing him back to the camp. "I want to bring him some food." Turning, I asked Dean, "When was the last time you ate?"

There was a pause, and when he did speak, he was quiet. "Don't remember. Been sick."

I sagged. Some part of me had hoped that I'd saved him from the infection. Obviously something was still inside him.

Roxie's muzzle dropped, pointing at the ground while her eyes bulged. "Are you serious? You want to bring him a damned picnic?"

"While we deliver the note to his sister. She needs to know he's not — a werewolf."

As Roxie sputtered, Eric stepped to my side and faced Dean. He crouched, digging the point of the machete into the ground and leaning his chin and hands on the hilt. "What kind of sick? Fevers? Nausea?"

"Yes. Am I a science experiment now?"

"A patient," Eric said. "And Caitlyn's friend, so thus mine. Have the sweats and nausea passed? When?"

Perhaps we could try to finish the healing I'd started.

"Last night. When I felt better this morning, I moved closer so I could deliver the note tonight." Dean sighed.

"My sister, Bettina, takes care of the chicken coup. I was going to leave it there."

Roxie, gun at her side, grunted. "I'm not helping."

"But you'll not report Dean? You'll let me and Eric bring food and deliver the letter?" As her expression hardened, I leaned in, forcing her to focus on my eyes. "Please?"

She glared at me. "Okay. You know I want to beat you with my staff, don't you?" From her expression, she might mean it. It lay four paces away where she must have dropped it while readying her rifle.

"Maybe when I get back from dropping Dean off some food." I smiled. "Not in the face?"

She blinked slowly and took a deep breath. "Definitely the face. I want to see the bruises for the next couple of days."

I hugged Roxie and whispered in her ear. "Thank you."

She sighed and gave me a short hug back, then pushed me away. "So, do we just continue our patrol as if nothing happened?"

Eric stood. "Do you at least have water?"

"Yeah," Dean said. "I'm next to a lake. It's not hard." He'd made a weak barricade of rotting boxes which had been stored in the shed. The rain had soaked the floor so it likely leaked.

"Stay put." I walked to the edge to get a better view. His bitten hand appeared darker, though he'd washed blood off of it and his jacket. "We'll be back with some food after it gets dark."

"Will there be a secret knock?" he asked.

"What?"

He shook his head and almost smiled. "Nothing. Too many spy novels. Thank you." He pulled a folded piece of paper from the inside of his jacket. "The note?"

"I'll pick it up when I bring the food. Then you leave. Right?"

"No regrets." He leaned back, his face slack.

I wasn't sure what he meant. "Don't give up," I said.

"I don't."

My comment had been meant to be comforting, but Dean's response had been sharp.

"Other than food, do you need anything?"

"Peach brandy? Shotgun shells?"

I closed the door to the shed. He didn't appear healthy, but at least he had some humor. I'm not sure how I would have handled his situation.

Storing her rifle and retrieving her staff, Roxie started ahead of us at a brisk pace. Eric retrieved his walking stick from the other side of the shed. I took a long moment, staring at the weathered boards of the doors.

Dean might leave after we did without waiting for food, but he had tried to hand me the note. He didn't know Roxie like I did. If she'd given her word to me, she'd keep it. We had never betrayed each other. I supposed she would consider my request to keep a confidence as cheating her out of a promotion. My actions had given her good reason to be mad at me. I'd owe her, big time.

Eric patrolled the shore as he had before. Roxie had already reached the next house, setting a quick pace. We rushed through the final section of the neighborhood and didn't talk again until we'd come to the footbridge.

"I'm surprised it hasn't rained," Eric said with a quick glance to the dark clouds overhead.

"Me too." The sky appeared close enough to touch the treetops.

He took the first steps onto the bridge. It had been repaired two summers ago, but the wood they'd used already had cracked and faded in the weather. The river below ran quicker here, and you could see it was shallow. The rain had cleared the water. In the dryer months, plants and muck clogged the area between the banks. I still liked the view.

Roxie snorted behind me. "You realize, if I'd shot him, we'd all get a promotion."

"Yeah." I knew it would eat her, and I was sorry.

As Eric reached the far side and waited for us, I stepped gingerly across the wood, avoiding the railings which had snapped near the middle and wobbled as I walked.

Roxie really wanted to run a unit, and I'd want to be in it. After all my blunders, she might not get a promotion during this inspection. The officers who showed up for their monthly visit always appeared to dismiss our magic, or perhaps they feared it. Tyrell treated us as important, while the military acted as if we were something they had to put up with. I couldn't imagine our units being used to liberate Columbia.

I reached Eric, who peered back over the water to the sheds where Dean hid. "Your healing might have worked, somewhat."

"He says that he can sense me."

"So, that was the feeling you had?" Eric turned with raised eyebrows.

"I guess so."

Roxie arrived as I spoke and began striding along the shore. "What do you guess?"

Our patrol would follow the shore, then return on the same path. "Those feelings I had about being watched. They might be my connection to Dean." The house, if not the sheds, were visible across the river. The sensation did seem to be coming from there.

"Then you'll know when he leaves. That's good." Her

tone was harsh, but at least she hadn't stopped speaking to me.

Our next lap of the patrol would take us to the interstate, and Roxie kept us at a swift pace. We reached the burned remains of the welcome center when the skies opened. By the time we made it back to the camp, the sides of the road were filling with water, and I couldn't help but get wet even inside my boots.

As we jogged for the camp, a trio of soldiers left toward town wearing their hooded ponchos, coated with something that kept the rain beading off. Each of them watched us carefully as we splashed through the deeper puddles.

A single soldier had replaced the unit teams at the gate, and he appeared as wet as me. When Roxie came through, he motioned to her rifle and she pulled the sheath and strap over her head. At least we didn't have to go to Tyrell's office.

Gusts blew rain under the balconies and into stairwells while sheets of water dropped from the roof. Eric headed off to his apartment he shared with Jordan, and I followed Roxie into ours. We both stripped before we'd taken a few steps inside.

"They should find us rain jackets again."

Roxie snorted. "Because there's so many left after the Sorrow."

In Civics they always touted the Savannah Charter's progress in manufacturing, but we saw little of it except for our uniforms. "Extra cloaks, then." Those too were made in Savannah.

My soaked coveralls from earlier hung from the kitchen cabinets, appearing no drier than when I'd put them there. Roxie's dangled beside mine, but I didn't dare ask her to use her magic to steam out the water. She didn't owe me any favors.

In my bedroom, I hung underwear and socks beside my

already wet pair and slipped into my last dry pair, leaving the socks for last. We'd tracked plenty of water into the room. The room was chilly, and they hadn't turned on the furnace. Dean would be wet and freezing too.

I grabbed a blanket and wrapped it around me, dancing back to the kitchen to beat Roxie. My water magic wasn't as good as my control over air or healing, but it worked. Using my heat magic might be disastrous.

I focused between our dripping coveralls and the otherness drew from all around me. Drawing water to the spot caused droplets to form, which became a trickle splashing onto the floor. I didn't have great control, but I tried to pull from the fabric more than the air. In the winter, it wasn't very humid anyway.

Squeezing the cloth proved they were drying, but not quickly. I stepped back and fought the weariness of stress and activity. The water rivulet thickened, splashing into a globe rising off the floor. I spun to find Roxie behind me, dressed only in underwear.

"You want a puddle in here?" she asked. Her ability with water far exceeded mine.

Our coveralls lightened, and I stopped focusing when the sphere of water moved for the door, drawing any droplets nearby. Roxie opened it a crack, and water streamed out to join the raging storm. I had to envy her control.

"You still mad at me?" I squeezed my almost dry coveralls.

"Why wouldn't I be?" She snapped hers down and headed to the living room to dress.

I frowned and followed. "I guess you should be. I hope I don't ruin your chance at promotion."

"Not reporting your abandoning patrol will ensure that. The stuff they don't know might get me demoted."

"They've never done that." I'd left the back of the coveralls partially buttoned and wiggled my hips in. The room still felt cold. "I wish I could bring Dean a blanket." I might try healing him some more.

"You saw the soldiers heading south?" Roxie reached behind her shoulders, buttoning the coveralls.

"I figured they were heading for town." A chill crawled to my neck. "Do you think they're heading along our patrol area?

"It was late, so maybe just around the school or some other task. They won't patrol at night."

I glanced out the back windows. The panes were smudged, but the storm let in no light. There should have been an hour of twilight left.

"Storm's letting up." The soldiers wouldn't have time to search all the buildings. If Dean left before sunrise, he'd be okay. "He's going to be wet and cold."

Roxie stood, staring at me. "You make a lousy soldier."

"I know."

She shook her head and stomped for her bedroom to finish dressing for dinner. "Let's hope they make these Specialist positions like you said. Make you a healer and save us from the trouble."

I thought about her comment even as we raced downstairs for the mess hall. The rain and wind had lightened, so except for my boots, I was dry when we entered. Selina sat at our table with the others, though her conversation appeared focused on Eric.

The odd glances from around the room told me the rumors were still grinding away. At least they weren't glaring.

I checked out plates as I walked. The roasted chicken would wrap easily in the napkins in the pockets of my coveralls. I was grateful we weren't eating fish. Dean wouldn't be getting any stewed carrots and onions. Taking extra wasn't allowed at dinner since we weren't permitted food in our rooms. I'd have to be careful around the others. Eric hadn't waited for me. I could have used him as cover.

"What a shit day," Selina said as Roxie gave her a kiss.

"You can say that again." Roxie didn't glance at me as I passed them for the back patio.

Water misted through the screen, but runoff trenches kept the patio from getting flooded. The aroma of grilled chicken caused my stomach to growl. The cook worked with his back to us, so I whipped out my napkins in a wad and threw the first on my plate as Roxie came out. She frowned but hung at the end of the serving table to keep an eye on the door.

The chicken had been quartered, so I wrapped three separate pieces and placed them into my coverall pocket at the waist. It would leak through, but I intended to hurry through dinner. I could skip the carrots.

"So," Roxie started in a conversational tone, "leaves are canceled again tonight." She eyed the cook when I jerked my head. "But, who'd be going out in this mess anyway?"

I would. I stuffed the last piece in my coveralls and tossed a piece of chicken on my plate. "Yeah. It'll be freezing with this rain." In the summer, I'd swum out to hang with Roxie and Selina before I'd turned old enough to go on leave. The little strip of water bordering us on the south would rise with the rain along with the rest of the river. I'd be drenched.

Selina watched me when we came back in and I ate my chicken off the bone. "Hungry?" In the winter months, she turned paler and her freckles faded.

"Famished." My word slurred with my mouth full. I was hungry, but more in a hurry than anything else. I had to get to Dean. The grease from the chicken would have soaked the cloth of the napkins by now, and soon my overalls.

"No carrots?" she asked.

"Tired of them. Now, potatoes I would have gone for."

Eric's eyes were tight, and his brow wrinkled. He had to know leave was canceled and probably wondered what my plan was. Seeing me rush to eat probably gave him the idea I'd be going anyway. I didn't expect him to take the risk.

Selina turned her focus on Roxie. "Anything interesting happen with you today? Jordan almost hit a rabbit with a rock. We had Sector E, and the animal was out on the old golf course."

Roxie turned from her chicken, careful not to look at me. "Boring and wet. I would have gladly tossed Caitlyn in the river for a little excitement." Because of me, she had to lie to her girlfriend. "Since leave is canceled, care if I come over for a bit?"

With her thumb, Selina stroked Roxie's ear and cheek. "Sounds interesting."

Roxie might be keeping Selina occupied for me, or just looking for a distraction from the stress I'd caused her. Either way, it worked, not that I believed Selina would be keeping an eye on me and catch me leaving the camp. Roxie had been clear she wasn't going to help me bring Dean food, but now I had to talk with Eric. He ate faster, perhaps planning to meet me upstairs.

I finished stuffing chicken in my face in record time and spun off the bench, checking my front for stains. The chicken bulged, but hadn't leaked through yet. "I'm going to crash early. I still haven't got my energy back."

"Just your appetite." Selina's tone almost sounded suspicious, but with everything going on, I couldn't trust my interpretation. She might have heard something on the stairwell, but not enough to know anything.

"Yeah, that's true." As I rounded the end of our table, my eyes flicked to the other units. I needed to get the food out of the mess.

Selina seemed about to say something else, but Roxie leaned into her. Black hair meshed into auburn as they kissed. I barged back into the patio and scraped my plate, trying to avoid appearing guilty to the cook. The storm had eased, but water still flowed off the roof. Beyond the fire of the grill, night formed a black wall on the other side of the screen. Returning to my quarters without getting caught was all that mattered.

When I came back out, Roxie had returned to her food and flashed a knowing, if not cold expression. Eric rose from the bench, finished with his dinner. He could meet me upstairs.

I caught a couple people glance at my waist as I dashed for the door, but no one called out. My boots clattered as I dashed up the stairs, using my memory in the absence of light. The rain made the cold air smell clean.

I stumbled inside our dark apartment and nearly slid. Feeling along the wall to the kitchen, I found the lantern, then scratched out a spark with the flint and steel. My heart had started to race leaving the mess; now it pounded in my ears. I planned to sneak across the waterway to the south, a small stagnant inlet of water.

Eric arrived as I wrapped the chicken portions into my towel. "I should go with you," he said.

I shook my head, carrying the bundle to my backpack, still empty and wet from my last excursion into water. "It was different when we were allowed to go out. If we had gotten caught, we could come up with a story. Caught outside the fence when leave is canceled, there is no excuse." I'd already gotten us in trouble when we abandoned our patrol.

"It's dark."

I zipped the pack and slipped an arm into the strap. "Not the best night for this. However, Dean hasn't eaten for two days from the sounds of it. Food, then get the message to his sister. He leaves. Simple." My comments felt cold and too logical.

In truth, I wanted to try healing Dean more. I wanted to save him. If I did, no one here would ever trust him, but he could go far away and start his life over. That thought didn't make me feel any better.

Eric swayed, frowning in the lantern light. "I should go with you."

Shrugging on the pack, I faced him. "I'll be fine. Go. I need to leave while everyone is still in the mess hall." I grabbed my machete and fastened the sheath to my belt.

As he opened the door, I turned off the lantern. When we stepped outside, I glared at the dark sky, but at least no one would see me. Without another word, I approached the stairwell, my eyes adjusting. I managed not to tumble down the steps, break a leg, and get caught with a pack full of chicken and a machete.

Rain pattered from the spent storm. The trek across the muddy training yard went easily enough, until I racked my shins against a low pole. Most of my vision relied on reflections. The silhouettes of the tops of the trees against the clouds didn't help me.

I found the water by sound. From previous experience, it was waist high at the deepest. Stepping carefully onto the muddy edge, I sensed the water as the otherness poured into me. In this case, I forced the water away from my path. It took more of my strength than I expected. Shaking from exertion, I stepped forward, boots sinking into mud.

I couldn't hold the magic for long. My next footstep sunk deeper and by the third, the mud sucked noisily when

I lifted my boot. Despite the cold, I found myself sweating under the coveralls.

When the mud inclined on my sixth step, I smiled, almost clear. Two steps later, I hit a root just under the slime, and I slipped.

Planting face first into the muck of the opposite shore, my hands dug wrist deep, my magic failed, and freezing water splashed in around my legs. Sputtering and blind, I freed my fingers and clawed up the bank. Soaked to my thighs, I emerged shaking off clods of mud. Using the somewhat clean inside elbows of my coveralls, I cleared my face enough to see.

I stood at the trail we'd patrolled this morning, except I could barely make out the trees and branches an arm's length away. Freezing, I needed to move. My body wanted to rest, but I couldn't. Branches surprised me and poked into my body, face, and hands as I stumbled on the path. More than one dug scratches into my skin. Roots and dead vines snagged at my boots. I navigated more from memory than light.

It wasn't until I made it to the first building that I could see the ground. From there, I knew I'd find my way to Dean. I just needed to feed him and get him on his way. My legs were stiff in the wet, cold, coveralls. Mud had caked on my front and in my hair. The rain had diminished to a drizzle. I was almost done. Finding the road back into the neighborhood made walking easier. Exhausted, I questioned my decision-making abilities.

I heard voices and crouched. Two men were talking to my left where I placed the school in my mental map. The sound ebbed and returned. A boot scuffed on asphalt. The soldiers were patrolling Bass Drive, or heading to town. For all I knew, they might be heading into the neighborhoods.

Standing, I was fairly sure I was the only one foolish

enough to be walking this far back. Pacing myself to their voice, I continued my journey slowly, letting them get farther down the main road. Eventually the two streets would intersect, but I didn't need to go that far.

They were gone by the time I reached the house. The sheds were both closed, but I recognized the area that smelled like a latrine. My shoulders loosened. I just needed to drop off the food and get the note. I didn't have energy to try any healing.

I let out a yip when Moonjir stepped from the side of the shed. "Lovely night for a stroll, Caitlyn."

Chapter Fourteen

Moonjir appeared as bright in the pitch of night as he had when we'd first met. His floppy ear dangled as he tilted his head, as if waiting for my reply. He'd walked out of the shadows on hind legs, but dropped to his haunches and one front paw as I stood gawking.

"You've got something" — he pointed a claw to the side of his face — "on your cheek. Your gold hair has seen better days, too."

My heart was racing, and my chest heaved with heavy breaths. Still, I reached a mud-smeared hand as if to straighten my hair. "I fell."

He dropped his paw to the ground and sat watching me. His bright tail fanned out behind him, impossibly tall even when curled. "That's good. I thought this was some strange human tradition I was unaware of. I'm fairly well versed in most of your kind's behavior."

Despite our rather loud conversation, Dean had not come out of his shed. He might have left, or he was sick. "What are you doing out here?" I asked, lowering my voice.

"Well, whatever I want, it seems." He leaned forward, raised his paw to the side of his mouth, and whispered.

"He's been snoring up a storm until now. I think we woke him."

Goosebumps raced along my arms. I had no idea what Moonjir wanted with me and certainly didn't trust him. He hadn't appeared to anyone else. "What do you want with me?"

Moonjir smiled and tapped his nose with a black nail. "There's the question. I want you to move up in this world. You've painted a pretty picture here." He swept a paw back toward the school and camp. "Very little is as it seems. When there is no visible path, which path will you take? There are two ahead of you: theirs and yours."

I blinked. "What?"

He dropped his paw to the ground and sighed dramatically. "Which part didn't you get?"

My jaw dropped. "Any of it."

The door to Dean's shed opened slowly and his eyes were on me. Tightening his jaw into sharp lines, he pushed his head out to see Moonjir.

The annoying pink and blue cryptid smiled at Dean, and waved. "It emerges from its slumber. That stick is going to be fairly useless; I'm not a piñata."

Dean pulled the broken handle from behind his leg where he'd been hiding it and stepped out of the shed. "Makes me feel better, anyway."

"You're far more dangerous without it, but it suits you. You've got that whole leather jacket warrior thing going on." Moonjir nodded to me. "I guess we'll be on our way now."

I flicked my eyes between Moonjir and Dean. "You're going with him?"

Dean raised his eyebrows, obviously not appreciating that idea.

"Oh worlds, no. Paths. I've mentioned them, haven't I?" He stood on his hind legs again. "We've all got our own.

Sometimes we create bonds; other times we break them." Moonjir bowed with one hand flourishing in an arc. "You've done well here, Caitlyn. I'd say humane, but caring for someone with whom you have no connection is almost inhuman, statistically."

I frowned at Moonjir's comments. It had not been the first time he'd mentioned paths and bonds. Dean took a step closer to me. His movements were graceful and measured with his focus on the bright cryptid. Dean's demeanor was almost protective.

My already soaked coveralls and Dean's leather jacket dotted with fresh sprinkles of raindrops. Moonjir's fur didn't have one damp spot and did not stir.

"Perhaps you could just leave?" I asked Moonjir.

He tilted his head again, ear flopping. "Of course. Until our paths cross again." Moonjir took two steps backward, disappearing behind the shed.

Dean moved quickly, crossing in front of me and padding to the side to see along the shed. His head jerked to the other shed and his neck craned as if trying to look over the short buildings. He motioned for me to stay put and crept quickly to follow Moonjir.

I could hear blood pounding in my ears as Dean disappeared. The light drops falling everywhere made enough noise so that I heard no footsteps. In a second, Dean came around the other shed, walking straighter, but with a scowl.

"He's gone." Dean studied me. "What is he?"

I raised my hands in the air. "He won't tell me. I've only met him once before, a couple days ago."

"Just one more thing." Moonjir stepped out from the spot he'd disappeared a minute before.

We both jumped in surprise. I stepped back. Dean leaped in front of me with his makeshift club raised. I blushed slightly at his heroics.

Moonjir raised his hands, as if to show he posed no threat. "Easy there. I just wanted to mention that this might not be the best place to be — come morning. In case you two were planning to settle in for the night."

Before I could answer, Moonjir stepped back behind the shed. Dean redid an entire lap around the sheds, appearing with a scowl when he finished.

"Can't you just. .." He waved his club as if a wand. "Do some magic on him?"

I started pulling off my pack. "Tried last time. Didn't work." Moonjir seemed harmless enough. Confusing and a bit startling, but he hadn't done anything threatening.

Dean paced a searching lap around us. "Do you think that was a threat?"

I pulled out a napkin full of chicken, leaving my towel inside with the remainder. "About not being here in the morning? I agree. Another patrol will come out, and the soldiers are out tonight. I rarely ever see them out in the dark."

Dean took the chicken, paused, and pointed toward the house. "There's an overhang on the side. We can get out of the rain for a minute. Thank you for the food." He took a step then turned, locking my eyes with his. "Thank you, for helping — before. I never said it."

He had a broad nose compared to me or Eric. His cheeks and jaw were strong. Dean was possibly the most attractive male my age between the camp and locals. Before our incident across the lake, he'd acted too cool to notice me. Now, I flushed at his attention. He could still be a werewolf, and he had to leave.

"It's wet." I pointed to the sky then closed my eyes, trying to blot out the memory of my ever so witty response. "Obviously." Pack in hand, I marched for the house. "Just ignore me. It's been a long couple of days."

Dean smirked as he walked with me and peeled back the greasy napkin covering the cold chicken. He had to be starving.

"You're welcome," I said belatedly. That would have been the appropriate response, had I not been flustered by his attention.

I had a simple plan. Feed Dean so he could leave, then deliver his note. Once I did that, my life would return to normal with Roxie and Eric.

We stepped onto the deck and the wood complained, weathered and nearly rotted. The overhang had been made of concrete and though the rain had made it underneath, a rusted steel bench was dry.

"It'll hold us." Dean sat, dropping his club and biting into the chicken.

The bench appeared sturdy, a rare find. "Do you take all the girls here?" I sat, conscious of how close we were.

"Mm-mm. No." He swallowed and pointed across the river toward hulking silhouettes of two large buildings. "The brick house over there with the round tower. No leaks except for the west side." Scraping meat off the bone with his teeth, he peered at me over his meal. I couldn't tell if he was joking. Probably not.

Suddenly I remembered he might be a werewolf. His teeth digging into flesh stirred a panic, and I forced myself not to jump. Moonjir had unsettled me. I wasn't here to lounge around with Dean.

He recognized the fear in my face. "Hey, you should go. Get safe. No regrets. I understand."

I forced a breath. "I'm sorry. If you were dangerous, it would have happened already."

Dean stared at the ground as he spoke, chewing. "I'm not right. I know enough to get away from people."

"Do you think I could heal you some more? How do you feel?"

"Achy. Tired. Hungry." He paused between a bite. "Or do you mean do I want to attack you with irrational rage?"

I stiffened. "Do you?"

His lips curled at the edges of his mouth in a smile, but he didn't turn toward me. "Attack might be a strong word, and certainly not in rage."

I flushed, extremely conscious of his proximity. My throat dry, I swallowed, and tried not to imagine how kissing him might feel.

Dean chuckled. "Probably a really bad time to flirt." He turned his face toward me but didn't move closer. "Sorry. You look like you've been through hell to bring me a piece of chicken, and I'm being all cool and cocky."

I touched my hair, caked with mud, and brushed the front of my smeared coveralls with dirty fingers. He couldn't have actually been flirting with me when I was coated with muck. My mouth hung open, trying to imagine how I appeared.

His single laugh barked into the night. "I barely recognized you, but I knew your voice."

I snorted out my own laugh and leaned to avoid making more noise. The absurdity of sitting beside a werewolf worried about my appearance struck against all the tension I'd been dealing with for days. Trying to keep quiet, I sounded like a coyote with hiccups.

Dean broke into a low chuckle accented with snorts which just set me off more. "Oh my god," he said, "stop. They're going to hear us."

Ignoring the dirt, I clamped a grimy hand over my mouth until we settled down. I had needed a release. With a sigh, I pulled my pack to my boots, dug out more chicken, and handed it to Dean.

We hadn't made that much noise, but Dean would have to leave after he ate. I wish we had met under different circumstances. Moonjir had been right about Dean not being here in the morning.

"So, you're okay," I said.

"I don't feel like attacking people," he said seriously, then a sly grin tugged at his lips. "Any more than normal."

I rolled my eyes. "After you eat, I want to try and heal you some more."

Dean nodded, tossing chicken bones out to the dirt. "We never knew you could do that — healing that is."

"It's not as common as it should be."

"You know, we all watch you practice. Even my grandpa and aunt. They won't let Bettina off the property."

"Watch us?" I'd seen the locals walk by the fence and gawk; everyone had. "Yeah, when you walk by."

"Oh, way more than that. The novelty's worn off now, but in the summer we used to sit on the other bank and see you doing all kinds of things. Down by the interstate, too."

"You sit in the bushes and watch us?"

Dean shrugged, unwrapping a second piece of chicken. "I think the lightning is the freakiest. You're never there. It got a bit spooky when your people killed some pigs."

I nodded. *Freak.* Some of us remembered the witch riots, but I couldn't forget the labs. The locals in Santee barely accepted us.

Silently, Dean devoured the food.

"You should save the last for later, if you haven't been eating." I shook out the napkin from the first piece, but it would take a bit to wash out the grease.

His mouth full, Dean nodded, and I stood. The rain had stopped, and what fell came from trees or the roof. It took less than a minute for him to finish. "Thank you." He tossed out the bones and handed me the napkin.

I wrapped it with the other in my pack and motioned for him to remain seating. "Will you let me try and heal you some more?" If he hadn't turned, but just gotten sick, he might not even be infected. I had felt the wrongness before, but maybe it was gone.

Dean had a confident demeanor about him. His words so far had been direct and rational. His expression grew cautious, and I thought for a moment he might refuse. "Okay. Never give up, right?" He raised his palms questioningly.

I moved to stand directly in front of him with his eyes even to my elbows. Placing both hands on his neck, I found the otherness around me and called it in. The first moment of a healing there's a connection between me and the patient. It only took a second before I sensed the infection within him. Before it had been in his blood, but now it oozed out of every cell inside him. Nothing remained untouched, and even the otherness I'd gathered balked, wanting to abandon him.

Dean hissed out a breath. "Damn."

Healing never hurt though it did cause a sensation of heat or itching. "What's wrong?" I didn't stop.

"I feel crappy."

Pushing against the wrongness, I tried to bring his body back to normal. *Human*, I thought. "Give me another minute." Unlike usual healing, the effort wore on me quickly, and for the first time in using my magic, the otherness acted sluggish and resistant.

Dean wretched and pushed me away. Partially chewed chicken sprayed on my stomach and chest. The sound and the acrid sent had me gagging as I staggered back. He dropped off the bench onto his knees and coughed at the ground.

I couldn't save him. He wasn't human, but maybe not

fully werewolf either, since he hadn't turned. If I'd worked harder in the beginning, or if Eric had been there to help, we might have cured him, but not now.

When I reached for his shoulder, I swayed with vertigo. My knees folded and I fell backward onto the weathered deck. "Are you okay?" I asked.

He shook his head, saliva or bile dripping out of his mouth. The coughing slowed, and he spit.

My eyes widened. Infection occurred when werewolf fluids entered the blood stream, but I only had scratches on my face and hands. I raised my fingers away from the slick leftover vomit on my coveralls. They'd never touched it, but I was wet from the storm, so I couldn't know if something had splashed.

I rolled over and wiggled against the wood, wiping off what I could.

Dean chuckled, then groaned. "What are you doing?"

I flushed and stopped my squirming. "Werewolf fluids. You're not healed." I had to leave. I'd done what I'd come for and failed. He just had to give me the note. "You need to go."

"After that little bit of fun, I don't know if I can even stand." He was trying, and not too heartily. Trying to heal him had been a mistake.

The energy I'd lost on the attempt had me feeling every bruise and scratch. I shivered from the thought more than the cold. My coveralls stank. I staggered when I stood. "I'll help you get to your feet, but I can't touch any vomit. I've got scratches, and if your fluids get in my wounds and blood, then I'll be infected."

He almost had his footing, but wobbled. "How do you know?"

"We learn that kind of stuff at the camp." *Trained*

freaks. I positioned myself to his side, unsure if I had the energy to help.

I tucked my fingers under the armpits of his jacket, digging in and pulling up. He was heavy in a solid, muscular way.

"How do they know?" he asked.

"I. .." Memories of the labs came to me. Peers who went off for a procedure and disappeared. We were studied for our abilities. They might have done the same to normal people. "I guess they tested on people."

He rose and I steadied him. "The government, the military?"

"I'm not sure which." I released him, holding my hands out to catch him if he dropped.

"Same thing." He swayed but stood.

It wasn't exactly true, according to what I learned at Civics class, but I wasn't about to argue. "Are you going to be able to make it?" Where would he go?

Dean snorted. "Not now. I can barely stand."

"You can't stay here." Moonjir had sounded too sure, as if he knew something. We were awfully close to the school. "At least get to the other side of the river."

He took a step and faltered, nearly falling. His arm waved toward me for that quick moment, as if to grasp me for support, then he righted himself. I'd have to help him.

"Maybe if we get you to a building where it doesn't leak." Where Dean brought his dates. "You could leave after a little sleep." There were hours before the sun rose. Nights were long in the winter.

"We?" he asked. "You carrying me?" His skin had paled, but still had its tan, olive tone.

"You can lean on me." I threw his uneaten chicken back into my pack and slung it on. "Just no fluids."

His smirk and chortle made me blush. He pointed at his

club. "Would you mind? I'd fall right over if I tried to pick it up."

I handed it to him before sliding my arm under his and onto his back. He held my backpack. "Let's do this." I might have failed getting him fed or healed, but at least we could get him a little farther away. Once I got him settled in, I'd head directly back to the camp. The note I'd keep for another night. I had to wash and not turn into a werewolf, then sleep.

He took a faltering step. "You know we'll have to cross that footbridge."

"I do. We'll figure it out. I know your little getaway house where you bring your dates." We started to move quicker, in sync. "Don't get any ideas."

"Don't worry. I feel like I'm going to die, and you smell like puke."

Chapter Fifteen

The next morning, Roxie woke me by sitting, or bouncing onto, my bed. "Hey, Sunshine. How'd it go last night?"

I hadn't slept enough, and the blankets weren't keeping me warm. Imagination or not, I could still smell Dean's puke. My voice was a hoarse crackle. "Did you bring your rifle? Shoot me." After I told her what happened, she might consider it.

"Your coveralls hanging in the kitchen look a little wet."

I shifted to press my knees against her, hoping for warmth. "I swam across." I'd been exhausted and planned on washing my coveralls anyway.

"Yeah, that was totally the right move." Roxie leaned into my legs. "Selina was asking a lot of questions last night. She's suspicious that we're up to something. But Dean's gone, right?"

I shivered and pulled my hands out from under the covers to study the scratches. "I made him sick, trying to heal him."

Roxie took a minute to restate her question more assertively. "Dean's gone, right?"

"Moved him across the river. Oh, and Moonjir showed up."

"Crap, Caitlyn." She could have been commenting on either of them as she jumped off the bed to face me.

"Dean's over in Sector C. You know the brick building with the tower? He brings his girls there."

"This is not a date. What happened with Moonjir?" I couldn't remember if she'd said his name before.

Some of the scratches were still wet looking, and the one on my left wrist appeared pink. "He just babbles." I pressed on the cut, bringing out a drop of liquid and then blood. Turning into a werewolf would end with me back at the labs. "Moonjir did suggest that Dean not stay in the shed, though."

"At least *he* had sense." She nodded toward the scratch. "Why are you messing with that?"

I slid my hands under my blanket. Roxie needed to know my concerns even though she might shoot me. "This is the second time I felt the werewolf infection. In his blood first, and then everywhere. When I tried to heal him, he puked on me." Swallowing, I waited for her to catch the implication.

"Did it — get in your blood?" Her tone started concerned, and ended in a harder note.

"I don't think so." I needed her to accept that, so I could ask Eric for some help. My head was foggy.

"That's not good enough." Her voice was angry now. She had to make a decision none of us would want to make.

If she reported me, they'd want to know how I'd been exposed. "Rather than start a big fuss and reveal what I've been doing — could we wait a little bit?" I'd have to tell her my plan. "Until we can get with Eric alone."

"Why?"

"I want to work with him and see if I'm okay. If not, we can try healing."

"Healing?" Roxie turned to study my blank wall. "You said it didn't work with Dean."

"I need to know." My heart started racing. I couldn't tell her that I might have a fever. "Just wait to report me until after I get him to work with me."

She spun for the door. "I will get him right now. We're not waiting." Her boots stomped the whole way out of our apartment.

I crawled out of bed and found my other coveralls, still damp, and pried into them, shivering as I did so. Roxie had left the lamp lit against the early morning darkness. The furnace pipe still had some heat in it, so I leaned on it while I waited for Eric.

They came in whispering in hushed voices, and Roxie started when she saw me. Eric rubbed his chest, unblinking. He approached as she stopped midway into the room.

"I'm probably just being paranoid." I showed him the scratch on my wrist. "Dean puked on me when I was trying to heal him."

"I don't know what to look for." He swallowed twice after his statement.

"You'll know. I'll know. If we find it, try and help me?" I was asking a lot from both of them.

He nodded slowly, then knelt in front of me.

"We might be late for breakfast." I smiled.

His lips curled, but he couldn't even fake it. His nostrils flared as he took in a deep breath and placed his hands on the sides of my temples. I put my right hand on my wrist and drew the otherness from around me.

I couldn't feel him. My stomach churned when I searched my blood. It was wrong. Not as wrong as Dean's had felt right after the werewolf bit him, but not right either.

Eric's eyebrows drooped and his bottom lip tugged in. "Crap."

Closing my eyes, I spoke calmly. "Help me. Try to heal it. Maybe together." Without waiting for his response, I pushed at the wrongness, trying to drive it out like in an infected wound. We'd both done that multiple times.

The room felt cold, freezing, despite the warm pipe on my back. Nausea roiled in my stomach, and my head began to hurt just behind my eyes.

"You're burning up," he said.

"Don't stop." I'd rather die from a sudden high fever, if you could, than end up a werewolf in a lab. I was trembling.

My pulse pounded at my throat, and my ears rang. The infection fought back against me, but I knew Eric was there and strong. My right calf cramped where I had it folded under me, but I didn't move.

"It's fading." Eric sounded hopeful.

My throat grew tight and I wanted to cry. My body shook, beyond trembling. Muscles in my arms spasmed and locked along my shoulders. I opened my lips to breathe, and a deep inhale hurt my lungs. Every part of me ached.

My eyes were open, but the room had gotten darker. The pain in my head split my skull, and I sobbed. At some point, my hand slid off my wrist. I had no energy to help Eric, and the sounds of Roxie's voice echoed faintly and indistinctly. Sweat soaked my hair at the back of my neck, and tears poured down my face.

I flinched when the mouth of a canteen touched my lips. When the water poured, I drank. My vision was blurred. Roxie held it. She'd been crying too.

Eric lay on the floor behind her. "She's going to be too weak to go downstairs." He giggled. "I'm too weak." Eric's tone had a sense of relief to it.

I choked on the water, and Roxie moved it away. "Did. ..?"

He rolled toward me. "I think so. You blacked out near the end."

"We can't be sure." Roxie's voice was hopeful yet unsure, not harsh. "I've got to head down, or Selina will be here checking on us. Eric, you should go too. I'll make something up about you, Caitlyn. However, this is not over."

I was drenched inside my coveralls, and my sweat reeked sharp and acrid. "I can make it there." Pushing with my heels, I sat straighter.

"The way you look?" Roxie scoffed. "That would take more lying than I'm willing to do. I dried out your coveralls from last night. Wipe and change. I smelled cornbread cooking. I'll smuggle you a piece." She placed my canteen beside me. "Drink."

Eric groaned and sat. "Help me up, while you're here."

They left me against the wall, and it took a few minutes and half the canteen before I stood. Eric seemed sure about the healing. Even my scratches were gone. Together, we could have saved Dean. My legs wobbled as I climbed out of my clothes.

I turned in the direction I knew Dean was. The sense I'd felt before was there, if lighter from the additional distance. Fresh tears ran down my cheek, partially because I knew we could have saved him completely, and because I was an emotional wreck from the healing. He should have been gone by now.

When Roxie brought me a piece of cornbread, I could hear the rain outside. "I told Selina you were being dramatic over sniffles from yesterday's rain. Make sure to wipe your nose a lot." Her brow furrowed. "I can't completely trust that you're okay. You know that, don't you?"

Deflated, I nodded. "You still think I might turn?"

Her lips tightened. "I don't know. Can you be sure you won't?"

With a sixteen-hour minimum, it gave me until around 1300 in the afternoon. "What do you want to do?" They could tie me up, but Selina or one of the officers would notice me missing.

"We've got gate before lunch. I'll be watching you. We're on patrol at 1300. Sector A again, if you can believe it. Everyone's complaining about the schedule. Selina warned that we might be crossing with soldiers as well. I think they're searching the buildings, but I didn't push for details."

Dean would surely be gone by then. I had his note to deliver under my mattress. "Will you have a rifle again for patrol?"

Her lips tightened. "I will."

"Make it a clean head shot if I turn." I smiled weakly.

"Okay." She sounded far too serious.

When we did our run that morning, I trailed behind at a jog, but otherwise I kept up. The rain came in drenching waves throughout the day. My strength returned little by little even though I was a mess at training.

In the afternoon, we headed out on patrol in wet coveralls. I was tired but not sick. Dark clouds threatened above as we started down the trail.

"He's still there," I said.

Roxie stabbed the ground with her staff. "They're searching buildings. Working their way outward. He's an idiot."

"He *was* sick." Maybe Dean had gotten worse. He could be unconscious. "We can check on him."

She grabbed my arm. "Stop it. No. You'll let this go and be done with it."

I stared at the leaves. "I. .." My excuse trailed off. She was right.

"We do our patrol and duty. Nothing else." She snorted and started walking again. "If he's fool enough to hang around, that's on him."

"Let's hope he keeps his mouth shut, if they do catch him." Eric offered me a wry smile.

"He won't say anything." I could tell from the little I'd interacted with him that he would never willingly get me in trouble. He was too honorable and stubborn. Why hadn't he left?

Roxie's tone was unsure. "You better pray he doesn't."

"Lucky we have Church class tomorrow." Eric tried to make light of it, but I'd put them all at risk.

When we got to the first building, a red slash had been painted on the door. Each structure in the neighborhood around the school had been marked, whether house or building. It continued and included the sheds where I'd first met Moonjir and where Dean had been staying last night.

We stood in front of the sheds for a moment. Moonjir had been right. I peered across the river to the brick house. Dean was still there. He needed to leave. Roxie caught my eye and glared.

I sighed. "I'm not going to —"

She snapped, interrupting me. "That's correct. We aren't." Her expression softened. "How are you feeling?"

Her rifle remained in its sheath on her back. I thought of my same questions to Dean last night. If all this weren't happening, he might have been fun to hang out with.

"I'm okay, just tired." I had the same doubts as her that the healing wouldn't be enough and I'd turn. What was I supposed to do other than wait it out? She wouldn't let me hurt anyone. I didn't feel like I was changing. "Let's go. This is depressing."

Her tense demeanor could be either annoyance with me or waiting to see if the healing had worked. If it failed, I would become the enemy.

We had proceeded to the next house when a man in a camouflage vest and a ratty baseball cap saw us and started running from the south toward us. Roxie stepped out ahead of us, and we all veered our paths to meet him. An older man, he panted heavily as he ran.

"I saw him. The Valdina boy who was bitten." He flailed an arm to the west, toward the land that jutted out with the buildings across the river and the brick house where Dean still hid.

A chill rose up my neck, and I froze. Eric glanced at me, then across the river. Roxie stiffened, remaining focused on the local. Nausea twisted in my stomach.

A rowboat had been pulled onto the shore, the man's I presumed, and a gust of wind rippled the river. No one moved on the opposite shore.

"Where was he?" Roxie asked. "Exactly." My chest hollowed when she reached back for her rifle.

"You can't see from here. On the far side of the build-ings. He saw me. Ducked down and tried to hide, but I know him." He swallowed visibly. "He wasn't a wolf." I could hear the unspoken word "yet" and the fear in the man's voice.

"Get back to town. Take your boat." Roxie pointed upriver where the locals had built thin wooden walkways as docks. "We'll take care of this."

He appeared happy to comply, running for his craft. Roxie turned and glared at me. She took long sharp strides toward me, forcing Eric to double back.

"I'm going to assume this a safe sighting, since there is water between you and the hostile. Eric and I will return to the base where we will report the sighting and that you remain hidden here to monitor." She was giving me a chance to warn Dean. Her voice lowered, though her glower never diminished. "Make sure the locals don't see you. Run and keep hidden if you spot anyone."

I noted the fisherman's position at the shore and nodded. "I'll be quick and waiting here when the soldiers come. Thank you."

Without a word she turned and slowly walked toward the main road. They'd have to jog the last portion to make their story appear valid.

Before the man had climbed into his boat, I started running. Most of the way I'd take the roads and hope no one else was on them. The weather might help. I'd been tired, exhausted, but my pulse raced as I reached Huran Lane.

When I intersected with Bass Drive, I paused just long enough to make sure there was no one to witness. The sprint down to Pinckney Road took seconds, and I kept full tilt until I reached the wooden footbridge. I ignored its rattling boards as I hurried across and barreled toward the houses.

Dean was returning with a canteen from the water's edge when I arrived. Annoyance flashed, but I avoided chastising him. My breath was ragged. "You've been spotted. The soldiers will be here."

His skin was ashen and darker around the eyes. "I'd rather they shoot me at this point." He stunk of acrid sweat and vomit. "I was just leaving. I've been sick."

My attempted healing had just made him worse. "Leave, please."

He smiled, appearing grimmer in his attempt. "You're worried about me."

"Yes. Where will you go?" I needed to run back, not say goodbye.

"Northwest. Burned-out maintenance building at Lake

Shore Campground. No more of your healing. I need to rest. Bring me some beef if you can. I'm not a big fan of chicken."

I paused, considering the possibility, then shook off the thought. "Go. Please don't get caught." My feet shuffled, knowing I should run back. "Can you make it? They'll be tracking you."

He shrugged. "I can hide my trail." His posture sagged. "How long do I have?"

"Minutes." Fighting my desire to say more, I turned my back on Dean and started to run.

I knew the campground Dean referenced. It had been a year since our outer patrols had included that area. We'd moved across the lake. Before Camp Sparta, there had been a fire through the whole area; the trees survived with blackened trunks.

I barely made it back. When Tyrell and six soldiers arrived, I hid in the dead brush with a good vantage of the opposite shore. My legs trembled with exertion and exhaustion as I crouched, trying to appear attentive. After the healing and the run, I could have slept on the wet ground. Worse, I worried Dean had not gotten enough warning. He'd been right that my healing had done more harm than good.

Tyrell's scowl grew as he approached, peering across the river. "Get back, now. Clinic. You never should have stayed. Be ready to report tonight."

"Yes, sir." It would not be a pleasant evening.

Chapter Sixteen

Roxie and Eric met me halfway into the compound. "How are you feeling?" she asked. Her rifle was gone, so she'd have to club me with her staff if I turned.

"Dead on my feet, but nothing else."

I couldn't read her expression, but she nodded. "Clinic, then eat. Tyrell wants reports from all of us when we get back."

The distant sound of younger voices came from behind as the students were running back to camp from the school. They were always noisy in the evening, and our patrol had been cut short enough to be here when they arrived.

We turned and my friends escorted me to the clinic, the chatter growing louder as the kids reached the gate. Other than the Youth Guard practicing at the air and fire ranges, the compound was empty.

"I reported to Selina already. She's suspicious." Roxie nodded toward the north gate.

"Thanks, I'll avoid her." I couldn't help but search for the sense of Dean, but he was too far away — or dead.

"Until dinner," Eric said. He smiled and would have

said more, but we were close to the clinic. "Wash day tomorrow, thankfully." He scrunched his nose.

My coveralls smelled musty. If the rain continued, it would be a little more difficult. I flashed a weak smile at Eric; he was trying to keep me from focusing on Dean or the trouble we'd have with Tyrell.

As we stopped at the door to the clinic, Roxie's lips tightened. "See you in the room, afterward." She still seemed to worry that I would turn.

Despite my own concerns over my healing and the impending report to Tyrell, I worried most about Dean. Not only was I connected to him through my healing, but I felt responsible for him. Even knowing the trouble it had caused, I would still choose to try and heal him if I had it to do all over again.

The clinic proved as embarrassing as ever, and after I scrambled back into my clothes, I headed upstairs to Roxie.

"Thank you," I said as I closed the door behind me.

She eyed me from the living room, standing with her hands on her hips. "He's gone?"

"I warned him, and I don't feel him anymore. I made him pretty sick trying to heal him the second time." I drained my canteen.

"I don't care, as long as he leaves. If this all came out, I can't imagine what kind of trouble there would be." Relaxing her stance, she dug her hands through her short black hair.

"He's really sick. I hope they don't catch him." I glanced at my pack, drying under the furnace pipes. "Dean said he'd be going to the campground by the lake. I think he meant that big square building made of tin that fell during the fire. He's going to be starving."

Roxie flinched, then her eyes tightened. "This needs to end. Look at the risk you've put us in already. I can't even report another sighting of the new cryptid." She moved toward her room and spun. "Whatever else you pull, I'm not helping. Today was it."

She had done more for me than she would for nearly anyone else. Roxie lived by the camp's rules. I'd caused her to abandon them all for my fixation on Dean. "Thank you," I managed before her bedroom door closed.

When it came time for dinner, we lied to Selina and our unit. Other Youth Guards came by the table, and Roxie retold the fisherman's tale, carefully leaving out my part in the story. As the rain started again, I waited for a soldier to call me to Tyrell's office.

I was sitting with Eric in my living room while Roxie was gone with Selina when a knock came on my door. The soldier gestured to follow him when I answered. "Sergeant Major is ready for your reports." He had seen Eric and waited for us both to exit.

Roxie stood on the balcony, and Selina watched from her doorway. The rain blew away from our building with the storm winds coming from the northwest, where Dean hopefully hid.

Roxie went into Tyrell's office first while Eric and I stood alone outside.

"Lousy weather," Eric said. "Doesn't look like it'll be getting better anytime soon."

I kicked my heel against the wall. "I'm not going out tonight, don't worry." In good weather, it would take an hour to get to the campground. I hadn't grabbed any food, anyway.

"Of course not, that would be foolish."

When Roxie reappeared, we both jumped. She pointed at Eric. "You're next." Taking a deep breath, she shook her head at me. "He's furious."

She left me alone and squirming against the wall. I couldn't hear through the window.

Eric came out after a much shorter period and grimaced playfully. "Your turn." The door had been left open and he didn't say anything as he peered at the rain and began jogging back to our quarters.

Tyrell stood with his back to me, staring at the map of Santee and the surrounding area. "Report, Soldier."

I stammered through the part I was sure he'd already been told about the fisherman. He turned to face me when I lied about hiding in the bushes and watching the far shore.

"It seemed like forever before you came, but it was probably only a few minutes. I never saw any sign of anyone over by the buildings."

He studied me for a long minute, then swung his gaze across the walls and maps.

"I was stationed in Savannah when the Sorrow was happening — I never lost anyone to a werewolf. The people here had it much worse. Did you know the frequency of those Taken was higher here, closer to the cryptid zone?"

My mother's scream echoed in my head. "I didn't know that."

"The Sorrow took everything from me," Tyrell said. He faced the Santee map again, jabbing a finger where Dean had been hiding. "Most were lost during the riots. The people here had different problems. We're stationed here to make their lives easier."

Dean wouldn't be causing the locals any problems. "I understand, sir."

"One of their own has been bitten and is likely hunting nearby. We're focused on the town tonight but will be expanding our search outward tomorrow." He glanced back at me as if checking on my reaction.

Keeping my face expressionless, I focused my eyes on

the town and resisted peeking at the large unpopulated area to the west and the campground. He wasn't yelling at me that staying behind had been foolish. If anything, Tyrell seemed reserved. Under my coveralls, goosebumps rose on my arms. I didn't know whether Dean's family had mentioned my visits or if he questioned what happened today. I had to be careful.

After a moment of my silence, he continued. "Then we'll start moving our search out to the lake. Man or wolf can't survive without leaving a trace. We'll find Dean, unless he moves deeper into the cryptid zone."

The image of Dean's wolf corpse hanging on our fence gave me a shiver. My expression must have flinched as his forehead furrowed. I took a quick breath, trying to find a viable reason. "Why would he come back here? So close?"

"Maybe family, maybe some other interest."

Tyrell couldn't mean me. "Did he have a girlfriend?"

"We've asked around. His friends say he didn't have anyone specific." His words were easy and measured.

Had he talked to Buck? I tried to keep my breath slow and deliberate. "Then maybe family."

"Perhaps. He lost his father to a werewolf, and his mother was taken. Boy's had a rough run of it through the Sorrow. His little sister is beside herself. All that's left is their grandfather and great aunt." Tyrell patted me on the shoulder and I jumped. "Well, if you come up with anything else, I'll be here. The search will coordinate through this office."

When I headed outside, the rain had drained to a drizzle, and the moon lit the clouds into a fuzzy haze. The air had a crisp scent to it, and if it were earlier in the year, I'd guess we would be getting snow. Dean had to be freezing. I needed to warn him about Tyrell's search.

I scoffed at my thought and jogged toward my barracks,

dodging under the balconies where I could. If I went out, Roxie would kill me. Eric would kindly tell me how bad an idea it was. It would be nearly impossible to navigate to the campground in this weather.

Still, I stopped by Eric's quarters and knocked. Jordan answered, grunted, and let me in.

"Is Eric. .." I stopped as he stepped out of his room. Punching a thumb over my shoulder, I gestured to meet outside and he nodded.

We walked over to the stairwell and sat. "How'd it go?" he asked.

"That's the weird part. He wasn't angry with me."

"Yeah, Roxie had to say it was her decision. She took the worst of it. With me, he pretty much confirmed that."

"I feel bad."

"You should." He smiled to take the sting off the comment. "I'm glad he's gone."

"Tyrell walked me through all the plans to find Dean. It was odd. Dean might only have a day or two before the search reaches him."

Eric frowned. "I wonder why Tyrell would discuss that with you. Do you think he knows something?"

"I've begun to think about the trail I've left talking with Buck and visiting Dean's house — twice."

"Yeah, not good. Now we lie low, right?" He waited for me to respond. "Right?"

"They're going to find him."

Eric buried his face in his hand. "Where did he go?"

"The campground, where we used to do our outer patrol. There's a burned-out maintenance building."

"The whole forest is burned. You really shouldn't do this. What if you get lost?"

"I know." I hadn't made up my mind, until I could talk with Eric. "I can't sense him anymore."

"I can't sense you, either." He had an impish smile working.

"What?"

"You connected with Dean in a strange way when you healed him. Well, I healed you, and something was definitely wrong, but no connection. Maybe he had the pure infection, and you disturbed it with the first healing, so what he passed on was — changed. You might never turn, and I'm glad you haven't. That's why I think we're not sensing each other."

I remembered reaching my blood and thinking it wasn't the same. "You might be right."

"This is what they should be studying at the labs," he said. We all had scars from our times there; his were physical and ran in two lines on each side of his back above the hips. He hunched forward, staring at the steps. "It's about half a mile to where he was hiding from here. It'll be about a mile to the building you're talking about."

"Which is why I can't sense him."

"But you will, about half way there at the least. Coming back is the problem."

"I was thinking the old trail might still be there." Patrolling regularly left paths which we followed.

"Probably."

I paused. "You think this is a good idea then?"

He snorted. "Hell, no. I think it's a horrible idea, but you'll do it anyway."

Two hours later, I walked through the remnants of a blackened forest, fairly lost, before I sensed Dean. He waited for me outside the bent ruins of a mammoth building. Slanted to the side, the square opening had been mashed into a triangle. The pitched roof leaned until it rested parallel to the ground. There would be room inside, but some seriously odd angles.

He needed a shave. His eyes were deep and bright. Dean leered for a moment at my arrival. "I'm going to take this the wrong way." His voice was tense even as he tried to joke.

I blushed. "I need to warn you." Moving closer to the remains of the tilted building, I let it block some of the frigid wind.

Despite the cold, he had taken off his jacket and draped it over his shoulder. Other than jeans and boots, he wore a threadbare, button down, blue and green checkered shirt.

His head whipped as if he heard something. "Seriously, you need to leave. They're coming."

My face warmed. I hadn't come out here on some crush. In different circumstances, it would have been interesting to hang out with Dean.

"That's what *I'm* warning *you* about." He didn't need to treat me like one of his local girls when I had serious reasons to come out here.

Dean shook his head, glancing out into the darkness. "No. .."

I stiffened, the miserable day weighing on me. He hadn't even apologized for puking on me and making me sick as well. I'd say my piece, and he could take it or leave it. "The soldiers won't be out here for a day or two, but they *are* doing a systematic search."

"Well, the werewolves are almost here. I can feel them. It'll be sooner than a day or two. You need to leave." Dean pointed back into the woods in the direction I'd come.

He swiveled, leaned forward, and sniffed. "Wait." He straightened. "Too late — get inside!"

Chapter Seventeen

"What do you mean, too late?" I squawked out the last word.

A pair of howls echoed across the forest. One came from ahead of me behind Dean. The second yowl from my left caused me to whirl. They were both distant, deep in the woods.

Dean hardened his jaw and glared into the darkness. "They've scented you."

"How do you know?" I'd assumed his connection with the pack was a loose sense, like mine. Obviously there was more. "How far away are they?"

The faint hint of a moon above the clouds did nothing to light the blackened forest. Werewolves' mottled white coats would stand out.

"I don't know." Dean's voice nearly growled.

I glanced toward the nearest tree. If it had been dead and dried out in the middle of summer, I might have been able to ignite it. My only weapon would be wind, and they would be on me before I could do anything in this darkness.

Another werewolf bayed closer, and I retreated a step.

I'd made one mistake after the next, but I knew coming out here was the worst.

Dean spun, glaring first at the triangle opening in the metal building then at me. His focus trailed to the ruined structure behind me. Without warning he twisted me around, grabbed my hips, and lifted me in the air. "Grab on." He was surprisingly strong.

I scrambled to get both arms, then a leg, onto the roof. It groaned slightly at my weight. He shoved my butt just as I got leverage and launched me onto the flat metal surface. Wood from inside had ripped through the metal in places. Snags tugged at my coveralls.

Heart pounding, I rose to my feet carefully as the metal creaked. I could see the lake behind me and to my right. The forest remained pitch black.

"Three of them," Dean said. "Ahead, to my left and right."

A breeze fluttered in the trees, and a growl drifted with it from the lake. I shifted, peering at the darkness to my right. "What do they want with you?"

"I can't read their minds." His tone had become throaty and hoarse. "Certain cravings and sensations."

Panic climbed my chest as I teetered on the edge to peer at him. He'd dropped his jacket and produced his club, but he was still human.

A werewolf snarled from ahead of us, and the indistinct form, a shadow in the already dark forest, shot toward Dean.

The otherness raced to me as I called to air and blasted a gust at the wolf. Leaves burst from the ground just behind it. The cryptid veered from the glancing blow and then leaped over ten feet at Dean.

He moved nearly as quickly, sidestepping and swinging his club in one graceful movement.

The werewolf slammed into the slanted wall with enough force to make the whole structure complain. Lurching forward, I waved my arms in a circle and managed to fall back, instead of onto Dean and the werewolf. The cryptid appeared so much bigger than those rotting on our camp fence.

A hazy shape flew in from my right toward Dean's back, and the otherness raged to me. Sitting on the wet metal, I managed a larger column of wind than the first and aimed it into the massive creature's trajectory. It crumpled with a growl, rear legs folding to its head, then I slammed a second wave into its neck and chest.

The werewolf flew higher than the building I sat on. Rolling in the air, its legs stopped moving and spread wide and stiff. When it was arcing to the ground, it struck a blackened tree trunk with its hind quarters. The yelp made me wince as it spun wildly from the impact.

Dean cried out in pain and anger. When I turned to see him, I instead caught the glimpse of the leaping werewolf from my left. It had cleared the leaning building easily. It would land on the angled roof, and its momentum would send it into me.

My magic threw the air between us, but too close. It did stop the wolf as it reached the angled eave, but thrust by the same gale wind, I rolled over twice. As graceful as ever, my face planted into a mat of wet leaves cradled in a groove of the roof. The metal against my chin vibrated as nails scraped.

I franticly blew and brushed debris off my face, turning for the next attack. My magic might have a chance, if I could stop falling. Dean screamed low and throaty below. It turned into a howl. My skin chilled. If he turned, I hoped the Dean I knew would remain inside.

I was too far from the water to run. Dean might die,

even as a werewolf, trying to protect me. Anger rose in me. I had put him in this danger.

Nails whined on the tin roof and the building swayed, threatening to fall. The wolf I'd thrown off leaped over the eaves. Twice my size, it arced high enough that it would land directly on me. All my rage went into my wind. Air rushed past me. A bone snapped, and the beast yowled as my blast impacted. The mottled mass flew into the trees.

Shaking, I peered over the edge.

Dean had turned. I hadn't saved him from that.

His fur was a shiny gray, silver. He wriggled inside his clothes while fending off his attacker. Boots already discarded, his pants were nearly off. The checkered shirt had torn, and he rolled, trying to free himself of it as the werewolf lunged, tearing only cloth.

My ears rang as my pulse pounded. I gripped the sharp metal edge of the roof. There were four werewolves now, not three. Still, the one attacked him, as if intent on killing him. They certainly weren't working together.

Shadows moved to my right as the werewolf I'd originally attacked returned. They sprinted at an impossible speed. Fingers tightening on metal, I drew a wealth of bellowing otherness and all the air around me to throw it in a massive, broad gust.

Rushing wind shoved me sideways and closer to the edge as my gale blew loose branches, leaves, and the approaching werewolf tumbling into the dark forest. My strength ebbed from using so much magic.

Silver-furred Dean had still not freed himself from his shirt. His antagonist darted in for bites, but each time Dean managed to fend it off with a snap of his own. Sharp white teeth flashed, and the mottled wolf would leap back. Even though he might turn on me if he survived, I wanted Dean to live.

Nails scraped on metal, and I spun. The wolf I'd blasted off the building had obviously survived. It hadn't leaped onto the flat roof, and I couldn't see it.

As I gathered the clamoring otherness, I shifted to my elbow, sliding off the edge over Dean and the werewolf. Frantically flailing, I managed to make it worse, and the canopy overhead slowly tilted in my view. My back scraped on sharp metal as I slipped upside down and sideways.

Both wolves snarled and snapped below me, oblivious to my situation.

I managed one hopeless grip on the edge with a finger dug into a shard of exposed wood and the resulting torn metal. The pad of my fingertip tore as my legs and hips slithered off, but I didn't release my hold until the full weight of my body fell toward the fray below. I'd be dead in seconds.

The drop was short, and my last attempted grasp had righted my body. The musty scent of the wolves' wet fur filled the air. The dark forest remained indifferent to the snarling squabble.

The heel of my right boot landed on the hind quarters of the massive werewolf who had attacked Dean. As it reacted, moving aside, my body tilted back. One leg outstretched, the other hit wet leaves and slid.

I slammed onto my back and coughed out my breath.

The beast wasted no time to attack. A gray shadow with hot breath and glistening teeth, it lunged for my exposed neck.

My right hand moved up in a feeble gesture, as if I might have the strength to hold it back. The otherness roared into me from the air and the ground below. As my fingers pressed through coarse hair, I felt the magic flow. Through touch, I knew what was right for a body and what was wrong. The body and organs fell to the torture of my fear. Like healing, my magic and body reacted without conscious thought. I'd killed this way once before.

The werewolf grunted before it died. Its corpse carried all the weight and momentum of its attack as it slammed onto my chest. The deadly teeth slid beside my neck, and its last foul breath gagged me. I scrambled, whimpered, and pushed my way from underneath it.

Old memories returned, with the dead tech draped over my young body. It had taken me much more effort to get out from under that corpse.

Dean had finally freed himself from his shirt. On his forearm, blood soaked his silver fur. As he shook out his body, he towered over me, standing on all four legs.

I froze, the dead werewolf draped over the bottom half of my body. "Dean." Part of me knew that I'd protect myself and kill him if he attacked. I'd be infected again, and he'd be dead. "Don't."

I had failed.

His eyes were gray with flecks of red. He panted, mouth open and teeth exposed.

"I'm sorry," I said. "I wanted to heal you."

Dean leaped and I squealed. My hands shot up to protect my throat.

His arc took him over me, not at me. Dean's silver fur took what little light came from the clouds and shone. I shrunk away from his body and watched the tail, arrow straight, fly over me.

A werewolf howled behind me, then gurgled and whined.

Squirming to turn, I pressed against the bent building behind me.

Dean's muzzle had turned dark with blood, and the other werewolf writhed on the ground.

I shook against the metal, cold and bleeding, but not

bitten. He had saved me. The werewolf had been approaching from behind me. Dean and I stared at each other.

He shook his head, and his fur puffed behind his wolf face like a mane. Dean let out a low growl and raced away, toward the last werewolf.

I trembled as I dragged myself away from the wolf I'd killed. I was alive, but I had killed again.

Dean, the human part of him, was inside his wolf form. He could have attacked me but had protected me instead. Would he return to human form or remain a wolf? Either way, he needed to leave before the soldiers arrived.

Snarling and growling sounded from the direction I'd thrown the wolf. They fought. I stood, unsure whether to help Dean or run.

I could sense him, stronger than ever. They were moving away. His jacket lay by the ruined building.

Exhausted, I stood in the cold, staring into the darkness. The sounds of fighting grew distant. He was moving away, chasing the werewolf.

I couldn't stay.

"Good bye, Dean." Would he remember my warning about the soldiers and leave?

Chapter Eighteen

When Roxie returned to our apartment, I was awake, staring at the ceiling. She had stayed the night at Selina's, and I'd spent much of it awake and crying. Failing to heal Dean was part of my misery. Worse was my foolish need to know he was okay dashed against my more rational hope that he'd followed my warning and left. I couldn't pull myself together.

My door had remained closed all night, and my room was frigid. I rose and washed again. Dried blood tinged the water a faint pink, but I'd healed my finger. The walk back to camp had taken forever.

We would have shifts at Christianity classes today and turns at the washing tubs for our coveralls and underwear. Normally Sundays were a pleasant social break in our routine when we worked together using our magic to fill water and heat it. I wanted nothing to do with it today.

The front door closed behind Roxie before I finished dressing.

It was too dark when I exited behind her. I didn't want to socialize around breakfast this morning. I knocked on Eric and Jordan's door.

Eric opened it, dressed. "You look like crap," he said.

I agreed with a tilt of my head and shrug. "Head out back?"

"Of course." He returned into his apartment and came out with his canteen.

We walked down the stairwell and around the building in silence. The cook scraped on his grill and glanced at us when we rounded the corner. The scent of fire and the aroma of frying potatoes hung in the air. I led the way to our riverside pavilion. "Dean turned."

Eric sat beside me. "Damn. Sorry." His lips tightened. "How do you feel?"

He could have meant emotionally over Dean, or physically over my earlier infection. I assumed and answered the latter. "The infection's gone. I tore my finger." I raised the pink digit with no sign of last night's damage. "I might be a little different, but not the wrong we felt during my last healing."

I grew hungry at the aroma of cooking food. The trees still lost errant drops of water, but it wasn't storming.

"So, he's gone?" Eric asked.

"I don't know." *Would he have just stayed there?* "He saved me." My mouth twitched. "We were attacked. I. .." I didn't talk about the tech I'd killed at the lab. Eric didn't need to know that I'd done the same to a werewolf. "Dean could have bitten me easily, but he jumped over me and killed one of the werewolves instead."

"Maybe your healing changed him so he's not one of their pack. It might have given him some control. That's good, right?" He smiled, as if everything was okay now.

"I guess." I pulled my hair back, considering a braid. "That's even more unfair. He can never live with us, but he's not one of them. What if he doesn't leave and the soldiers catch him?" My throat thickened, but I refused to cry. I had to assume that he'd survived against the last were-wolf since I'd blasted it a minute before.

"You can't control that."

I couldn't, but wanted to go check on him anyway. "I won't do anything foolish." I made the promise more to myself than for Eric's sake.

He chuckled. "Too late."

I swung lazily at him. "Roxie's still pissed at me."

"You know her. She'll cool down."

Inside the mess, lanterns had been lit, and a couple shapes moved inside. Selina would get our schedule for the day and be there early. She took all of it, the camp and being a Youth Guard, so seriously. I just preferred it to the labs, or being at risk among the townspeople for being a witch or freak. Once Dean was off everyone's mind, including my own, I could go back to our routine.

When the cook began serving the food, Eric and I went inside via the screen door. Jordan came out, surprised to see us. "I wondered where you went." He spoke to Eric, not me.

Scooping out some eggs, Eric smiled at his roommate. "I heard we were having potatoes. Wanted to be first in line."

I followed them, grabbing a napkin and heading back inside. Selina and Roxie were talking with Leslie by the front door; all of them studied me as I made my way to the table and sat with my back to them. Trying not to let my imagination take hold, I focused on my breakfast. After using so much magic and not getting enough sleep, I was starving. The potatoes were seasoned with onion and almost crispy.

Eric sat across from me, his eyes flicking toward Roxie and Selina. "I wonder what the gossip is today."

If Roxie had said anything about what I'd been up to with Dean, Selina wouldn't be gossiping but reporting to Tyrell. I started to respond, but he stiffened and flicked his fingers at their approach. Roxie and Leslie headed straight for the back patio. The room was filling, and the murmur of conversation had risen.

Selina smiled as she paused at the table. "Easy day today." Her head tilted. "Caitlyn, you look tired."

"Didn't sleep well." I shoved potatoes in my mouth.

Yaz came running in, and Selina joined her at the growing line for the morning meal. Some of the others offered us greetings, but I could still catch them watching me. Whatever rumors they had going on, I was sure they didn't come close to the truth.

When we received our schedule for the day, Roxie leaned against Selina. Like any other Sunday, the morning was Christian studies and washing. I tried not to appear suspicious when Selina assigned us Sector C, the patrol that would search around the brick house with the tower. The schedule still had not been sorted out. Units weren't going on outer patrols. Roxie seemed less angry and more indifferent toward me, which was worse.

Gratefully, it didn't rain during our washing. Those who could control water reasonably, such as me, Eric, and Roxie, filled bins from the river. Yaz helped, but she spilled even more than me while Roxie's streams arced gracefully from river to the waiting containers. Jordan and Selina heated the water in the tubs made from steel barrels cut in half. We all took turns washing spare coveralls, bedding, and towels with the rare soap which the camp provided.

I tried to engage Roxie. "With all the rain we've had, I don't know that my coveralls need a washing."

"Soap helps."

"Yeah, I guess it helps get the smell out." The shore was too crowded to discuss Dean's vomit. The stench had remained even after I swam across the short bit of water to the camp that night.

We worked together with water and heat to dry everything before folding our piles and heading back to our quarters. Roxie hadn't warmed much, but she hadn't ignored me or been outright hostile. I owed her for my mess with Dean. If I could control myself from trying to check on him, we'd be done with it.

The students were out of school today and joined us in Christian studies. Young and restless, they ogled us, though rarely tried to interact. The only ones they talked with were their peers who had aged up to join a patrol, such as Yaz. She seemed to enjoy the attention.

Well before lunch, Roxie, Eric, and I were on gate duty when unit leaders started congregating outside Tyrell's office. Selina was among them. Eric noticed first, then we all watched. The carcass of the dead wolf hanging on the fence bothered me more than usual. I couldn't get the reek out of my nose. The vision of Dean's silver form hanging there caused me to shiver.

My stomach churned. "Do you think they found him?" I asked.

Roxie scoffed. "I doubt they'd announce it to unit leaders. They haven't before."

With nothing else to do, we stared at the administrative building. I couldn't decide if I wanted to see Dean to make sure he was okay or confirm he'd left. No, I wanted to see him.

The smartest move would be to let it go. He might just remain a wolf. According to our classes, werewolves could return to human form, but rarely did.

Eric leaned beside me on the fence. "I assume these new positions mean we'll be taking on more outer patrols. Do you think they plan on using us to clear out the cryptids?"

"It's part of our long term mission," Roxie said.

"Yeah, but I always thought they meant the military."

"Which we're supposed to be joining." I thought back to Tyrell's pep talk. "As observers, Tyrell said, but that was just a test. I got that the end goal is we'd be part of the military."

"There's a sci-fi book I read like that." Eric smiled. "I'm not looking forward to it."

Selina exited Tyrell's office. We watched as she made a straight line for us.

My pulse began to rise. What had the meeting been about? I turned to Roxie. "You didn't say anything to her, did you?"

Roxie swore. "After all I've done? You have no right to ask. I should have told them all from the start."

I sagged and tried to keep my face expressionless. Tyrell had said something to Selina, and now she came for us. What if they caught me? Did I care?

Her face grim, Selina strode toward us with a determined gait. She stopped directly in front of me. "You took food with you the other night. Guess what they found at the building where this Dean boy was lurking?"

Chicken bones and a napkin, I thought. "I don't know."

"The next morning, you were sick. Were you bit?"

"No."

"But you've been helping him, haven't you?"

I stared into her blue eyes. They were wide and intense. If I told her the truth, she'd probably drag me off to Tyrell. About to deny it, I faltered and swallowed.

My shoulders sagged. I'd done what I could to save Dean and left the evidence behind me. I didn't want to be a soldier killing cryptids. The camp and promotions didn't matter anymore. I admitted to Selina's suspicions. "Yes."

Eric turned away. "Crap."

Selina glared at Roxie. "You knew."

I'd just dragged my friends with me. Selina would have to do the right thing, no matter our friendship. Roxie wouldn't get her promotion.

"No," I lied. "They were covering for me, but they didn't know why. It started after I fell in the river. Dean was there, and I tried to heal him. I did, partially. He didn't turn. I went looking for him, and Roxie and Eric got caught chasing me when I abandoned patrol. When the fisherman spotted him, I let them leave, then ran over and warned him. It was all me." Glancing at Roxie, I swallowed. "She knew I was up to something, and we don't keep secrets. That's why she's mad at me."

Selina studied the three of us, focusing mostly on me. "Where is he?"

"I don't know." They could punish me, but I wouldn't give up Dean.

"Did he bite you?"

I marshaled a scoff and lied. "No. I told you, he didn't turn." Selina would need to report this; I hoped I could keep Roxie and Eric clear of the backlash.

She turned to stare at the ground. I didn't dare glance at the others. Selina sighed. "It will look bad for the unit if Tyrell finds out." She raised her head. Her blue eyes bored into mine. "So, it's over?" Her question was more of a command. "Tyrell doesn't need to know. They'll find Dean on their own."

I nearly laughed with relief, then subdued my expression. "All over. He's gone." As if cutting the strings between me and Dean, I slashed the air with my hands.

She spared one last glance at Roxie before she turned and headed for our barracks. We didn't even peek at each other as she walked, afraid Selina would turn and see us.

Roxie spoke first. "That was extremely stupid."

"Yeah," Eric agreed.

"It worked." Tucking a stray hair behind my ear, I waited, but neither of them responded. *I hope she believed it.* My heart ached to check on Dean, but Selina would likely be keeping a tight eye on us now.

We had a break for lunch before our patrol, and I spent most of the time arguing with myself about Dean. I couldn't sense him, but that only meant he hadn't gotten closer. Selina ate quietly while Yaz chattered with Eric and Roxie about a game of soccer planned for the afternoon, if the weather held.

We got an extra three hour period off from training on Sundays. Mine wouldn't be until before dinner, and I considered sleeping.

I perked up when Yaz mentioned the soldiers searching for Dean. ".. . West of Bass Drive. They're doing a house by house search. They got pulled from their other patrols."

"Where?" I asked. Cringing, I tried to assume a lightly curious expression, but Selina didn't even glance at me.

Eric lips were tight as he pointed south. "From the town's intersection, west through the golf course."

They wouldn't be close to Dean's hiding place at the campground. The Youth Guard didn't patrol that old golf course. It was considered town because a few people had opted to live out there. I kept my relief hidden. If Dean hadn't left yet, they wouldn't be working their way out to him today. "Out by the green pond?"

"Yep." An unreadable expression covered his face. "They cleared all of Sector C yesterday and again this morning. Then they moved to town."

I listened to their conversation as I returned to my food. Dean had a reprieve, but they'd move to the campground eventually. He had to have left, but he had been bleeding after the fight. What if he was hurt? I didn't dare try to heal him. I studied the cornbread on the table and adjusted my napkin on my thigh before taking another piece.

Half an hour later, I walked Bass Drive with Roxie and Eric, and two pieces of cornbread in my pocket wrapped in a napkin. They'd still issued Roxie a rifle, and I hoped she wouldn't shoot me when I told her about my plan. The clouds were a light gray but still covered the sky. A light breeze pushed from the north at our backs with the scent of soggy leaves.

"You're going to hate me," I said.

Whipping her head to face me, Roxie stopped in her tracks. "Then don't."

"I have to."

Each of her words were crisp. "No, you don't."

"I could go tonight, but I'd move faster in the daylight."

Her face darkened and her lips curled. "Why do you have to be so selfish?"

"Because I care about someone other than the Youth Guard?" I cringed at my own anger. "I'm sorry. I just want him to survive this. He didn't ask to get bit."

"It's not just about what you want. We're supposed to be a team. We used to be." She gestured to Eric and herself.

"If it were one of you, I'd do the same. More. He doesn't deserve this."

Eric rested his hand on my arm. "Going out there, *again,* won't necessarily help him. It does put us at risk if someone catches you. That's what she means by selfish. I'll cover for you if you choose to, but you'd do us all a favor if you let it go."

Roxie glared at both of us now. I'd made up my mind. Admitting some of the truth to Selina had released some kind of permission for me to move forward. My friends could still plead innocence with only a slight risk of not reporting me. I pointed down Bass Drive to the entrance to

Pinckney Road. "I'll meet you where we take the other road for Sector C. They're going to be busy in town today."

I didn't wait for an answer and ran down the road. Roxie might choose to report me, but I doubted it. Drawing crisp air with each breath, I raced for the footbridge leading to the other side of the river. There were no fishermen or soldiers milling about. The birds and squirrels darted from my hurried approach. I'd have to keep a quick pace to not make us late.

Dean might not even be at the tilted, burned building, and the others would believe that for the best. I had a hard time accepting his fate. He couldn't stay near Santee. If he was wounded from the fight, we'd see what we could do to heal him better. Wind ruffled the water.

A weathered house stood past the path to the arched footbridge, and I slowed to a jog. Across Pinckney Road, dense brush, pines, and some leafless trees led to the woods. In that forest, I caught a flash of pink that caused me to stumble over my own feet and nearly fall. I stared for a moment, then turned toward the bridge before glancing back again. The color could only be Moonjir, but why would he spy on me and not come out?

I walked onto the bridge and stared into the water, as if merely waiting. A glint of metal flickered in the brush where I'd seen pink a minute before. Already breathing heavily from exertion, my pulse rose. From the side of my vision, I caught a gleam again, as if from metal. Someone, not Moonjir, hid in the bushes. If it were one of Tyrell's soldiers, then they suspected me. I turned, walking back along the bridge.

Moving away was someone. In the woods, a motion caused another dull reflection of the clouds above. The shape was surely a gun worn over the shoulder.

Tyrell had stationed someone there, or they had

followed me. Confronting the soldier would only highlight my involvement. Either way, I couldn't run into the woods alone and lead them to Dean. Thunder rumbled from the north. Sighing, I turned at the road and headed for Roxie and Eric.

Chapter Nineteen

When Eric spotted me approaching, his eyebrows raised. Roxie just frowned.

"What happened?" he asked.

I waited until I reached them, turning to peek behind me. No one followed. "There's a soldier hiding in the woods by the footbridge. I don't know if they're just watching the area or followed me."

"You think Selina told, after she said she wouldn't?" Roxie's voice held a sharp edge, but for whom I couldn't be sure.

"I don't think she would," said Eric.

Selina had been my closest friend for years, and a lover, but she took her duty seriously. I couldn't know for sure. Surely they'd come out and grab me — or would they wait for me to return to camp? "They might just be watching that access point. It *is* close to where Dean had been hiding."

Thunder growled, and we all started back on patrol. Gusts blew wet leaves, and the scent of rain came with it. The weather wouldn't hold.

We watched the woods when we approached the footbridge. Under darkening clouds, I couldn't be sure if the soldier was still there. Paranoia had my neck tickling as we continued. I'd take my chance in the dark after everyone went to sleep.

The patrol was awkward; Eric tried to keep up the conversation while Roxie brooded and I plotted what might be my last trip out to see Dean. If the soldiers were watching me, I'd have to be careful. Leaves outside the camp were still suspended, so they very well might guard the bridge tonight. If they caught me outside the camp, Tyrell would surely suspect me.

The rain hit halfway through patrol. It was the heaviest downpour so far, with lightning often illuminating our way better than the dim clouds. By the time we returned to camp, we were all soaked. The guards didn't escort me to Tyrell, so I assumed Selina had kept my secret.

I stripped in our apartment and hung my soaking coveralls beside Roxie's in the kitchen. She said nothing as she headed for her room to change for dinner. The walls shook from the wind and thunder.

Our dry coveralls were misted with the storm's spray as we went downstairs and into the mess. The other Youth Guards were less attentive than they had been, as the allure of the rumors had died. Selina, however, bored holes in me as we made our way to the back patio. Roxie left me on my own as she diverted to kiss Selina. Eric entered the front as I went out the back.

The chicken had an herbal aroma with garlic. Eric joined me as I served myself sweet potatoes. Rain and gale-force winds sprayed water inside the screens to hiss against the cook's grill.

"River's going to rise. I'd hate to be out in this." He winced at the comment, perhaps remembering I'd be worrying about Dean.

Lightning lit the trees out back. I'd be soaked in the first minute out in this. I was still going to check on Dean. "Maybe it'll let up soon."

He stopped me from heading back in and pulled me into a hug. I fought a sudden sob. "It's going to be okay," Eric whispered. "We'll get through this."

Roxie came out,and her pleasant expression dropped into a frown. I held onto Eric with one hand, watching her face. She'd forgive me eventually.

When I returned to the table, Selina studied me despite odd glances from Jordan and Yaz. "How was patrol?" she asked.

I slid onto the bench beside Yaz. "Boring. Wet." My tone sounded too stiff. "Did you get soaked too?"

"We did," said Yaz.

A flash of hardness crossed Selina's face. "Everybody did."

Eric took the space on the other side of Yaz, leaving the spot beside Selina for Roxie. "I thought the sweet potatoes were finished."

"Supplies came in today." Jordan stabbed toward the front of the building with his fork. "One of the trucks."

The Savannah government rarely used the diesel trucks, except to bring in new personnel or for the officers when they came for inspection. I'd gotten a ride or two, but it was rare. One of the drivers had let Selina and I hang on the back when they'd come through the gate. We'd been so much younger.

Roxie set her plate down with a smile for Selina and a blank glance in my direction as she sat. Her eyes widened as the door to the mess hall closed behind me. I turned to find a tall soldier marching between the tables, seeming to head directly toward me. My skin chilled.

His eyes were focused on me and he stopped in the aisle. "Cadet Caitlyn?"

I swallowed. "Yes."

"You're needed for a report." He noted my plate. "Apologies for the timing, but they want you to come immediately."

My legs trembled, but I rose. "Okay."

The rain drenched us between buildings, and we stopped not at Tyrell's office, but at the cryptid classroom. The soldier opened the door and tilted his head in a gesture for me to enter.

Tyrell, Gayle Simmons, and a pale officer stood at the back of the room waiting for me. The door closed with a click, and I started. The soldier had remained outside. Panic tightened my chest. Selina had betrayed me.

"Caitlyn, this is Major Burris. He's here to get a first-hand report of the cryptid you saw." Tyrell stepped forward, beckoning me. I'd frozen at the door.

"Alleged," the major said. "You must understand, we cannot take the word of a young girl on this matter."

I laughed in relief, then blushed in shame for assuming Selina had turned me in. "I'm sorry, sir." They didn't have to believe me. "I *am* supposed to report what I see. Beyond that, I can't control what you do with the information."

He had tiny dark eyes and heavy jowls, like some of the townspeople. Major Burris was not fit and trim like the soldiers or Tyrell. His pudgy finger pointed to Gayle's desk. "You can't think we'd believe this?" I assumed he pointed at the drawing she'd made from my description. When I didn't respond, his expression turned darker. "We don't appreciate humor like this."

"Why would I lie about this?" I asked.

Gayle's expression had remained unreadable, and Tyrell studied me, as if expecting me to confess. The major's lips tightened. "Perhaps you thought it would get you a promotion. I understand you have dropped behind the others in your age level."

I didn't care about the upcoming inspection or my rank, not after all that had happened over the past few days. "If I wanted some new stripes, I'd have come up with something a little less ridiculous, don't you think?" My tone had risen. I was wasting my time and hadn't gotten to finish eating over this.

"Sir," Tyrell corrected.

I closed my eyes for a moment, then calmed my voice. "Don't you think, sir?"

Major Burris took a step closer to me, but there was a reluctance, as if I were tainted. "There are those of you who wash out from the camps, you know. Not all of you are capable of being soldiers. We can't just let you back among the normal population." He studied me with a sense of malice.

If he meant going back to the labs, I couldn't handle that. I gritted my teeth, not willing to be afraid. "Yes, sir."

"And yet, you won't retract your report? Admit to your lies?"

"I will do whatever you command me to do, sir." I pointed to the picture on Gayle's desk. "If you wish me to lie about what I saw, then I will tell you I made it all up. Sir." The vision of being put on a truck and shipped back to a lab flashed through my thoughts. I would run before they could put the collar on me. Camp Sparta had taught me how to fight, if nothing else.

Major Burris stepped away, as if from a snake, and shook his head at Tyrell.

"Dismissed, Cadet." Tyrell hadn't stood up for me. I didn't know the man any more.

"Yes, sir."

I headed for the door, hoping I'd make it back in time to salvage my dinner. My stomach churned at the thought. The soldier waited outside and glanced in when I came out.

My arms shook as I walked back, whether from anger or fear; both boiled inside me. A week ago, I'd been comfortable with my life; now, I couldn't understand how I could be comfortable at Camp Sparta. The rain poured on me between buildings. Students laughed from their dorms on the floors above. I walked, letting the cold water drench me.

Ahead, one of the Youth Guards raced up their stairwell, avoiding the worst of the gusting downpour. They were still at home here. I didn't belong. The major's accusations stung, though he didn't matter to me. What hurt worse was Gayle and Tyrell standing by and letting him be abusive. No one believed me.

I came to the last building where the Wolf Squad and other units had their barracks. Stopping at the door to the mess, I peeked in through the window. Ben and some of the Hounds stood at the end of our table talking as they sometimes did.

Turning, I peered at the gate, but the sheets of water blocked any view of the guard there. I walked to the end of the overhang where waterfalls dug holes in the ground. The practice grounds were gray mist. The storm swallowed any hint of the river. No one could see me if I left now.

Selina might come searching for me to find out what had happened.

I only heard the door when it closed behind Roxie. She wore a worried expression. "Everything okay?"

"No." Drawing a deep breath, I spoke quietly. "Some major came by to tell me I was full of shit. Doesn't believe me about Moonjir. I don't care."

She stepped forward and spoke quietly. "I'm sorry."

When her arms pulled me in, I cried, and she held me tight. "I was scared. .."

We rarely spoke of the labs, any of us. It gave me some comfort that she worried about me, even after all the trouble and concern I'd caused her. "I'm sorry, too."

"Don't apologize. I get caught up in myself and forget what you're feeling." She separated us, wiped my eyes, and smiled. "Go. I'll tell Selina what the issue was and tell her you went to sleep. Go get wet, meet with your werewolf, and make sure he's okay."

Chapter Twenty

I couldn't see the edge of the inlet of water which separated the camp from the forest. The whole river had swollen, so of course I slipped on mud and landed in the water feet first. Pulling at the otherness, it roared and joined with me to push a path through the five or six paces of standing water. My boots sunk with each step.

"Crap." I slipped on the far side and dug my hands wrist deep into slime.

The rain poured off my shoulders and arms as I picked my way slowly through the dark forest. I found a branch to help me navigate and made it to the back of the school. The streets were flooded, but easier to navigate than the trees and brush. The only real worry I had was where I'd seen the soldier. When I came to the spot on Pinckney Road where I'd seen the spy, I strode into the brush, smacking my way through with my stick.

"Hello?" No one was there. I had no idea what I'd say if I were caught, but I wasn't leading them to Dean.

It was slow and difficult in the weather, but I made it over the bridge and into the far woods.

As before, I sensed him a good distance away. He

hadn't left, and I feared he was too injured. There was also the possibility that he'd turned for good and hunted even now. The thought didn't deter me. I trusted him for some reason.

The trees blackened around me, and the rain eased as I neared what I believed to be the campground. The clouds still did not let much light through, but the sheets of water had stopped.

The silhouette of the tilted building sprang into focus when I arrived. A shadow in a human form separated from the darkness, and Dean walked forward to meet me.

A shred of blue-green shirt was tied around his forearm. Dean's bare chest was solid and better formed than any of the Youth Guard, but he'd previously made a living rowing. I swallowed, trying not to ogle.

Stubble shaded his chin. "It's dangerous to be out here." His eyes were dark. Rain matted his hair and glistened on his skin. "Why did you come back?"

"Why did you stay?" I asked. He had to be freezing.

He lifted his arm. "I've slept most of the day. I was going to grab my boat and leave before morning if the rain let up." Dean led the way to the slanted opening. The dead werewolves were gone.

The storm leaked inside with steady dripping, but he'd piled cardboard on a dry section as a bed. His jacket was rolled like a pillow. A musty, foul odor hung in the air. "Aren't you cold?"

He shook his head. "Not that bad. I've stayed dry until I sensed you and went outside." Dean sat at the edge of the cardboard and patted it to offer me a seat. The rain thrummed on the metal roof.

"It'll get wet."

"It'll dry. Sit." He rubbed his face. "You never answered my question."

I sat, closer than when he'd been a silver wolf. "I needed to know you were okay. Did you chase off the last one?"

His face tightened. "I killed it." He clenched his fists. "It wasn't like hunting when you need food. I just couldn't help but want it dead." Dean let out a short, bitter laugh. "I've always hated werewolves. They killed my father."

"I'm sorry."

"It still should have bothered me to kill out of rage, but it didn't. I tasted their blood and liked it. It was. .." He fell silent.

"What was it like?" I wanted to reach out and comfort him.

"Like a dream." He shook his head, almost violently. "I could have hurt you. Some things seemed real, but my thoughts and emotions were a haze; even now they're off." He touched his face, as if confirming it was still human. "I could hear your magic. Can you hear it?"

I called the otherness to bring heat into the broken building from outside. A dangerous plan considering my inabilities with heat, but I did hear the roar. "Yes." If I warmed us, I didn't feel it. "I don't know if I'd noticed it before." I thought about our training sessions. "I don't think I've heard anyone else's." I shivered in the cold.

Dean shook out his jacket, then leaned in to drape it around my shoulders. "You aren't afraid of me?"

"You saved me." I pulled the leather close, drenching the inside. "What will you do now?"

"Leave." He closed his eyes and touched his nose. "I don't know if I can live like this."

It broke my heart to hear the despair in his voice. I wanted to hold him and let him know it would be okay, but it wouldn't ever be okay. "I'm so sorry."

He stiffened, pulling away. "No regrets. I'll be fine."

I shivered as the chill dug into unused muscles. "I'd

offer to try and heal your arm, but that didn't work out too well last time."

He laughed, seeming to appreciate the change in topic. "I ate raw fish today; really not looking to puke that up." His smile waned. "I do want to thank you for helping. I never really have. Whatever you did, it changed me enough that I was never part of their pack. I don't have the urge to go slaughter anything, though I would kill for a steak." Dean studied my eyes. "I owe you everything."

My teeth chattered as I spoke. "I couldn't *not* try. I just wished it worked."

"You're freezing," he said.

I nodded and he slid closer to me, pulling me against his warm chest. He smelled like a sweeter version of his leather jacket. His hair rested wet on my forehead. I let go of his jacket and put my hands on his sides; his skin was hot compared to my chilled skin. "Cold hands," I said.

He didn't respond, and when I pulled my head back, he studied my eyes, then lips.

Until that moment, I hadn't really wanted him to kiss me, much.

Dean swallowed and wet his lips. The cold air seemed far away. My mouth opened and he leaned in carefully and slowly. His skin was fire against mine, and his lips firm.

Heat flushed through my body — a different kind of magic. Our mouths pressed firmer, hungrier. My hands clung to his back and rubbed along the lines of his muscles. His hand cradled my neck, then slid along my collarbone.

A familiar ache rose, and I wanted his fingers on my skin.

Dean yanked himself away from me.

I fell back onto the cardboard, stunned.

He jerked, swallowed a guttural whine, and then growled as he began to turn.

My heartbeat, already fast, raced, pounding in my ears.

His beautiful face contorted and silver fur sprouted from his olive skin.

I froze. He'd already lurched away from me. Now, standing on both legs, his pants began to loosen and slide. His muzzle formed with a gurgling howl. Dean dropped to the ground on all fours and shook out a thick silver mane. My breath caught in my throat. He was terrifying and beautiful.

His eyes reflected the light from outside and glinted flecks of reds and golds. He growled deep in his throat as he wriggled free of his clothes. Tugging at the bandage on his arm with his teeth, he ripped it off.

I finally took a breath.

If he attacked me, I wouldn't call the magic. I had put us in this situation.

My classroom learning flashed in my head. Heavy emotions could cause a werewolf to turn. Usually anger or fear were the cause, so I should be flattered, but I would have preferred that we were still kissing.

Free of clothes and bandages, Dean studied me with dark intense eyes. He snarled and leaped, easily clearing my prone form and launching into the dark woods. He howled as he ran.

I touched his jacket, remembering his smell. We couldn't have love. The passion would drive him to change. My throat thickened, and I pulled his jacket around my shoulders. Tears burned at the edges of my eyes. I curled on my side, fighting sobs.

Chapter Twenty-One

I'd given up on waiting for Dean and gone back to the camp barracks, leaving his jacket behind. Roxie was at Selina's, so I washed as best I could, wrung water out of my coveralls, and crawled into bed. I woke to Roxie's gentle push on my shoulder.

"Am I late?" My eyes were glued shut and my throat was dry.

"Yeah. I checked in on you, then dried out our coveralls. Late night?"

Thunder rumbled outside. "Early morning." I peeled an eye open and sat in frigid air. The apartment had felt warm when I'd come back. I could still feel his lips on mine. Digging fingernails into my bare thigh, I kept the tears at bay. "It was horrible." *And wonderful*, I thought.

Roxie sat on the bed. "What happened?"

"He changed again." I brought both arms into the chill air for her to examine. "He didn't bite me. He kissed me — that's what made him turn."

Her lips pursed and she touched my hand. "I'm so sorry." A smile crept onto her face. "Good kiss, I guess."

I snorted out a chuckle. "It was."

"So, what are you going to do?" Roxie glanced aside, not meeting my eyes.

"He was planning on leaving this morning. I may have screwed that up."

She let out a shaky laugh, as if relieved. "I hope he does. They've got to search out there eventually. You warned him, I assume." Her tone drifted back to a sharper, serious note.

I nodded and climbed out of my bed. "I did. You're not mad at me anymore?"

Roxie let out a heavy sigh. "Eric helped me accept your behavior. I'm your friend, first and always. I can't hold it against you because you want to help — or get kisses." She smiled. "You're not off the hook. I can be mad at you and love you at the same time."

I raced to get dressed and grab my canteen as the storm battered at the back of the building. Roxie waited for me, and we stepped onto the balcony to find Eric and Jordan standing at the railing. They were watching a local man in a yellow jacket and a soldier jog across the grass toward the administration building. In the darkness, I wouldn't have noticed him if it were not for the bright colors.

"What's going on?" asked Roxie.

Eric pointed. "He came to the gate looking upset. The soldier let him in."

The chilly wind blew the rain away from us, but the mist drifted in. Roxie headed for the stairwell. "We can ask Selina about it."

When we got downstairs, Selina studied me as if I might turn into a werewolf there in the mess hall. We walked across the room, and Roxie split from us to head to the table while I hurried to the back patio. The storm blew rain through the screen, and the cook leaned against the wind.

Eric and I came back to the dining area as a soldier stepped into our mess.

"Unit Leaders with me," he barked and headed outside, letting cold wind whip through the open door. Our lanterns flickered, causing an ominous effect as Selina and the other leaders stood from their breakfast.

Eric and I waited with plates in hands watching the commotion. "News from the town?" he asked.

Dean was far from the town, at the campground. Still, my breath tightened. The other werewolves were dead. *Could there be more?*

While the rest of the room and Yaz chattered about the intrusion, Eric, Roxie, and I ate solemnly, exchanging glances. I had difficulty tasting the eggs. Lack of sleep and an excess of emotions had left me punchy and prone to imagining disasters. I was grateful when Selina and the others returned.

She sat, peering at me. "There's been a silver wolf spotted by highway six. Obviously not a werewolf, but we're going to be careful while the soldiers hunt it."

I blinked and held my breath. She kept her eyes on mine. Roxie and Eric focused on their food.

"Are there silver wolves?" Yaz asked.

Selina nodded slowly. "Dark gray, but the sun wasn't up when the man saw it. Swears it was silver-white. Either way, run is canceled, so we have an hour of free time. No one leaves the compound." The last sentence she said slowly, eyes locked with mine. "Patrols might be canceled as well, but we'll get instructions before then." She began detailing our roster for the day, or what the schedule had been.

I had martial training again at 1000 and we had gate at 1300. Our patrol was Sector B, which was all woods and closest to the sighting of Dean. Why had he ranged that far, and why hadn't he turned human yet? He might never change. I doubted I'd have the chance to ask him. He'd planned on leaving this morning. I needed him to be safe, but couldn't deny the desire to see him one more time. Unable to finish my food, I stumbled into the gusts of the patio and cleaned my plate.

Selina appeared beside me. "We need to talk. Your apartment." She spoke quietly, and handed me her plate before leaving.

She likely guessed that the silver wolf was Dean. I scraped off uneaten food and went through the motions of rinsing the plate before leaving it in the soak for the students to finish. The storm howled at me, and all I could think about was Dean. They'd be hunting in the wrong place, if he went back to the campground or left. What if he didn't? I dropped a plate in the sink and soaked my sleeve retrieving it.

We left Yaz hastily finishing her breakfast. Roxie followed me, and I whispered to her and Eric about Selina. Jordan scowled at me suspiciously. Eric flashed a worried smile as he headed for his apartment, leaving me and Roxie at our door. As we entered, she rubbed my back, trying to be encouraging.

Selina sat in one of our chairs. Her blue eyes followed us as we entered. She waited for the door to close before she spoke. "Is it him?"

I nodded. "More silver than white."

Her lips twitched. "So he *has* turned. You lied."

My skin rose with goosebumps. I was horrible at keeping secrets. "It just happened last night. Truly. We kissed, and —"

"You said you were done." Selina raised a hand, stopping my response. "I need you to be done." She pointed to the other chair.

I sat while Roxie slid to the floor. "I need him safe." My

voice wavered and I swallowed the lump in my throat. "Away from here. He planned on leaving this morning."

"Where is he?"

Panic boiled in my stomach. Selina had said she wouldn't turn him in, but she could change her mind. "West, in the woods." Technically, it was true.

She held her hand out to Roxie, focusing on her for a moment. "You should make sure he left. Where did he plan on going?" Her eyes remained on her lover, not me.

Flustered, I paused. She wanted me to sneak out again. I had expected a rebuke for last night. "I don't know. North?"

"Across the lake. He still has his boat, I imagine." She added the last bit as an afterthought. "Make sure he gets on it and leaves." Her head tilted to watch me. "You met with Major Burris. I heard he was here to see you about Moonjir. They don't believe you. None of them."

She meant Tyrell didn't believe me. That had been evident when he didn't come to my defense. "I guess I can understand. It *is* pretty strange."

Selina let go of Roxie's hand. "You *are* telling the truth, right?" She leaned forward.

Lightning flashed outside. *She* didn't believe me. *Did anyone?* "Yes. It would have been easier if I never mentioned it."

"Like Dean." Her tone harsh, she waved off the comment. "Make sure he leaves." She stood, peering at me.

I stood and faced her. "Just to be clear. You want me to break the rules?" I found it hard to believe.

"Again. Yes. You seem quite capable of it." She smiled and touched my shoulder. "Once he's gone, we can forget all about this. You can sneak out while Eric and Roxie are on patrol."

"What if patrols are canceled?" Roxie asked.

Selina lifted a shoulder in a partial shrug. "I'm sure Caitlyn will figure out a way." She took two steps toward our front door, then turned her head. "Did anyone know about your trip out last night?"

I didn't glance at Roxie. "Nope."

Smiling, Selina left us.

I faced the closed door, Roxie to my side. "That was odd," I said.

She stood. "Maybe not. You were her closest friend for a long time. Selina has a harder time forgiving you, that's all. You've risked her position by keeping her from reporting this. I can see why she wants Dean gone. I do."

She didn't mean her words to hurt, but they did. So did everyone thinking I'd lied about Moonjir. I patted my canteen and forced a smile. "Civics class 0800."

As our instructor reiterated the Savannah Authority's mission to unite America under our Christian doctrine, I worried about Dean. The emphasis on clearing the godless cryptids from the northern and western zones as a mandate made me squirm. I slunk in my seat as he rehashed the Sorrow's history with werewolves as the horror from the north, which we were here to combat. The storm outside rattled the windows, bringing starts from the younger members.

Whatever Selina's reasons were, she was right; I needed Dean to leave. I'd probably find him gone, but at least I'd know for sure.

Chapter Twenty-Two

When the pounding rain lessened on the windows, they let us out of Civics early. Outside the storm had eased to a drizzle, but the wind still gusted on occasion.

Three diesel trucks passed outside the fence toward the military base, causing everyone to cluster under the balcony. There were a half a dozen soldiers in each, four riding under a tarp in the back. They gawked at us as much as we did them.

For Dean? I thought. My heart started to race. "Why are they here?"

Eric saw my concern and rested his hand on my shoulder. "Takes a day to get from Savannah to here. Another to send the message."

It still could have been about Dean. I was curious. "I've got martial training next, after break. Maybe I'll head over now, since the storm let up."

He held back a laugh. "Makes perfect sense. I've got water training, but I think I'll take that break anyway. See ya." Eric lightly pushed me forward.

I waved at Roxie and headed for the north gate. At this time of the morning, the guard was a soldier, disinterested in my reasoning for heading over early as he let me through. The last truck ambled down the broken road ahead of me. The men in the back peered at me with unsettling grimness.

If they had been sent to Santee to hunt Dean, why not drop them off in town? Then again, like Eric had suggested, they probably had been on the road for a while, so they wouldn't know where to search. They'd have to check in.

The soldier who opened both gates to let the trucks into the base waited when he saw me coming up the road. I jogged the last bit as he held one open. "You're early," he said.

I pointed to the sky. "I'd rather sit here dry. I don't think the storm is done."

He nodded. "It ain't." His shadow of a beard reminded me of Dean, and a wave of sadness poured over me.

Outside of the two Jeeps which they kept on base, there were five new vehicles. Four were trucks and one was as big, but enclosed. I recognized the style from those that littered the roads and parking lots around Santee.

Major Burris stood beside the new arrivals, talking with another officer who I'd seen before, a tall, pale man with a tiny mustache. I avoided both of them, veering toward the closest building. The one I needed was behind them. My evasion didn't work, as one of the new soldiers said something, and the whole group turned in my direction. I walked faster.

The major yelled out to me. "Hey! Over here."

Reluctantly, I complied; it was my fault for being nosy. The trucks reeked of burning fuel. The soldiers crawling out of the vehicles were all armed with rifles over their shoulders and had packs as if they intended to stay for a while.

"Attention, Soldier." The major's uniform had droplets

forming from the light rain, but he hadn't been soaked in the earlier downpour.

I stood stiffly. "Yes, sir."

The other officer left to identify the leaders of the new soldiers. They all kept watching me. The group clustered on the edge of the crumbling parking lot.

"What are *you* doing here?"

"I'm scheduled here, sir." I listened to the other officer as he discussed a briefing, but not the specifics.

"Waste of our resources. That'll change. Did Sergeant Major Tyrell send you?" The way he spoke Tyrell's name had me believe he did not like our camp leader very much, unlike most of the other soldiers here at the base.

"No, sir."

"Well, he's supposed to meet us here. Dismissed."

"Yes, sir." I headed for the building where we held martial training. Footsteps sounded behind me as the soldiers were dismissed as well.

The major's demeanor toward me brought back memories of the lab where some of the scientists ordered us around with visible disdain. I'd taken it to heart, until Tyrell brought me to Camp Sparta where they promised we'd be useful and productive. My belief in that concept was waning. I reached the door to the building and turned enough to gauge how far back the soldiers were. Their glares made me uncomfortable. I'd wanted to see what they were here to do, but that had been a mistake.

"Blondie." A rough male voice spoke, making my skin twitch.

I didn't turn or hesitate and let the door close behind me. Inside was comfortably warm. The building had an acrid scent of oil. I hurried for the gym downstairs.

The door opened behind me, and one of the soldiers called out, "Witch!"

I ignored them, continuing to walk deeper into the empty, expanded room. The rain had started again, pattering at the back windows and glass doors. I'd expected the usual instructors, but I was early. Following the soldiers and coming early had proved to be an increasingly bad idea.

"Maybe they'll let us clean out some of the freaks on the way to Sumter."

Cringing at being called a freak, I stiffened, but strode toward the far wall. Even the townspeople thought of us that way, according to Dean's story.

Footsteps ran behind me, and a man with a low voice called, "What are you doing here? Why aren't you back there locked inside with the others?"

I glanced behind at a young face and strawberry blond hair. His ugly expression included a smile of sorts. A larger soldier jogged two paces behind him while the others watched with amusement. I ignored them and kept walking.

"Hey, witch. You don't belong here with us humans." He reached for my shoulder, and I dodged forward, turning to face him.

They'd made enough noise that I expected someone to come out. The room hadn't been prepped yet for whatever the instructors planned. I was awfully early, though. "I'm here for training. It's on my schedule for today."

"Training?" The larger man laughed as he spoke. "I thought you were all voodoo and shit. What kind of training do you do here?" He hadn't shaved for a day or so, and hairs were thickest near his ears and his jowls.

The two men had stopped two paces from me. I wasn't backed against the wall, but I felt confined. "Martial training. At least once a week." My voice came out a little loud, perhaps hoping our instructor would hear and interfere.

They both laughed. "We can help with that. Never tossed around a freak before." The bigger man tapped the other on the shoulder as he spoke, and they grinned at each other.

"No thank you." My chest tightened. They wanted to hurt me.

Behind the other soldiers, I recognized one of our instructors, a bald man named Mathews, but he hadn't moved forward. How long had he been watching? I side-stepped, trying to catch his eye. He seemed to be content to stay put and not help. I was on my own.

"I insist." The larger man lunged at me while the strawberry blond jumped to my side, stopping any escape.

I barely considered the size of the room as otherness roared to me. A short gale, all the wind I could gather from the room, slammed into the smaller man. He toppled against the larger soldier. Windows in the back shattered from my change in air pressure. His pack rolled under him awkwardly as he hit the floor. I staggered back.

The big man swore, stepped over his friend, and grabbed me by the throat before I could dodge. Panic swept through me at his touch. Then, rage burned inside me as I glared back at him and circled my fingers around his wrist. I was in control. His grip tightened, cutting off my air.

Before when I'd killed the tech and werewolf, I'd reacted in panic; now, I acted with precision. The otherness growled to me and I sensed the bonds between the millions of elements contained in my grasp and beyond. Bones connected to tissue and even deeper bonds formed between the components of the seemingly rigid structure. There were so many points which could fail and ruin the whole.

Suddenly brittle, the bones in his hand crumbled against the pressure of his own muscles. Tendons detached and snapped along his arm. He shrieked from the pain. His ruined hand slid off my throat. I could breathe.

The room exploded into chaos. The soldiers yelled

questions and demands. I could hear Mathews barking for them to stop as weapons were being drawn.

A gale surged in through the windows I'd broken. Rain glittered on the floor and a wet leaf tumbled.

Over a dozen soldiers were focused on me. I had nowhere to run before they would have their guns out. I couldn't bring in enough air through the windows to stop all of them. They would kill me.

Chapter Twenty-Three

The two soldiers in front of me were in various stages of their reaction. The man whose hand and wrist I'd ruined had crumpled to one knee. The other knew something had occurred, though he didn't know exactly what, and tried to scramble away from me.

The remaining soldiers were yelling. As sidearms were pulled from holsters, I crouched behind the bulk of the big man. He stunk of stale alcohol and musty clothes. Mathews had reached the main mass of soldiers, but there were too many for him to get their attention.

The gym had several support columns large enough to hide me, but too far away for me to run to in time. Their bullets would be faster. I'd created a disaster, all in an attempt to find out if they were here to hunt Dean.

I drew the otherness to me and gathered the air in the room to my will. My jaw tightened as I braced myself. The large man started to shift away from me. As wind swirled through the remaining soldiers toward me from the farthest reaches of the gym, I turned toward the closest support column. My focused gust slammed into my back and legs, jettisoning me forward.

Two gunshots rang out, echoing oddly in the enclosed space where I'd manipulated the air. I tried to keep the wind constant, but it slipped off my right side to spin me to face my adversaries. Hands and weapons raised, they were trying to follow me. A third shot sounded, louder than the first ones.

I slammed into the floor and slid. Two more soldiers fired, and the cracks of their guns echoed loudly in my ears. They were yelling, but it sounded distant. Scrambling, I shoved myself against the concrete pillar, as trapped as I had been before.

The broken windows were only six or more paces away, but if I tried the same trick to blow myself out the building, I'd as likely shred myself on the shards of glass in the frames as slam into a wall. Curling into a ball, I wrapped my arms over my head and waited.

They were arguing, or at least the instructor was. The shooting had stopped. I recognized a new voice as the major's, and he bellowed demands.

My stomach churned as the soldiers claimed I'd attacked them.

The instructor Mathews offered a weak response. "It was a misunderstanding."

Anger boiled inside. Tyrell's belief that I had lied. The threat of the soldiers hunting Dean. The disdain Major Burris had for me. *For a witch, a freak*, I thought. All of it burned through me. I stood. Not caring if they fired, I stepped from behind the support column.

I pointed at the large man coddling his now purple right arm. "He put his hand on my throat and choked me." I included the strawberry blond man. "They attacked me while the others watched. Ask Mathews." Guns were still pointed at me, but they didn't fire.

Mathews glared, lips twisting. "A misunderstanding."

The major appeared almost pleased. "Take her into custody."

I stiffened, but not one of the soldiers moved forward. A few of them glanced at the swelling purple hand dangling from the big man's arm. A couple of the men had expressions that told me they would rather just shoot me where I stood.

Major Burris reddened as he bellowed, "I said, take her."

"No," Tyrell said. I hadn't noticed him behind the others, but he stepped around the cluster of soldiers. "Lower your weapons. Cadet Caitlyn, you're confined to your quarters. I'll call you in for a report sometime this afternoon."

The major's face was pink. "You don't have the authority."

Tyrell faced him. "You know I do, this side of the bridge. I'm not even in your chain of command, so technically the one without authority here is you, sir." He glanced at me and motioned the instructor toward me. "Escort her out the gate, Sergeant Mathews. Put those weapons away." The last comment he made with a snarl toward the soldiers, and they slowly complied.

I waited for Mathews to approach and weapons to return to holsters. "Let's take you out the back," he said.

Glass crunched under our feet, and the storm had turned ugly again, blowing rain in our faces through the broken windows as we reached the back door. I followed the instructor into the storm while my emotions churned between relief, anger, and lingering fear. The major and Tyrell were arguing loudly as we left.

I never should have come. Roxie and Eric were enjoying their break and would be heading to water and heat training, if practices weren't canceled due to weather. The soldiers hadn't come to hunt Dean, but if they did, there were enough to spread to the campground. From one of their comments, they were headed to Sumter, a city north of Santee according to Tyrell's maps. They still might be drawn into the hunt first.

My laugh caused Mathews to glance back at me. I was off duty for the day, with Tyrell's outrage planned for the afternoon. He'd be furious. I couldn't know what he'd do to me. Either way, I didn't care about his consequences anymore, and it left me free to go warn Dean.

I strode faster, caught up with Mathews, then started to jog along the side of the building. "Let's go."

When I reached my apartment, Roxie was dry and prepping to leave. "I'm going to go warn Dean about him being spotted and the new soldiers."

Her eyebrows drew closer and her mouth slackened for a moment before she spoke. "You've got martial training this morning."

I laughed, collecting my machete. "Oh, I got some in with the help of some jerk soldiers. I'm in quite a bit of trouble. Confined to my quarters until Tyrell can yell at me for ruining one of their hands."

Roxie gaped at me. "What?"

I patted my canteen and machete sheath. "I just don't care anymore, Roxie. They hate us. Tyrell just wants to use us. At the rate I'm going, they'll probably want to send me back to the lab." I flinched at the idea of a collar around my neck again. "I'll die before that."

"Wait." Roxie followed me as I headed for the door.

"No time. I've got to get going. Please, if anyone asks, I'm confined to quarters." I turned at the door. "Or not. Don't care." Her expression of shock didn't change as I gave her a quick hug and left.

I raced through the rain in the middle of the heat

training range. The gate and guard weren't visible from where I was, thanks to the storm. Smiling, I ran toward the small inlet of water separating the camp from the beginning of Sector A.

The otherness howled as I drew it in and took hold of the air behind me. Fatigue nibbled at my energy; I'd used too much magic already. When I reached the muddy bank, I timed the gust to push me from behind as I leaped in the air. My new trick wasn't perfect. In fact, I landed short of the other shore, splashing knee deep, but it had been close.

I started running through the woods to the neighborhood behind the school. Everyone else would be at their training for three hours. Tyrell might send someone for me by then, but if I was quick I'd make it back unnoticed. I slipped on a section of wet leaves and found a bruise from my antics at the gym.

It took me until after I'd passed over the footbridge to realize that there might be an instructor stationed at the heat practice area when I returned. "I don't care," I panted. The magic I'd used, the lack of sleep, and emotional turmoil had left me exhausted and numb. Long before I reached the burned woods, I'd slowed to a jog. The storm gave no sign of easing.

I sensed Dean ahead and knew he would feel me heading toward him. The prospect made me smile.

Shirtless, but in human form, he waited for me in front of the ruined building. What had he done with the dead werewolves? The air smelled of storm and soggy leaves, nothing more.

His expression was grim. "You shouldn't be here." The bite on his arm had scabbed to a pattern of dark dots.

I frowned, not expecting his response. "Why not?" There were lots of reasons, but what was his?

He stared into storm and shook his head. "Because of what happened?"

"After the morning I've had. .." I snorted and walked into the building. "You're my least worrisome option. I had to warn you."

Dean's forehead furrowed. "What happened to you? What do you mean?"

I sat on his cardboard bed, conscious of his leather jacket and remembering our kiss. Pulling my knees up, I wrapped my arms around my legs and rested my chin atop them. "There's new soldiers in camp. I didn't know if they were here to search for you or not. I went to the base, and they tried to attack me."

He knelt on one knee, keeping his distance. His nostrils flared and his eyes were hard. "What do you mean, attack you?"

"They were calling me witch and freak, then they wanted to fight. I hurt them." I shrugged. "I'm in trouble now."

His fists clenched, knuckles pressed against the ground. "How can you be in trouble?"

"I'm the freak, remember." I regretted the comment. "Anyway. There's a good chance they'll search out here before they head to Sumter. You promised you were going to leave. Someone from town saw you this morning." He must have been a wolf all night. "Did you choose to stay a wolf?"

He turned away. "I was angry. It's unfair that I can't even —" His eyes flicked to mine. "You know."

"Kiss me? Yeah, that sorta sucked." I blushed, but smiled.

We stared at each other awkwardly. "You want me to leave?" he asked.

No. "You have to. They'll hurt you otherwise. This isn't

far enough away." I'd likely be caught, and who knew what punishment Tyrell would devise. There had been accidents, but no one had intentionally used magic to hurt anyone except for a push of wind here or there. "I don't know if I'll be able to come back. No one seemed to care that the soldiers were going to hurt me. They even shot at me."

His face hardened again. "Leave. Come with me. I can take care of you."

My eyebrows raised. "Take care of me?" The idea of leaving with him wasn't as disturbing as I might have thought it would be.

Dean's lips twisted. "I don't mean like in a macho way. I could teach you how to fish and trap, so we could eat. My boat is right here, hidden just off the lake. Packed to go. You could be yourself and not worry what they think." He blushed. "It's a bad idea. Sorry."

If anyone had suggested leaving the camp a week ago, I would have laughed. My friends were as much family as my mother, Grandpa, and Marjorie. "I don't want to be a soldier."

His head tilted and his lips pursed. "Does that mean you want to leave?"

I studied his brown eyes; they appeared almost hopeful. He wouldn't want to be alone. His lips tightened and relaxed, and I remembered the kiss. The only one we would ever have. "Sort of." I had the two options at the moment. I could go back and face the consequences, which might mean getting sent back to the labs. Hurting a soldier had been foolish, but what choice had they left me?

My other choice would be to go on the run with Dean. We could find an abandoned house and make it livable. Someplace with fresh water. I blinked, actually considering it. "But I can't. I couldn't leave Roxie and Eric."

He nodded and forced a smile. "Of course. They're your friends."

"More like family." I drew in a breath. I'd rested enough and would need to get back if I wanted to try and sneak in without getting in more trouble.

"Family," Dean repeated. He stood and stared out into the storm.

The leaks from the roof dropped rain into puddles, mostly at the corners. This would likely be his life now. He'd left his real family behind — his sister. I hadn't delivered his note for Bettina. Shame flushed my cheeks. "I'm sorry," I said.

He shook his head without turning to face me. "Don't be."

I suddenly wanted to hold him and comfort him, but we shouldn't do that either. Passions would eventually arise. If they didn't try to send me back to the labs, I'd deliver his note. I would die before going back to wearing that collar.

Dean turned, smiling. "You should get back, before you get in more trouble. I'll leave in the morning, when it's still dark. Don't come back out."

Chapter Twenty-Four

I was drenched to the skin and crying when I reached the inlet to the camp. No fires lit targets, so I assumed practice had been canceled. Not caring, I swam through frigid water instead of trying to use my magic. It quelled the tears at least. Lightning marked the eastern clouds, and thunder rolled close behind.

Roxie and Selina waited for me at the apartment.

"Oh," I said.

"Tyrell sent me to make sure you were in your quarters." Selina wasn't scowling as much as I would have expected her to. "He's concerned about what you did to that man."

I started stripping out of the freezing clothes. My jaw ached as I gritted my teeth. "He had me by the throat."

"They said you broke the windows first, blew one of them over." Selina rose from the chair, approaching me. Her voice still hadn't risen in anger.

I wrung water into a waiting pail. "They cornered me, threatening to hurt me."

"The instructor said he only saw you attack them."

"He's lying, but they hate us." I shivered.

Her tone grew colder. "Fear us. Now, more than ever. Tyrell will have to do something."

"Send me back?" I didn't have to say where. We'd lived the first two years at the camp waiting to be returned to the labs. "Maybe put me in the cage they keep for werewolves?" We'd all seen it behind the administration building.

Selina took too long to answer. "I don't know. Something."

I should have left with Dean. Tying my soaked coveralls, I took down the slightly drier pair and headed for my room and towel. "I don't care anymore."

Roxie stood and shifted restlessly, offering a wavering smile.

Selina followed me into my room. "Were you with him, just now?"

"Yes. I told him about the new soldiers. He was leaving right then." I lied with my face under my towel rubbing uselessly at my hair.

My pulse had risen slightly at her implications about Tyrell's impending punishment. He would have to do something.

When she didn't respond, I flashed her a smile. "Truly."

She laughed and sat on my bed. "You have no idea you do that, do you?"

"What?"

Her eyes were on her hands pressed against her legs. "You say 'truly' when you lie."

I trembled, tossing the towel onto the bed with my coveralls and headed for fresh underwear from my trunk. "I'm not lying." Sagging, I felt myself want to say the word. "Fine. He's leaving soon." That was loose enough to be near the truth. "We argued, somewhat." I changed, my back to her. "He wanted me to leave with him."

Turning around, I swallowed as Roxie had come to the

doorway. Selina remained sitting on my bed, faced away from me. Roxie's mouth hung open. "Are you going to leave?"

Tears tugged at my eyes as I grabbed my overalls. The apartment was freezing.

"When?" asked Selina.

A knock sounded at the door, and Roxie turned. She frowned, but left to answer it before I could respond.

"I didn't say yes." Shame flushed across my face. Not saying no felt like betrayal to Roxie. "I'm not heading back there."

Eric's voice came from the front door. Selina stood and headed back into the living room as I buttoned my coveralls. The back of the Wolf Squad patch held cool water, a wet spot on my chest.

"What's going on? I heard. .. Is Caitlyn okay?" Eric asked.

Selina glanced at me, then spoke. "Caitlyn's trying to decide if she's going to run off with Dean."

I wilted at the comment. Eric and Roxie were family. I couldn't leave them.

Eric rounded the corner. "Because of the thing with the soldier?"

"I hurt him." I said. No remorse or guilt twinged at the mention. I might have avoided the consequences and done something different, something less drastic, if I could do it over. It was done, though. "Now I have to be punished."

He rubbed at his ear. "Are you afraid they'll send you back to the labs?"

I gave a light shrug. "Yes. I won't go."

Selina sat with a sigh. "They have tranquilizers for us. You know that."

Roxie hadn't taken her eyes off me. "They killed the werewolf when they tried that."

"Yeah. I know." Selina sounded exasperated. "This has turned into a major shit show. Tyrell will have to do something." She smiled. "If it were me, I'd give up Dean to get in good graces. You, though, you'll likely run away with him tonight."

The three of us stood silently at the doorway facing Selina. Tyrell had to have a better punishment than sending me back to the labs. Selina was right in that I would rather run than give Dean up. Would she give up Roxie? I didn't ask.

"Patrols are back on for this evening. Roxie and Eric will have to man the gate without you. Tyrell expects you here when he gets done briefing the soldiers at the base. They'll be moving on Sumter when the rest of the troops arrive. If he's not done with you by the time patrol starts, I'll send Jordan with Roxie and Eric."

"Done with me?" I asked.

"The punishment will either be a demotion or. .." Selina tilted her head.

Roxie sputtered angrily. "They can't send her back to the labs."

Selina leaned back. "It's been done, just not at this camp. Caitlyn won't be given the choice if it comes to that."

"No. We can't let that happen." Roxie swung her head between us. "I won't."

"What choice do we have?" Selina scoffed. "If we fight them, we'll all end up running off with Dean."

"What?" asked Eric. He hadn't heard my earlier conversation.

My pulse had risen. "Dean asked me to leave with him." My throat was thick. "I can't leave you, though."

Selina stood. "You might not have that decision, if Tyrell decides he can't trust you." She cocked her head, studying each of us in turn. "Your best option might be leaving with Dean."

Eric covered his head with his hands, and Roxie leaned into my shoulder, hugging me awkwardly from the side.

I shouldn't consider it. However, I would fight to the death before I'd let the soldiers take me away. Was there a difference between leaving and fighting? It might mean death either way. If I fought and won, I'd still have to run. I could choose my path.

I shifted Roxie closer with one arm and pulled Eric in with the other for a hug. "I think I have to leave." He cried at my words.

My statement calmed my racing heart. I would have expected it to terrify me. Leaving meant losing my friends. "I don't belong here," I whispered.

"You do." Eric choked. Roxie said nothing. Of the three of us, she was the most practical.

I glanced when I heard Selina rising and walking across the living room. She studied my pack and contents spread along the wall under the furnace pipe. "You're going to need supplies," she said.

Eric tensed, but Roxie released us and turned. Selina was right, but I couldn't go rummaging now, or they'd suspect I was running away.

"We can't get you any weapons." Selina pulled back her hair. "I'll get a cloak and hat from storage and an extra flint. Roxie, head to the infirmary and get what supplies you can. Tell them it's for your pack. Don't take much. Eric, see if you can sneak some food from today's lunch." She headed for the front of the apartment. "We'll meet back here."

When she opened the front door, the storm blew a gust into the apartment. Roxie left a minute afterward while Eric wiped his face.

"I don't want you to leave." I'd dragged down his usually bright demeanor to pure misery.

"I screwed this up. I've never fit in right here. I'm not a Youth Guard. The only thing I'll miss is you three. You're my family." My mother had let the soldiers take me. She'd been terrified of my magic. Eric, Roxie, and Selina had been the family I'd chosen. "I'm going to miss you every day." I smiled and pushed him toward the door. "If it's fish, don't bother getting me any."

When he stepped outside into the weather, I sagged and fell into a chair. Tears burned my eyes. I had to stay strong. So far, I hadn't gotten them in trouble and planned on keeping it that way. Selina surprised me with her support and more by offering to get me extra gear. Packaged bandages and tape from the clinic were most precious because they were manufactured before the Sorrow ruined everything.

I scavenged everything from my room. Besides clothes, I had two thick paperback books from one of the abandoned houses. I couldn't fit my wet overalls inside, but I'd bring them. I touched the Wolf Squad patch; it would be my only link to my friends.

Eric returned first with more cornbread than chicken. "Wouldn't it be better to see what Tyrell plans before running off? We could help you escape if they do try and lock you up; take you away."

I shook my head. "Too risky. This way you can say you knew nothing. If you helped afterward, *you* might end up back at the labs. I won't chance that." My decision seemed so clear now. Dean would teach me how to survive outside the camp, and together we could fight off the cryptids. My friends would be safe.

He slumped into one of the chairs as I hid the napkin of cornbread into a side pouch. "I'd rather risk that than have you gone. It won't be the same without you." His tone was mournful.

"Yeah, you won't be getting into as much trouble."

"I like trouble." He offered a weak smile.

Thunder sounded the moment before Selina returned. She carried a folded cloak and hat wedged under her arm. "It's getting worse out there. At least no one will see you leave. I can't even see the gate from here."

I accepted the cloak and beret. "Thank you for helping. I know you don't like breaking the rules."

She shrugged. "I'll take it as a win if you get away safe."

The cloak had gotten misted, but otherwise it would be dry and hold the worst of the rain off my pack. The beret might not even stay on in this weather. "You won't get in trouble for these?"

"They don't monitor us." She put her hands on my shoulders. "I'm going to miss you. We had a lot of good times, didn't we?"

I beamed. "The best."

Her expression withered. "If it weren't for Dean. .." Selina turned away.

Roxie came a minute later and began pulling rolls of gauze and a tape from her pockets. She even managed a partial tube of antibiotic cream. "I made a little mess when they wouldn't give me more than a roll of gauze. The rest I had to steal while she was distracted." She smiled as she handed them over, then her lips tightened. "I'm going to be pissed at you for leaving. You know that."

I carefully tucked her items in my pack. "You'll forgive me, though."

"Maybe not this time." She grabbed me in a hug, pausing my attempt at packing.

Eric joined us, then Selina. She waited a moment

before she spoke. "You've got to hurry. If a soldier comes from Tyrell, you won't be able to leave."

Eyes stinging, I untangled and finished packing. "You three are the only good thing about this place."

When I finally left with my cloak draped over my pack, I couldn't help but cry. The rain came in gray sheets, and the practice field had turned muddy and dotted with large puddles. I approached the inlet quickly, bursting into a sprint when I could see it, and summoned enough of a gust to plant me face first into the soggy bank on the opposite side. I'd have to practice my wind-assisted leaping skills, or at least the landing part. It could come in handy.

I worried that Dean had left early, under the cover of the storm, until I could sense him ahead. Even though my chest felt hollow from leaving my friends, a light smile crept onto my face. We could never be lovers, but I wanted to be with Dean.

Someday, we might find a way of curing him. Eric and I had been able to keep me from being infected.

The rain had eased, or it wasn't raining as hard on this side of the river when I crossed into the burned forest. The tops of the evergreens were small and scattered, letting in some light from the gray clouds. I spotted the silhouette of the slanted building before Dean's darker shape came into view. Shirtless, despite the chill, he leaned against a portion of the ruined wall. His eyes glinted in the dim light.

He smirked as I approached. "You changed your mind." Rain had matted his hair and soaked his jeans to a dark blue. The scent of fish hung in the air. His arm still had tiny scabs from the werewolf bite. I ached to try and heal it. Now wouldn't be the time.

I shrugged, but the cloak and pack probably made it unnoticeable. "I did." Had he expected this? Stepping under the angled opening, I got out of the worst of the rain.

Water beaded off his face and chest, but he only turned his head. "You sure about this? I don't think they'd be very happy if you go back after a couple days." His shadow of a beard made him look older. "We don't know what to expect. I planned on heading to the north end of the lake. There's fish and too much marsh for them to patrol."

A red feather flicked against his chest. I flinched when the light gunshot echoed through the woods nearly at the same moment.

Dean smacked at his front and swore. Even as I turned to search the blackened woods, I saw the red-tailed dart land among the pine needles. I'd heard of tranquilizer darts and their description, but never seen one. The shot still rung in my ears when a tiny flash lit among distant brush, and a dart slammed into my armpit. The second pop seemed small, not like a real rifle.

I staggered back, though it didn't hurt too badly until I moved my arm. My heels scuffed in the dirt, and I landed on my butt inside Dean's building. He barely growled as he began to shift. His pants loosened and the back of his arms sprouted silver fur.

I'd been followed. It had been raining so hard that I hadn't checked the forest when I went over the footbridge. They could have been hiding there.

Metal clicked against the outside of the wall near Dean, but he already had gone to the ground, trying to wriggle out of his clothes.

I grabbed my dart and yanked, surprised when it ripped flesh. It had hit along my side, but I didn't feel drugged at all. Anger surged in response to the pain. Warm blood trickled down my side.

Another shot nearly sent a dart into my face, and I rolled to the ground. Dean had freed himself of his pants and fully formed into a wolf. Rain beat on the roof, but I heard no voices or any more shots. The pack on my back hung heavy, and the cloak was pinned under my thigh.

"Dean, run. Run away!" I yelled as I winced and crawled away from the opening.

The soldiers had killed a werewolf with a dart before, but I didn't know the details. Maybe they had hit it in the face. They weren't very good shots.

Dean bolted straight ahead, toward the woods where I'd seen the shot come from. "Run away!" Could he understand me when he was a wolf? If he were safe, I could try and escape later. Maybe they would focus on me if he got far enough away. *No.* I knew they'd hunt him.

Swiveling, I nosed toward the low slant of the opening and peered out at Dean loping into the forest. No one seemed to be there, but I heard another pop. I pulled at the otherness and sent the air after him. If he were closer, I could create an air dome over him, protecting him from my wind. Instead, I formed it into corridors on each side of him and I slammed gusts through the brush ahead of where he ran. A shape in camouflage tumbled among flattened bushes and a warmth flushed through me in satisfaction.

Dean needed to run. He might not be able to think clearly as a werewolf. My pulse raced and I pushed to stand, rocking the creaking walls. I stepped outside to a commotion where he'd run, but I couldn't make him out.

"Hey!" Tired, I forced another gust into the area, relieved to see Dean's silver form leaping.

A reflection glinted over the brush. Two or three pops sounded, much quieter than the others.

I could hear voices and jogged toward them. My side hurt, and blood stuck my coveralls to my upper arm. The next blast of my magic exposed two soldiers with clear shields, which I had never seen before. My heart dropped when I saw an edge of white fur wriggling on the ground. "Don't!"

Dean should have run. If he could think clearly, he might have believed he was protecting me. If I hadn't come out here, none of this would have happened.

"Caitlyn." Tyrell called to me from my left.

I stumbled, dropping palms to the ground. "Don't hurt him."

Though he wore a holster, his arms were raised. "We have to capture him. You need to come back with us." I couldn't see the expression on his face, but his voice was soothing, like before I'd made him angry.

"I won't go to the labs." It took effort to drag myself back to my feet.

"No. I won't send you there. You can't be blamed for your emotions. You need to let go, though."

I peered at the brush where I'd seen Dean. Blasting into the growing group of men there might harm him. "What did you do to him?"

"Just tasers. He's alive." Tyrell had been walking slowly toward me, and he wore a comforting smile. "Sit for a second." There were more men emerging from the brush behind him, weapons drawn.

I could attack them, but it wouldn't save Dean. Standing, I swayed from exhaustion. Perhaps the tranquilizer was working. I drew in otherness and dropped to a knee from the effort. My body did feel wrong, and I tried to heal it, but I barely had the strength or focus to do anything. There was more than the drugs in my body. Some leftover from Dean's infection seemed to survive, altered in some way.

It didn't matter. I'd failed. After everything I'd done, and all the risk I'd put my friends through, I hadn't saved Dean.

Chapter Twenty-Five

I woke drifting through the forest with rain splashing down my cheeks. Groggy, I opened my eyes, water dripped in, and I rolled to my side.

"Shit," a man's voice called out from my feet as I toppled to mud and leaves. His boot caught my calf and he dropped something on me as he stepped away.

I spit out dirt and pine needles and pushed myself up. A makeshift stretcher of rough branches and cloaks rested on my legs. A pair of black boots backed away from me.

Tyrell spoke as he gently pulled on my arm. "Easy now. We're almost back to the camp."

I rose to my knees, eyes flicking to the soldiers ahead and behind us. We were on Pinckney Road near the foot-bridge. "Dean?"

His voice hardened almost imperceptibly. "He's gone ahead of us."

"He's alive?" Using the back of my sleeve, I wiped my mouth and felt the wound under my arm stretch.

"Of course. Do you want to walk?"

The soldier in front of me had his hand resting on his holster. He wouldn't want to carry me awake. "Yes." My pack and machete sheath were gone, but my canteen hung at my belt. I reached for it. "Just thirsty." I wanted to hate Tyrell for what they were doing to Dean, but he was being kind to me. Maybe the drugs still had me groggy. I knelt, already drenched, and drank heavily. Meanwhile, I gathered the otherness and focused on healing my armpit and purging the drugs in my system.

I was tired. It would have taken them at least an hour to carry me this far.

Tyrell held my arm gently when I rose. "Are you good?"

"Yeah." My legs trembled, but held me. I took a step and then another.

The first soldier let us pass, then fell in behind us. Tyrell kept a hand under my left arm for a few steps. "I don't think you understand how important you are to us."

My brain wouldn't clear. *Dean.* I had to think. "I'm not a very good soldier."

He chuckled. "You might be selling yourself short on that, but you are part of the reason I wanted Specialists. Having a healer in each squad, such as yourself or Eric, would make the Youth Corps that much more powerful."

"Youth Corps?" The term had never been used before.

"Over seven hundred strong at this point. When your squads start working with our regular military, we'll be unstoppable." We took a few steps in silence before he continued. "It will change the way citizens regard you."

Freaks. I glanced back at the two wary soldiers behind us. "I don't know if being better at killing will make us any more popular."

"You mean the new soldiers at the base who you had a run in with? They've had some bad losses lately, so they're on edge. An integrated squad of Youth Corps would help ease tensions, and we intend to start next month with

Sumter." The storm gusted heavily down Bass Drive when we turned onto it.

I'd probably made his plan a bit more difficult considering Moonjir, Dean, and the soldier at the gym who I'd mangled. What would I do about Dean? First, I had to know what they planned. "What will happen to Dean?"

"He'll be sent to the Reevesville lab in the morning. They won't kill him. He's different, from what I gather. I hope in time you'll be able to report everything so we better understand the situation." He raised a hand to stall me responding. "Let your emotions settle before we discuss it."

I didn't want to settle into anything. Dean would be at the camp overnight. I could sense him. I might still have a chance to do something. Tyrell might expect that. "What's my punishment?" I asked.

He studied me. "For getting emotionally involved with Dean or defending yourself against bullying soldiers?" Tyrell shook his head. "For optics and politics, you'll be demoted. Maybe I'll have you wash dishes with the students. I don't really think you care about rank anyway."

"You're right." I needed him to believe I cared about the camp. "But I'm not excited about washing dishes." I wiped water out of my eyes. "If you're serious about training us as healers, then we need to have more practice time."

Tyrell scratched at his jaw. "There are biases to overcome with that. If we had more people willing to be healed, we would have more practice. The soldiers are ordered to report issues, but they hide them."

I could see the gate between sheets of rain. Hopefully, none of my friends had been caught helping me, but I certainly couldn't ask. He had to wonder about the cloak. "I guess my reaction at the gym isn't going to help that."

"No." He shook his head. "It won't."

"Maybe let me and Eric go into town and try to get

some people to let us help." My mind had cleared from the drug and my heart rate had risen.

A smile flickered across his lips. "We'll see. It sounds like a promising idea." He stopped within sight of the gate. "Understand that we need to put this Dean business behind us. He'll be gone, and you'll have to work through your feelings."

I stared at my feet and added a pathetic tone to my words. "He won't be killed?"

"No."

The worst part was, I believed him. What Tyrell couldn't fully understand is I'd rather die than go back to the labs. I certainly would risk my life to save Dean from that. "I'll try."

"All I can ask." As we entered the camp, the soldier at the gate stood stiff.

I was slightly surprised the Youth Guard weren't on duty. It couldn't be that late. Dean was ahead to the right based on my sense of him. They probably had him at the administration building in the cage they kept there.

When the gate closed behind us, it shut with a final and constricting clang. The rain was heavy but lighter than earlier in the day. Tyrell led me straight for my building across crumbling asphalt and puddles in potholes. On the way, I spotted a soldier posted in the wet grass. His position was in clear view of the inlet I'd been crossing. With Dean here in the camp, it didn't matter.

Tyrell watched me ascend the steps. "We'll talk in the morning."

I flashed a sad smile and continued my charade. The first thing I needed to do was find where they were keeping Dean. My pulse sped with each step toward my apartment.

A frowning soldier stood beside my door. The storm threw a gust of wind onto the balcony and misted him. I paused halfway on the second set of steps, staring at him wide-eyed. His expression didn't change, nor did he bark any commands at me. The implication was easy enough to decipher; I wouldn't be leaving my apartment tonight, at least not without an escort.

I slunk to the door and stepped inside. Roxie and Eric were sitting in the living room. I didn't bother getting out of my wet coveralls.

Roxie stood, eying me. "Selina came by to report that they'd captured Dean. The camp is on lock down."

I pointed to the front door as I approached. "There's a soldier outside."

She nodded. "We're supposed to bring you dinner here and keep watch. After we eat, Selina's assembling the whole unit in our apartment to discuss everything."

Eric gestured to my coveralls. "Get out of that, we can dry it out." His lips pursed. "I'm sorry about Dean."

"I need to free Dean." The words sounded weak now after seeing the guard at my door.

Roxie swore and spun away from me. "You can't save him." Her words were a sharp knife.

"You can't," Eric agreed in quieter tone.

My throat thickened, and I stumbled toward my room. I started to close the door, but there was no window and I hadn't lit a lantern. Despite our conversation, Tyrell had no intention of relaxing his guard. Dean would be carted off, likely before we even woke in the morning. If Dean had left days ago, this wouldn't be happening.

"Get out of those clothes. Rest." Roxie had followed me in. Her initial sharp response had softened. "We'll dry them out, get you some food, and stay with you tonight."

"My own personal guards?" I regretted the comment immediately. The soldiers were watching me, so I couldn't do anything anyway.

She just chuckled. "Lousy at it since we were your conspirators. Selina seemed nervous, but she said no one seemed to suspect we were helping you."

I was grateful for that. My friends didn't need to get in trouble with me. I crouched to untie my boots. Exhaustion made me dizzy. "They're going to bring him to a lab. I get demoted."

"Better than you joining him at the lab."

I stripped, Roxie collecting pieces as I peeled out of them. I wasn't embarrassed in front of her, but I frowned as I took off my underwear. "All my clothes are in my pack."

"They didn't bring it here. Selina might know where it is. I'll check at dinner."

I didn't even have a towel. Crawling into bed, I pulled dark green blankets over my head. The door clicked closed. Thunder rolled outside. My brain spun ridiculous plans to escape and free Dean, but they were as fanciful as any dream I'd ever had.

Startled awake, my eyes opened to lantern light flickering on my walls. I sat as Roxie walked in with a plate and the aroma of chicken grilled with herbs. My clothes were folded and piled on the corner of my bed.

"I wasn't sure if you were awake. Selina will be here with the others in a few minutes. She wants to have a unit meeting."

I slid out the opposite side of the bed and began dressing, glancing at the open door. "Do you know where they are keeping Dean?"

Roxie didn't answer. When I turned, she was glaring at me. Lips tight, she placed the plate on the floor and spun to head back into the living room where the lantern shone. I caught the patter of rain on windows.

Muffled, Eric spoke. "She still upset?"

Roxie's voice was loud enough for me to hear clearly. "If

you mean is she still obsessed with Dean, then yes."

"It's not something you just get over," he said. "You'd be the same way if it were Selina."

I left my boots off and grabbed the plate to join them. The furnace hadn't warmed yet, so the rest of the apartment was as chilly as my room. Eric sat on the floor watching me while Roxie stared out the back windows into the darkness.

My cheeks flushed as I watched her stiff back. She didn't turn as I sat down beside Eric. "I'd rather die than let him be taken to the labs."

He tilted his head. "I don't think they're going to give you that opportunity."

The storm rattled the windows in front of Roxie, and she turned away without meeting my eyes. "No, they're not. Selina says they'll be on the road before first light. They would have left last night, but the roads are dangerous."

I suddenly imagined myself waiting at the roadside and flipping the truck with wind. It might be harder than I thought, and Dean could get hurt.

Her face tight, Roxie took a seat in one of our chairs. The chicken was good, though I didn't appreciate the carrots that accompanied it. I was hungrier than I thought.

Eric leaned over, touching shoulders. "We'll get through this."

I didn't know how. My mind had searched for any number of ways to free Dean, but they didn't seem plausible, especially without help. My friends had risked themselves numerous times already, and obviously they weren't willing to do it again. I couldn't ask them to. It would kill Roxie to get demoted.

The front door opened, and chilly wind gusted in as Selina, Yaz, and Jordan entered. I peered into the night but didn't see a sign of the soldier guarding the door. Turning back to my plate, I ignored Jordan's smug glare.

"How are you holding up?" Selina asked me as she strode in, taking the other chair.

I mumbled through a bite of chicken. "As well as can be expected."

She rolled her eyes slightly. "Tyrell informed me of his decisions. Along with being demoted, you'll be placed on my patrol so we can work closely together." Her eyes flicked to Roxie and Eric. "Jordan will take your place."

My throat thickened as I swallowed. Perhaps Tyrell suspected Roxie and Eric of helping me. The three of us enjoyed our group. He might not know that the transfer hurt worse than any demotion.

Everyone appeared surprised, but no one said anything. Jordan sat beside Eric, and Yaz flashed a smile as she dropped next to me.

"There will be no patrols the next two days; half as many in the upcoming weeks. New rosters will reflect more practice time and increased martial training." Selina pursed her lips. "Tyrell is considering an outreach to the towns-people for those with an innate ability in healing."

I raised my eyebrows. I'd expected him to be placating me when he'd said he would consider my suggestion. My proposition had been half-hearted as an attempt to make him believe I'd accepted my fate. That hadn't been neces-sary, it seemed, with the extra soldiers watching me.

"Outer patrols will be continued with mixes from all units, cadets and above."

That would exclude me, but I took some solace in Jordan's sudden frown.

Selina held back a smile as she continued. "I'll be joining a temporary unit for the military push to Sumter. Roxie will be in charge while I'm gone."

Roxie straightened in her chair. "Okay. Who will be in this temporary unit?"

"Mostly unit leaders." Selina studied us. "Questions?"

I had none, mainly because I didn't care. My thoughts scrambled back to Dean at every break, but I still couldn't come up with a way even out of the apartment.

Jordan squirmed as if he wanted to say something. Selina studied him and then spoke. "Caitlyn's disciplinary action is Tyrell's choice. The other units will hear about much of this; it is unavoidable, and there will likely be anger among some of them. I'll not tolerate cruelty in my unit. No snide remarks or bullying. She's gone through an emotional response, however misguided, and needs to be safe in the Wolf Squad."

Yaz patted my leg and I smiled at the display. She was young enough that she'd never been to the labs. When her and Jordan's magic had developed, they were whisked off to the school without witch riots or electric shock collars. They still missed their families, but they hadn't experienced what most of us had.

Lightning flashed behind the building, creating shadows. The thunder came quickly after it. The area behind the administration building would be a nightmare for Dean hanging in a cage.

"Inspection is coming. Everyone will be reviewed and considered for promotion, except for Caitlyn. Tyrell will determine when to release her from the disciplinary action. You all have a short while to be on your best behavior." Selina's focus stayed on Roxie. "Give it your best shot. Next month we'll see a lot of changes as the army is preparing for activity here in the northwest, including a summer campaign to free Columbia."

"With the Youth Corps assisting," I added.

Selina's head snapped toward me. "Yes. Where did you hear that?"

"Tyrell's welcome home recruitment speech." I placed

my plate down a little harshly, carrots untouched. The light-ning earlier had sparked a plan. I wished I'd put on my boots before eating. At the moment, I needed to get into a tiff with Selina. "Will he be making you a Section Leader? He promised me a Specialist position if I played along here at Camp Sparta."

She flicked a glance at Roxie, then squared with me. "You need to show a little respect, after all you've done and the trouble you've caused."

Selina *had* helped me, but I needed to do something about Dean. "Yes, trying to heal someone from being a werewolf is probably against the regulations. I'm sure Talia would agree." She tried to talk, but I raised my voice. "We're all good little soldiers here and will kill whomever they tell us to."

Jordan sneered. "They're cryptids. How stupid are you?"

"Shut up you little shit," I swore at him and stood.

Eric reached for me, and I backed away, toward Roxie's room. My heart had begun to pound. They'd all tried to turn me from helping Dean since Tyrell led me back to the camp. None of them, except for Eric, realized I'd rather die than give up on Dean.

Roxie stood, palms aimed at Selina and Jordan. "Just stop. She's upset, and this isn't helping."

Selina face contorted in anger. "Always standing up for her. How do you think this turned into such a mess? I hope you're not planning on a promotion *this* review."

My chest hollowed, knowing how much those words would twist Roxie, but I needed to use this moment for the rest of my plan. "I'm done with all of you. Leave me alone." Spinning on my heels, I walked into Roxie's room and slammed her door. I sagged against it, the first part of my plan in place.

Chapter Twenty-Six

I waited at Roxie's bedroom door to see if any of them chased me in there. Eric seemed the most likely.

Roxie spoke, anger bubbling in her voice. "I can live without a promotion, but I'm going to be there for my friends."

Eric tapped on the door and I winced at deceiving him. "Leave me alone!"

A chair scraped, and Selina spoke. "Come on. Roxie, keep an eye on her, if you can manage that."

I hadn't meant to cause a rift between Selina and Roxie. The rain rattled the glass, and the storm raged against the trees by the river. Taking a deep breath, I studied the door which led to the rotted porch. We all knew enough not to go out there. The lock turned with a light squeak, but it couldn't have made much sound.

I pulled on the handle, but the door held. My unit was still speaking in the apartment, muffled as though they were moving for the front door. I leaned against the window and peered into the darkness. There would be no use going out if Tyrell had stationed a guard out there.

With a knee pressed against the wood frame for leverage, I pulled harder, not wanting it to yank it open and make noise. Slowly it began to budge. The bottom held, but once I had the top free, it gave way.

I could see into the living room at an angle, and lantern light flickered on the walls. Roxie was nowhere to be seen. She'd eventually come into her bedroom and figure out my ruse. I counted on her to not alert the others too soon, but that might be expecting too much.

The patio had been screened in at one point, and shreds hung in the top corner. Through broken, rotted boards, I could see to the extended porch which held our cook's kitchen. The rain gusted from the west, a few drops reaching the door. The ceiling, the floor for the third story, was in no better shape. I climbed out to the first plank, closing the door behind me. We'd investigated when we first moved in and let it be after I broke a board.

The section by the wall was the sturdiest. I pressed a foot out to the next plank and pushed on it. The wood resisted, then yielded with a dull snap at the edge of the cross-beam underneath. The next board was a longer reach, but I managed to crumble it.

I turned around and used the handle of the door to keep me from toppling backward while I dropped my leg into the hole I'd made. When I angled low enough, I grabbed soft wood under the window to brace myself and dropped my other hand to the support beam. Holding my breath, I shifted my other leg into the hole; then I fell through.

A plank shattered under my butt and then scraped my back. My fingers held for a brief second, and I faced a ground floor door with no lights inside. The tear under my arm, which I'd partially healed, screamed in pain. I lost my grip. With a thud, I landed on the concrete pad.

I groaned and crawled to the edge, peering into the darkness as rain fell in torrents off the roof. The ground dropped quickly to the river. My coveralls soaked through at my stomach and shoulders. Waiting, I studied the dim shapes of the back pavilion until I was sure there was no one there. The screened patio where the cook usually worked appeared empty as well.

Only three dim lights shone in windows of the buildings that curved alongside the river. Two were at the far end where the administration building waited for me. I could sense Dean there, ahead of me. I climbed off the mildew-slick concrete. Behind the pavilion, I dashed under the waterfall, but it soaked me.

The mess hall was pitch black and the cooking patio smelled of grease and wet ash. There shouldn't be anyone on the ground floor of our barracks at this time of night. If it weren't for me, nearly everyone would be in their beds.

Lightning flashed to the west, and I could see along the buildings clearly for a spare moment. The brush and trees hid the farthest buildings, but I saw no guards lurking nearby. I waited for my eyes to readjust. I'd have to sneak to the back of the administration building.

In socks, I stepped on a fallen branch and winced as it dug in. I shuffled, mainly through puddles, to the far corner of the building. No one waited in the area between my barracks and the next.

Lightning offered me glimpses again, and I passed the second building without any concern. The third and middle building was the school. The young students all slept in groups upstairs. As I passed their cooking patio, I had a clear view to administration where Tyrell's office was.

I'd only assumed the administrative building, and the sense of him was still in that direction. My heart pounded in earnest. I might have to hurt someone to free Dean. Thinking that far into my plan churned my stomach. They would surely guard him, not from me specifically, but in case he tried to get away.

The sky lit with two forks of lightning, and I saw the cage. It hung high in a tree behind Tyrell's office. Guns glinted from two guards standing underneath. It didn't last long enough for me to see Dean, or if he were in wolf or human form.

Still partially blinded, I stepped past the corner of the students' screened in kitchen.

Hands grabbed my coveralls from behind. My heart stopped and rain splashed in my gaping mouth.

Roxie pulled me to the ground and hissed in my ear. "Shit, Caitlyn." Her voice was sharp. "What are you going to do?"

My heart felt like it was going to explode from surprise. Water soaked even deeper into my backside and covered my hands pressed into mud. I stared toward the tree where I knew Dean was trapped. "Let me go." She couldn't stop me without making a scene. Maybe she intended to. "Please. I have to try."

A mottled shadow at the corner of the administration building shifted. *A third guard.* I hadn't noticed him, and he was the closest. She'd saved me from walking right by him.

Roxie spoke at my ear, her grip still firm on my soaked coveralls. "Four guards that we can see. Are you going to kill them to save Dean? They'd shoot you before you could get to them all."

I peered through the rain. "Where's the fourth?"

"Are you kidding me?" Roxie dragged me up, pulling me back as she did so. "That's your response?" Her tone changed to a worried pitch. "Tell me you weren't planning on killing them."

I didn't resist as she pulled me back, then gained my footing. "I only saw two. Where's the fourth?"

"One on each corner, two below." She spun me and walked me away.

Unsure how to get past them, I let her lead me. I hadn't seen the one on the far corner. "I didn't —"

She interrupted, finishing my sentence. "Think. You didn't think. Did you believe they wouldn't guard a werewolf?"

"I have to —"

"Get back to the apartment, the way you came in. I'll make a rope of some sort. The soldier thinks I'm getting water for our canteens."

I might be able to handle four guards, but with them spread out, they might get a shot off, which would bring more. Unless I did kill them, one at a time.

I hated that I considered that.

With each step back toward our barracks, I felt colder and increasingly empty. There didn't seem to be a way I could disable four soldiers without raising an alarm. I would die to save Dean, but I couldn't murder them.

I was surprised when we arrived at the backside of our barracks. My head whirled, trying to work out a way to overcome and succeed, but I couldn't. It made me want to curl into a ball, but I couldn't let go.

"Wait for me. The soldier is going to be suspicious. I might have to talk my way past him." Roxie raced for the front while I ambled for the concrete slab below our broken porch.

I passed under the waterfall listlessly and climbed with water pouring off me. I stared aimlessly toward the river. My situation had turned horrible and hopeless so quickly. A minute later the door opened above, and Roxie peered down with the lantern, disappeared, and returned with her blanket to drop as a rope. Exhausted and distracted, it took me two tries to reach her. I stood dripping in her bedroom.

Roxie threw her dirty wet blanket to a corner in disgust. "I'm done."

I stared, dazed and empty. "Help me."

"I've tried." Her expression of anger softened to pity.

"I need to rescue him."

She closed her eyes and turned toward her ceiling. "You can't."

"Not alone."

Her chin snapped down, dark eyes wide. "No."

"Please. There are only four guards. If you, and maybe Eric, could distract them to the front, I might be able to free him."

"Or get yourself killed."

"I'd rather that than not try."

"You can't mean it."

I did. My back straightened, and I peered into her eyes. "I do. The only thing holding me back is not wanting to kill those men. I can't do that. But I would rather die trying to save Dean than let them take him to the labs." I smiled, lopsided and quivering. "Please. Help me."

She closed her eyes again and held her hand to her lips. Rain glistened in her hair. When Roxie opened her eyes, she studied me with her mouth tight as if she were in pain. I caused her this agony and the tears which formed in her eyes. If I could do this alone, I would.

With a sharp inhale, she wiped her face, forced a fake smile, and shrugged. "What's the worst that can happen?"

I slammed into her with a hug, and after a moment she returned it and whispered, "You're impossible, you know that?"

"Yes." I pulled back from her. "Will you see if Eric will help? Between the two of you maybe throw a branch through a front window or something?" He had skill with wind, where hers was limited and unpracticed.

She laughed. "Of course. The nice man outside will not think *anything* is suspicious with me going out again and coming back with Eric."

"Tell the soldier I'm a mess."

"Well, you are." She opened her bedroom door and stepped out into the living room.

Excited, I followed close behind.

Near the open door to my empty bedroom, Selina stood. Roxie and I dripped water on the floor. There was no way to explain away what we were doing.

I dropped the guilty expression and straightened. "Selina, I'm going to do this, and I need your help."

Chapter Twenty-Seven

I waited for her tirade and prepared my excuses. My obsession to save Dean consumed me. If this were any of my friends, I would do the same. However, I hadn't been there for Talia. That sole thought sobered me.

Expressions of shock turned to anger on Selina's face, but when she finally spoke, she focused on Roxie. "And you agreed?"

"She'll get herself killed if I — if we don't help." Roxie took a step forward and stopped.

I could feel the chasm I'd caused between her and her lover. "Don't blame Roxie. I'm a horrible friend." My voice was firmer than I expected.

"I know." Selina turned to my empty bedroom. "Is Eric in on this?"

Roxie wiped her face. "I was about to go get him."

"I suppose that will be less suspicious, now that I'm here."

I frowned, somewhat stunned. "Are you helping?" She didn't respond, but tilted her head as if in pain. "They are going to suspect all of you." I meant her, since she'd come to check on us.

Thunder growled farther away, but the room remained silent as Selina stared into my room. She finally chuckled, and faced us. "Not a problem. I'll tell Tyrell that I think Roxie and Eric were in on it from the beginning. Maybe get a promotion right on the spot." Selina had to be joking, but my heart skipped.

Roxie's hands straightened, tensed, then balled. "Do what you have to. I'm not letting Caitlyn kill herself over this."

Selina waved off the response. "Relax." She stepped over to one of the chairs and dropped into it. "What's the plan?"

I drew in a deep breath and stepped closer. "There are four guards." Mentioning Roxie's part in this wouldn't help their relationship. "One on each corner of the building, and two under Dean's cage."

Clasping her hands in her lap, Selina spoke. "So are you going to try to take them all out at the same time? The three of you? Four, if I join in."

Did she think we were going to kill them? "No. I thought Eric and Roxie could cause a distraction out front and draw off a couple of the guards. I don't want to murder anyone. If it's just the two under the tree, I can blow them into the river. They'll survive." *Hopefully.*

"And you just walk past the guard out front?"

I pointed to Roxie's room, the toward the window over the porch. "I went in and out through her door already without getting caught."

Her eyes widened and she scoffed. "Okay, what's the distraction?"

"I thought they could blow a branch or two through the windows."

Selina laughed. "Roxie? She might be able to toss a few twigs."

I flushed at her animosity and started to respond, but Roxie spoke in a cold, even tone. "I can move a lot of rain though, enough to break a window."

"Okay, but have Eric toss something big against the fence. The guards will think something is trying to get through. They're concerned that the other werewolves will come for a member of their pack." Selina raised a hand palm up. "If he can knock a tree into the fence, that would be best. Then a branch into a window. And, the rain from Roxie."

I had never mentioned that the werewolves were dead, and it might prove useful. "Will that be enough to draw the guards away?"

"Not all of them. I'll go with you, in case you need a little help." She paused. "We should make sure we're just dealing with four of them. You couldn't have gotten that close."

She was right. I hadn't even noticed all of them. I glanced at Roxie before I asked Selina, "How?"

"Tyrell wanted regular reports on your status. I doubt he's at his office at this hour, but it'll give me a pretense to see what they've got stationed outside."

I tensed, but if Selina planned on telling Tyrell about our plan, she'd just go outside and have the soldier take me away now. It would save Eric and Roxie the suspicion that would fall on them if we succeeded. "Okay, but should you really help me? In the back of the building, I mean." Her ability with air was as poor as Roxie's.

"Emergency backup, in case it all goes to shit. I can't have them shoot one of my Wolf Squad, can I?" Selina smiled and pointed Roxie toward the door. "Go grab Eric. Tell the guard we're talking Caitlyn down from her hysterics."

As Roxie left, I grimaced apologetically to Selina. "Thank you."

Selina waved off my comment. "Eric explained it well. If this were Roxie, how far would I go to save her? You can't change who you care about." She yawned. "So, where will you two go, north across the lake?"

I started to say yes, but if Selina got in trouble, she might talk. Shaking my head, I gestured to the back window. "West where no one knows who we are."

"He can control it?"

"Yes." I flushed slightly, trying to remember what I had told her. I didn't need to detail about the consequences of our kiss. "After that one time."

She snorted. "Sounds promising. You might end up regretting this — someday."

Pulling back my reaction, I smiled. Selina's help had been a surprise, and I wasn't about to rattle her fragile cooperation. "What I will always regret is losing all of you." I didn't realize how much I meant it until my throat grew thick.

Selina blinked, then nodded toward the puddle at my feet. "You might want boots for this."

Chapter Twenty-Eight

I had one boot laced and was wringing out the other sock when the front door opened. My pulse, already rapid, sped until I heard Eric's voice. Roxie glanced into my bedroom as she passed and then waved Eric behind her.

Leaving them tugged at my heart, but it couldn't be helped, unless I wanted to leave Dean to the labs. Grimacing, I squeezed out what water I could.

"Think you can drop a tree across the road, into the fence?" Selina asked.

Eric cleared his throat. "I can try."

"Good. Then throw a branch into the front windows. Roxie will help. The plan is to bring the soldiers guarding Dean to the front. Caitlyn and I will free Dean."

I laced the second boot in the long silence before Eric answered. "Okay."

Roxie spoke as I stood. "We can go out the back with Caitlyn."

"The back?" Eric's tone through the entire conversation had been not reluctant, but not enthusiastic.

I stepped out, and he glanced at me. Clearing my throat,

I sighed as I spoke. "If you're concerned about getting in trouble —"

He shook his head and faced Selina. "Why are you helping? Won't this threaten you getting your Section Leader promotion?"

She pointed at me, then Roxie. "They'll do it without me. So would you. I'd have to tie all three of you up, if I guess right. Better that Caitlyn doesn't die in the attempt. I don't care what happens to Dean, or whatever he is now." Rubbing her face and yawning, she continued. "Yes. I may very well get called out on this, but I'll spin it best I can. Caitlyn is quite the handful."

Eric's head tilted. "They'll suspect me of helping, at the least."

"Yes."

The time it took for him to respond crushed me. He had to blame me for putting him in this position. All of them had that right.

"Okay. I'm in."

Selina smacked the arms of the chair and rose. "Then we're decided and committed. I've got some scouting to do. Give me a while and then meet me behind the next barracks. I'll update you on what we can expect."

We watched as she left. Eric took a deep breath before speaking. "Can we trust her?"

"I think so." Roxie spoke in a quiet voice.

If Selina wanted to turn us in, the soldier would have been sent inside. She wouldn't let us go through all this when she could end it before it happened and take the credit. "Me too."

Eric nodded, lips tight. "You two know her best." He stepped toward me and his eyes were wet. "I don't want you to leave, but I know you have to." His bottom lip tugged, fighting. "What am I going to do without you?"

I let him pull me into a hug and felt him release a single sob. My own eyes were clouding, and I could barely manage a whisper. "I will always remember everything."

Roxie joined us, her voice strained and pitching high at the end. "Good riddance, I say. Look at the mess you got us into."

"Maybe someday. .." No, I'd never be forgiven.

Eric's voice was thick, croaking. "We'll never know if you're alive."

I drew in a deep breath, holding them tighter. "I'll leave a message where I saw Moonjir. If we're close enough." We all knew that wouldn't likely happen.

Still pressed against my shoulder, he wiped his face. "Where will you go?"

We pulled apart and I sniffled. "I think the north end of the lake."

"Never seen it. Won't the soldiers be a problem?"

"Dean didn't think so."

Roxie smirked. "Be careful with him."

"No kissing."

"Exactly." She pulled her hair back, dripping water. "Ready for this?"

Eric jabbed a thumb toward the front door. "I'm going to go use the latrines." He winked. "Meet you out back."

"That's not fair." Roxie faked a pout, then smiled.

"I'll let you back up afterwards." His face darkened and he turned for the front.

We waited until the door closed behind him, then I let her lead the way to her bedroom. I took one last glance at the apartment. If this worked, I wouldn't be back.

Roxie was tying a knot in her blanket. "I'm taking your blankets."

"Least I could do."

She opened the door and let in the storm winds. Sliding

the knot under the door she shoved it to the hinge, and it stuck.

"Smart." I let her hold the door and grabbed the blanket as I lowered my legs over the edge. I still had to drop a couple feet, but it was a much easier landing than before.

As Roxie climbed, I stared through the waterfall from the roof to where I knew Dean waited. "Shit."

"What?" she asked.

"The cage." I assumed they had a rope or chain on a pulley tying it in the tree, and that I could work out. "It'll be locked." They wouldn't leave a key lying around. Tyrell would have that.

She nudged me to climb off. "Take the heat away. You don't do much heat practice, though, so you probably will need some time to get it cold enough."

I braced myself and passed through the sheet of icy water. "What good will making it cold be?"

She growled as she emerged into the rain. "Freeze it. Metal snaps. We need to find a rock."

"Are you sure?"

"I've seen your heat practice; it'll take a minute for you. I could do it in a flash, so could Selina."

Selina would not likely want to be that close to Dean. "It's my best shot." I peered into the darkness and water. "Yell if you see one."

"Thanks, but I'll whisper and point."

We started toward Dean and easily found a fist sized rock before we stopped at the meeting place for Selina. She crept down the side of the building as we arrived. Eric would have to do a loop around the latrines, but shouldn't be long.

Selina frowned at the rock. "You could just use air."

"For the cage," I said.

Her frown didn't fade, but she nodded. "I only saw three soldiers, but didn't go to the far side of the building."

"That's where he was." Roxie stared at Selina, as if trying to catch her eye.

"Here's Eric." Selina motioned between the buildings. "Say your goodbyes."

I swallowed and hugged Roxie. "Love you," I whispered.

"Love you, too." She pushed us apart gently and turned her face away.

Eric took a longer hug and cried again. "I will never forget you. Visit, if you can."

I couldn't promise that I could return. "Take care of Roxie."

He snorted, choking. "She's the tough one. You be careful."

"Thank you — for everything."

"Make it worth it."

Eric and Roxie left between the buildings, whispering with their heads close. They'd have time to get into position before I reached the point where the guard I'd missed could see me. Knowing he was there, we could keep hidden until they started the distraction.

I'd never see them again, no matter our plans for secret messages. My life at Camp Sparta would be over if I saved Dean.

Selina studied me, then nudged her chin forward. I guessed there would be no hug and no tearful goodbye. I crept forward into the storm to the patio where I could see the dark shape of the closest guard. Now, we waited.

Chapter Twenty-Nine

I crouched with Selina as thunder rolled from the north. The lightning had moved out toward the lake, so it barely lit Dean's cage.

Selina whispered close to my ear. "I'll stay at the corner of the building. You're on your own, unless I think you need me."

"Thank you for helping."

"Of course." Her voice, matter-of-fact, had a cool edge. "Didn't leave me much of a choice."

We'd been inseparable for the first couple of years at the camp. Friends had joined us in time, but it was us. Lovers had been the first wedge, duty the last. I'd never been built for the Youth Guard, and she'd been born for leadership. She might miss me. I would miss her.

I mistook the sound of Eric's tree for a heavy gust or distant thunder as it ripped free from the soil on the other side of the buildings. When it noisily crashed into the fence, I swore I felt the vibration in the mud.

The soldiers all turned. My focus was on the closest, a mottled shadow at the edge of the building. If he didn't leave, I'd have to take chances. He swung around, as if he might move toward the front, but remained. I forced myself to breathe.

The crash from the windows sounded like Eric and Roxie had taken out the entire front of the building. My soldier disappeared.

"Go." Selina pushed my shoulder.

Creeping with careful steps so as not to splash, I watched the other soldiers move. One ran to the far corner. Holding my canteen silent at my belt, I reached the edge of the building and leaned out to chance a peek. My guard had run to the front of the building and spun slowly, searching for danger.

I jogged toward the last building and the pine trees there. As I stepped toward him, I checked on Dean above. I could see him curled in a flesh-colored ball. They hadn't even left him clothes or a blanket. Anger tightened my shoulders.

The two guards stood at the far end of the building, closer than the werewolves who had been attacking Dean. I drew in the otherness and it roared to my call. Hit by two distinct gusts, both men flew like leaves toward the river. Even above the storm, I heard the satisfying splashes.

I raced to Dean's tree, a tall pine with barely a limb, and peered above. It was time to try Roxie's trick with heat, or the absence of it. As I expected, a long rope had been staked to the ground and looped through a ring affixed to the tree above his prison. The metal cage was made of dull gray bars, and black ones connected in a misshapen grid. I couldn't make out a door or hinges. Spinning slowly, I positioned myself near the rope, facing the building in case someone exited.

Just then, lightning arced from one boot to the next, and water evaporated in a puff of steam. My body locked. Pain racked my feet, and the world turned a tinge of red. Belatedly, I recognized the otherness whooshing. As I fell back, a shape stepped forward and I caught the grim smile on Selina's face.

As I hit the ground, water splashed from my stiff body. The rock bounced out of my fingers. The storm raged on, indifferent of my plight. Dean dangled above, his tan skin turning whiter and hairier.

Everything still had a red tinge to it. I could see the building but not move my head. Smoke rose from my boots, rising against the downpour. The top half of Selina stood at the edge of my sight, just right of my boot. I couldn't move my body, but it trembled.

Tyrell stepped out the back door and glanced between me and Selina. "I guess you were right to be concerned." He had a gun in his hand.

She approached him, motioning to the front. "I'd bet that Eric helped from the sounds out there. Maybe even Roxie. You can't blame them."

My brain thick and foggy, I closed my eyes and forced a breath. My jaw hurt from clenching it, and my legs trembled. Anger boiled in my chest. She had not only betrayed us, but set herself to be the one who stopped me. My right foot burned. Had she intended to kill me? How else could she get away with this?

"We'll check on them in a minute." His voice grew closer.

Dean snarled above us. He'd turned. Once again, I'd failed him.

"She attacked two of your men before I could reach her. They're in the water."

"They should survive." He had nearly reached me. "What a waste. I can't let her foolish actions threaten the Youth Corps."

My boots stunk, and the soles of my feet felt seared to the bone. Walking or standing wouldn't be happening. I kept my face placid, dead. My eyes closed, I pulled in the otherness, and focused healing to the bubbled flesh. Twinges threatened to force me to grimace. I kept my jaw tight. Magic was about movement. Moving air from one place to another. Bringing heat to one spot. With healing, all matter moved to the call as skin, blood, and cells moved back to their rightful positions. I endured a dull ache just below the searing agony, then the pain lessened. I breathed out in relief.

"She's alive," Tyrell said from above me.

"What?" Selina's boots squished in the flooded water, still some distance away. She did not sound pleased. The otherness growled. "Step back," she said.

His voice rose. "No. She's unconscious. I might be able to salvage all this."

"She's dangerous." Selina had been about to finish me to hide her deception. If we all corroborated that she was part of it, he'd know, and she'd never get the promotion. It hurt that she'd go this far.

I remained motionless except for slow, light breaths. He had to have seen my chest moving. My head was clearing. She'd kill me if she had a good reason. Muscles still tight, I fought exhaustion to focus another wave of healing through my body. If I had any energy left, I could surprise them both.

A gust blasted across me, and Tyrell grunted. I blinked open my eyes as he toppled back. Leaves and pine needles blustered around me. Roxie and Eric had to be here. They didn't know about Selina and her betrayal.

Pushing up on my elbows, I pried open my jaw to yell a warning.

Back near the corner of the house, Eric lit with lightning. Mid stride, it arced between his legs. It illuminated his face from below.

His eyes were wide in terror. Fists to his side, he spasmed uncontrollably.

I gasped as a flame sprouted at his left boot. His gray coveralls steamed and smoked. His eyes turned milky, and he toppled.

I choked a sob and couldn't breathe. I'd killed him as surely as Selina.

My shriek made no sound from a too thick throat. He'd died helping me. That wasn't supposed to happen.

Behind him, Roxie stared in horror at Eric's body. She'd never be able to forgive Selina or me. Her mouth hung open. She swayed as if she might fall.

Smoke drifted into the sky from Eric's corpse.

"No," I croaked. My plea never rose against the storm.

Roxie eyes were hard when she peered toward Selina. A snarl formed on her lips. The otherness began to call.

A gunshot deafened me.

Roxie's shoulder sprayed dark blood and she spun, falling out of sight.

Somewhere behind the smoldering corpse of Eric, my last friend lay.

Selina whirled toward me and Tyrell. I thought for a fleeting second that she might be concerned about her lover, but a cruel smile rose on her face when she locked eyes with me.

Anger obliterated any thoughts in my mind. I became part of the storm above as the otherness thundered into me.

My body felt lighter, like I might float up, defying gravity itself. Raindrops appeared to slow their fall, as if they might return to the clouds.

The entire sky, air and rain, raced from above — to me. I became the center. A living maelstrom. The strength of what I imagined a tornado poured from me and twisted at the edge of my clothing. As the wind hit the ground it shook with the force, and a wall of debris slammed outward along with my rage. The otherness was deafening.

Selina slammed into a tree and twirled in the air like a leaf. Her auburn hair disappeared into the darkness beyond Eric's body.

The windows of the building, every one I could see, shattered soundlessly in my ringing ears. Glass shards sparkled as they blasted away. Wood borders and roof shingles ripped off and flashed into the air. The trees around me leaned away, roots loosening.

Eric's body rolled from me.

I screamed, my voice drawn into the chaos. Whirlwinds sucked sand and water from the ground around me, the leaves already spent. The air swirled in a thickening murky haze.

If I had known Selina would betray us and kill Eric, I would have sacrificed Dean.

I wanted the entire camp to be obliterated under my raging storm. However, my energy and the storm began to abate. Strength faded, and my shouts became sobs.

Shakily, I stood scanning for Tyrell amid the wind and debris. I couldn't find him, even as my tempest subsided.

The ground under my right heel lifted, causing me to spin.

As the tall pine tree leaned toward the water, the rope holding Dean yanked out the stake. Roots flung dirt into my face as they were torn from the ground. The metal cage bobbed and bounced with his silver wolf form trapped inside.

The tree's fall stretched impossibly long in time. Roots popped loose. The trunk tilted farther over the river. The cage slid to the side, aiming for the water. In a futile gesture, I reached forward as if I might grab a root and stop it.

When the pine tree hit the lazy river, two huge waves sprang up. Dean's cage and his silver form danced with them, then sank.

Chapter Thirty

"Make it worth it" had been the last thing Eric said to me.

The root ball rose to my right, so I scrambled down the bank to the left. The trunk angled into the water, its green top barely visible. The rope, cage, and even the ring on the trunk were submerged.

I raced into the frigid water and dove into a swimming stroke with the tree to my right. The current had slightly more pull than usual, likely due to the rains.

Mid-stroke, my hand slammed into the metal of Dean's cage. I recognized his frenzied ball of white fur underwater. He would drown. Here, the trunk submerged under the dark river. Rain added to the mayhem.

I bobbed, trying to stand, rough bark at my elbow. With a frantic scramble, I threw one leg over the tree to sit atop it.

Risking Dean's sharp teeth, I grabbed a dark metal bar and leaned back, trying to drag it atop the trunk to lift a portion of the cage into the air so he could breathe. I didn't have the strength or mass.

Calling the otherness, I harnessed the water, trying to push him and his cage onto the trunk. Waves splashed into me, threatening to push me off, but they did nothing to save Dean.

His movements were slowing. He would run out of breath.

The rained danced on the surface as the current flowed around me. Hysterical, I held onto the metal with both hands and peered into the darkness for a lock or even a hinge. I couldn't see anything more than a hand's depth into the water. Dean was dying, and I held uselessly onto his cage.

I could hear the wind laugh over the ringing in my ears.

Gathering waning strength, I pulled in the otherness again, and pushed away the water where the corner of the cage was closest to the surface. Roxie would have been able to do this easily. I fought the oncoming current and barely created enough space for Dean's muzzle. As his nose twitched and he drew in air, his dark eyes were locked on mine. He was counting on me to save him.

The current was too much, and my strength faded. I lost the otherness.

My rage growled against it all. My stiff fingers ached, wrapped around the metal. If it were in the air, I might be able to freeze the bars, though I'd long since lost the rock. Underwater, I'd form ice. Still, I called the otherness, a shrieking stream of it to my hands, and focused on the metal.

A sensation akin to healing came through the touch. The metal was more varied than air, akin to flesh. Made of a multitude of elements, I could sense their differences and how they connected. Some bindings were more correct than others.

I made it all incorrect. Cracks formed and bonds broke. Some were the different metals they used at the joints, others were within the bars themselves. With every last shred of my energy I called in the otherness and tore at the metal from inside itself.

A joint loosened, and I readjusted my grip to force pressure along it. Another snapped open, felt in my connection to it. Somehow, Dean recognized what I was doing, and the cage squirmed in my grip as he forced his head and paws against the bars.

All at once, joints snapped in a dozen places and the cage fell into pieces in my hands. One section felt soft and malleable.

Dean wiggled free and broke to the surface, splashing and climbing over metal to join me on the submerged trunk.

With barely any breath, I gasped. "We did it."

Relief washed over me as Dean hung onto the tree, though most of his legs were under water. He panted and snarled, scanning our surroundings. His glance at me was sharp, but familiar. I didn't feel threatened.

I heard the otherness. To my left and four yards out in the river, a weak arc of lightning rose from the water to the clouds above. The shock hit my legs and wrists. My teeth locked for a second, but it passed quickly. I panned the shore for Selina and found her leaning against a tree, her left arm dangling oddly.

Selina straightened, and I heard the otherness gathering. The next bolt would kill me and Dean, half submerged as we were.

I reached for my magic as well, but had the strength for no more than a whining trickle.

The water near the shore bulged, then the river rose like a massive fist as the otherness roared. Only Roxie could have summoned so much. *She's alive.* I sobbed in relief.

The wave dove for the shore and crashed into Selina. It smashed through the windows on the bottom floor of the building, splashed the sides, and sprayed out to the sides.

Selina had killed Eric, but Roxie would survive.

I had to save Dean and make it all worth our sacrifices.

He took the initiative, growling as if to call for me, and dove into the frigid river away from Camp Sparta.

I held my breath and followed, hoping the opposite shore was closer than it seemed in daylight.

Chapter Thirty-One

When Dean slogged through shallow water toward the shadows of the shore, I knew we'd been pulled downstream, nearly to the lake. I barely had the strength for each stroke. The storm hid most of the noise, but I had heard shouting behind us. Roxie needed to be safe. I would return someday to make sure. Part of me hoped Selina hadn't survived Roxie's wave, but I knew she would.

I could never forgive her for killing Eric, even though I had a part in his death.

When my hand touched some underwater grass, I freaked slightly, then dropped my feet to search for the bottom. Pushing into muck on my tiptoes, I found footing and began to climb out of the water. The rain continued to fall, if a little lighter than before. The wind reminded me of the cold temperature.

Dean, his silver fur wet and clumped, shook as he waited for me. His eyes found light in the darkness and glinted. He was alive and free.

He'd fare better in this cold than I would. Tyrell would be searching for us, if soldiers weren't on their way already.

Dean probably thought the same, as he barely waited for

me to stumble onto firm ground before loping slowly into the forest. I could barely see in the darkness, but his silver fur gave me a guide. He'd change back to human, I was sure. Before, he'd been angry. I thought back to him hanging in the cage. He hadn't turned until Selina shocked me.

I stumbled regularly as I slid in muck or caught on a root. Each time he circled back, until I could rise and follow. The cold had my teeth chattering.

When we came to the familiar shape, I was only a dozen paces from the slanted building. We'd approached from a different angle than what I was used to. "We have to leave, Dean."

He stopped, eyes bright and studying me before he led us to the opening. His clothes were there. I flushed and grabbed them up, sodden as they were. When he changed back to human, he'd want something to wear.

Dean paused at his bed when I retrieved his jacket and bundled it with his clothes. When I moved toward the opening, his muzzle nodded in single nudges down.

"What?" Shivering, I rubbed my arm with my free hand. "We don't have a lot of time."

He made the motion again.

I hoped he'd change back to human again. It would be hard for him to teach me how to trap and fish like this. My thought flashed to our kiss, and I flushed. "What do you want me to do? Can't you just change back and tell me?"

He glanced out into the forest and growled as if in response. Maybe he couldn't change back until he felt safe.

"We need to leave, before they come here. It'll be the first place they'll look." Dean nosed the jacket. As my teeth chattered, I guessed. "You want me to put this on."

When I started putting on his soggy, but slightly warming jacket, he turned, heading to his bed. I was going to argue that we needed to leave, when he started digging at the cardboard. He grabbed a strap with his teeth, and pulled loose a pack.

"Got it." I stuffed his clothes inside without looking at the contents and slid the straps on my shoulders. "Now?"

Dean trotted toward the entrance, glancing back for me to follow. He'd mentioned a boat, and I guessed we'd be heading there.

"I don't really know how to row. Maybe you could change back?"

He loped toward the back of the building and I trotted behind. The jacket really did help keep me warmer, as did the pack.

"What do I do if the boat fills with rainwater?"

Dean didn't answer, of course. The glimmer of the lake became obvious ahead, and the trees grew in thickets. He brought us to a snarl of brush, and I nearly tripped on the edge of the upside-down boat as I came closer. The front pointed deeper into the brush. It would be easier if I flipped it right side up first.

"I'd really appreciate it if you would change now, before I have to learn how to row." The boat, a good ten feet long, was made of wood and heavier than I thought. Kneeling on one knee, I managed to tip it to its side. Oars slid under the seat, but stayed inside. A metal pail with a handle rolled out, tied by a rope. With a shove, I shifted the craft onto its bottom, then tossed the bucket inside. A net on a handle rattled on the floor, and a box was tied under a small seat at the pointed front. I didn't notice the fishing rod tied under the middle seat until I leaned back, trying to drag the boat. "This is heavier than me."

I'd seen plenty of these types of boats, some made of metal. The locals fished all year long. I never thought about dragging one around. The reeds of the shore were at least ten feet away. The boat had moved about a foot.

It took a decent amount of time, swearing, and energy to get it to the edge of the water. Dean waded out, as if urging me deeper. Grimacing, I stepped into the water and pulled the front. It slid easily now. Pleased with myself, I rocked the edge. "I've seen the locals row, but I really don't know how to do it."

The rain had lessened, and the winds didn't gust so strongly. The lake seemed to go in all directions from the shore. I pointed. "We go that way?"

Dean lowered his head in a single nod, then nosed the boat.

"Yeah, get going. I got that."

I crawled in, falling to the bottom when it seemed ready to capsize. The fishermen sat with their backs to the front, so I climbed onto the seat and fumbled for the oars. The boat did not feel stable even with the back stuck in the muck.

Dean hadn't gotten in. "Are you coming with me?"

He nosed the back of the boat. Maybe he wanted me out deeper. I put the oars in the little hooks on the side and pulled. We didn't move. I leaned back and tried again. The boat shifted, and Dean leaped inside.

As a wolf, he was quite beautiful. I had little else to look at except the darkness. On occasion, he'd nudge his nose to the left or right, and I'd try to point the boat more in that direction. I took the pack off eventually and put it at my feet between us. Rowing wasn't hard, but I wanted to sleep.

When Dean changed back into a human, he growled and whimpered. It happened fast, but the sliding bones, muscles and skin seemed painful. As his face became recognizable, he grimaced with teeth clenched. I stopped rowing, but couldn't do anything to ease his discomfort. I blushed when he finished, naked and kneeling in front of his pack. As a human, he was quite handsome.

"Can I do anything?" I asked.

Dean spit off the side of the boat and wiped his face. His voice was gravel. "No." Shaking, he fumbled in his backpack and brought out his clothes.

I stared to the side and started rowing, blushing as I did so. The boat rocked as he contorted to get dressed. I hadn't found socks. He sat on the back seat when he tucked his shoes on.

"Thank you," he said. "Before I forget to say it, I'm sorry your friends got hurt."

I thought of Eric's smoldering body and blinked away tears. Trading his life for Dean's hadn't been the plan. "Are you sure we're headed in the right direction? I don't know what I'm doing."

"Lock the oars, and we'll switch."

After a bit of explanation, I found myself sliding by Dean and nearly tipping the boat. I grabbed onto his arm, firm with solid muscle, and blushed at the contact with his skin. He was warm and had a rich, musky smell. As I slid onto the larger seat with a hot face, he sat and studied me with a smirk. "God, this sucks."

I assumed he meant that he would turn into a furry wolf if we kissed, then blushed deeper as I imagined beyond the kiss. "Yeah." Elbows on my knees, I shoved my face in my hands. "Why didn't you change back, once we were safe?" I needed to talk about something else.

His rowed with strong, sure strokes, and a crest of water rose in front of the boat. His chest swelled with each pull, and I focused on his eyes. "I can't change at will. I wanted to. I think knowing the soldiers would be searching for us kept me tense." He flashed a weary smile. "It's getting easier to keep control of my actions, though. I'm learning." That comment caused his expression to slacken and he shook his head.

"Where are we going? To the marsh?"

"Yep. I've been out there at least once a year for the past three, maybe four."

"What will we do? How will we live?"

We talked for a while as Dean explained trapping, both land and water. He discussed tributaries of the marsh and the various kinds of plants and trees we could expect. The conversation ebbed with my fading attention, and the steady splash of the oars became a lullaby.

I woke briefly when the boat scraped on a tree root. I'd curled up on the bottom, happy that the rain had ended. Dean dragged us onto solid land and settled to the ground at the front of the boat; I was content to return to sleep.

I didn't wake again until Moonjir spoke. "Silver and gold together, as expected. I see you finally chose a path, Caitlyn. You should have packed better."

The sun peeked through wisps of clouds and turned his pink and blue colors vibrant. His head tilted, exaggerating his bent ear. Behind him, trees grew on a peninsula or island while the lake continued around us, though thick with reeds.

Dean rolled over and crouched in a single fluid move. "What do you want?" He checked me quickly, then rose slowly.

Moonjir folded his arms, then raised a nail to his chin, staring at the clouds as if contemplating his answer. "World peace. I would imagine Karelian pasties have come a long way. Is mead still a thing? This world has always offered such delights."

Dean stood on a shore made more of roots than earth. "I meant, what do you want with us?" He squared his shoulders with Moonjir but didn't get any closer.

Moonjir's tail rose higher. "Oh my, nothing whatsoever. Don't get excited. Please. None of us want that." He smiled, and his fox face glinted with white canine teeth. "Just congrats on your move. Lovely neighborhood you've picked. A bit marshy for my taste, but plenty of fish." He gestured to his left, then behind. "Your neighbors are spread out. There's a lovely Tuathua enclave just north of here, and those brutish soldiers rarely come out this way, though that might change now, eh?"

I scrambled to sit straighter, ignoring the bruises. "The Tuathua are close?" Peering behind, I expected to see winged warriors bearing down on us.

"Less than a day's walk." His expression grew serious, and he squinted against the sun behind me. "You could make it before nightfall."

Scoffing, I climbed to one knee. "I certainly don't want to go there."

Moonjir shrugged. "Suit yourself. You seemed like the go make friends type, but I could be wrong."

Shakily, I exited the boat and balanced on the roots. "Not with Tuathua."

"Such bias. Friends are friends."

I'd lost my true friends. Stepping gingerly over the uneven shore, I put my hand on Dean's bare shoulder. "We'll be just fine on our own."

Moonjir flashed a smile. "Of course you will. It'll be paradise."

"Is that it?" asked Dean. His tone implied he was done with Moonjir.

"Oh, yes. Good luck on the new adventure and all that." He winked, turned, and walked toward the trees. When he stopped and raised one nail, Dean growled. Moonjir spun around with an apologetic smile. "One more thing. A warning. Those grouchy soldiers patrol this far on occasion. Best you keep hidden as well as you can, or make some new friends."

I gripped Dean's shoulder a little tighter, but spoke with confidence. "We'll be fine, just the two of us."

We'd love your review on Amazon, Goodreads, or anywhere!

Afterword

We've left Caitlyn and Dean alone in what they hope to be a safe place. Life in the Sorrow is never easy, but they have each other.

Alliance of Bonds and Storm: Book Two of the Sorrowborn Trilogy does not leave them on their own for very long. New friends, old enemies, old friends, and new enemies await.

Acknowledgments

Our common passion for Brandon Sanderson's work led to a love of characters who persevere despite their personal failings.

We appreciate everyone who supported and encouraged our project. Editors, critique partners, and beta readers have all been there for us.

Special thanks go out to Heather Norris who gave us our first review in her beta read, "I loved this book. The story was fantastic, and I love the characters. . . . I got attached to them enough that I cried . . .."

About the Authors

April Davis owns a bookstore in rural Florida, runs bookclubs, edits novels, cosplays, and reads a wide variety of genres.

Kevin A Davis travels nearly every month to convention and events as a speaker, vendor, and even staff.

Find us at
Sorrowborn.com

Also by April Davis & Kevin A Davis

The Sorrowborn Trilogy

Path of Sorrow and Wind

Alliance of Bonds and Storm

Home of Fire and Tempest

Sorrowborn.com

Grab some free short stories from Dean, Caitlyn, and Roxie set just before the trilogy begins.

Join the newsletter with the download of Dean's short story *Never Give Up*

https://dl.bookfunnel.com/d8rkbkphxt

or get Dean's story without a newsletter signup

https://dl.bookfunnel.com/v7szegjy27

Follow the links at the end of the story to download Caitlyn's story, then Roxie's

Also by Inkd Pub

The DRC Files A fantasy series by Kevin A Davis

The Khimmer Chronicles A fantasy series by Kevin A Davis

Spooky, horror, fantasy, science fiction, LGBTQ+, mystery, and explicit romance anthologies. Find them at InkdPub.com